WIDOW
LAKE

BOOKS BY RITA HERRON

WIDOW LAKE

RITA HERRON

bookouture

Published by Bookouture in 2023

An imprint of Storyfire Ltd.
Carmelite House
50 Victoria Embankment
London EC4Y 0DZ

www.bookouture.com

ISBN: 978-1-83790-424-2
eBook ISBN: 978-1-83790-414-3

To my amazing editor Christina Demosthenous for bringing the Ellie Reeves series to life!

PROLOGUE
WIDOW LAKE

2013

Amy Dean had made a lot of mistakes in her twenty years. Some of them her fault for being stupid and naïve. Some of them not her fault because she'd been thrown into the deep uncharted territory of the foster system by every adult in her life. Feeling unloved and unwanted, she'd blindly paddled through the muddy waters, sinking and flailing until she'd almost drowned. So many times, she'd imagined herself trapped by the ghosts that dwelled in the haunted lake, her grave unmarked, her disappearance unnoticed.

She'd learned the hard way to hang tough. To fight. To tolerate the ghosts and not allow the pain to destroy her.

But then she had Paisley and the world was filled with a bright beam of hope.

She stroked her precious two-year-old little girl's soft brown hair and rolled her aching shoulders as she tucked Paisley into the back of her beat-up VW and buckled her seatbelt. Today she'd cleaned houses for the "Ladies of the Lake"—that's what they called their little group. Three of them were nice and paid her well, the other an obsessive-compulsive control freak who demanded Amy redo things a thousand times if she saw a wrinkle in the bedding or found a speck of dust anywhere.

She wanted to quit that woman more than anything. But Paisley had to eat and needed new shoes and a roof over her head. Amy would do whatever it took, swallow her pride and work for dirt cheap to take care of her beloved daughter.

Yes, she'd made mistakes. But as she drove the short distance to Lake Haven Apartments, the complex which housed half the students at Widow Peak College, she heard little Paisley's soft breathing echoing in the back of the car and refused to call her a mistake.

Paisley was the best thing that had happened to her. After years of torment and anguish, Amy had a family. Someone to love. Someone who loved her back.

Someone who made her want to be better. To earn a degree and get a proper job so they could move to a nicer place and take vacations like real families did.

"We'll be home soon, baby," she murmured as she turned onto the road leading to the complex. She recognized a few cars belonging to other coed girls, although she hadn't made friends. While they indulged in party mode on the weekends and even during the week, she worked during the afternoons, had a child to look after and studied when Paisley went to bed. And truthfully, she didn't want to discuss her daughter with them. Too many questions. Ones she didn't want to answer. Her baby was her business and nobody else's.

Not that she minded staying in. A party was what had gotten her into trouble three years ago. That trash can full of hooch punch...

Her stomach roiled at the thought. Dumb. Foolish. Rum had short-circuited her brain and turned her into mush. The drunken blindness had robbed her. Then he took the rest. She hadn't cried out or fought. She was too far under.

Then six weeks later... the morning sickness began.

Dark clouds hung heavy tonight over the steep Appalachian Mountains adding a gloomy feel.

Inhaling to ward off the emotions that swamped her when she was tired and needed to sleep but had to hit the books, she parked, slid out and retrieved her backpack, hurrying to get Paisley from her car seat. Her sweet toddler had fallen sound asleep and clutched her blanket like a lifeline.

Paisley snuggled into her as she walked up the sidewalk. Nerves gathered in Amy's belly—the streetlight that had been broken for a week still hadn't been fixed and it was practically pitch dark. A noise to the right—footsteps maybe—made her jerk her head around.

The sense that she was being watched overcame her, making her hands tremble, and she dropped her keys. Paisley raised her head as Amy stooped to retrieve them, but she soothed her before getting them inside.

Thankfully she'd left the hall light on before she'd left, and she made it to the bedroom without tripping. As Amy tucked her daughter into her crib, Paisley opened her eyes for a split second and looked at her all sleepy-eyed.

"Night-night, baby," Amy whispered.

"Night-night." Paisley's eyes were already drifting shut. Amy kissed her soft cheek and adjusted the sound machine to Paisley's favorite lullaby, then turned to go back to the living room and tackle tonight's studies.

But the squeak of the floor in the hall made her freeze. Another squeak. Then breathing. Slow. Shallow.

Someone was in the house.

Fear clenched her chest and she turned back to scoop up Paisley and hide her in the closet, but the breathing grew louder and louder. Then someone jumped her from behind.

She screamed and fought, desperate to throw off her

attacker but he knocked her to the floor and jabbed a knife to the base of her neck.

And then there was pain and darkness...

She reached out for her daughter... had to save her... but the world tilted into nothing, and when she heard her baby cry, she knew it was too late.

ONE

WIDOW PEAK

Ten years later

Twelve-year-old Lorna Bea Jones paced the confines of the small dark, room, her heart thudding with fear.

Finally, the monster who'd taken her had left her alone. She sat huddled in a ball in the corner and stared at the locked door. For a long time, she held her breath and listened for his footsteps to return. Seconds ticked by. Minutes. Maybe half an hour.

Horror stories of men kidnapping young girls raced through her mind. She shivered and stood, restless and terrified as she tried to block them out.

Maybe he wasn't coming back. At least not tonight.

So where was she? Why had he taken her? What did he plan to do to her?

Did her daddy even know she was missing? And what about Nana? She hadn't seen her grandmother when the man dragged her down the steps at the cabin.

Nervous energy pulsed through her, and she crossed to the window to look outside. She was in the mountains somewhere.

Tall, sharp ridges jutted out and climbed toward the sky. She'd heard about this area. About the Appalachian Trail with wild animals, dangerous steep drop-offs and woods so thick that people got lost in them.

The giant massive trees shrouded most of the light. Tree branches swayed in the wind. Their limbs reached out like monster hands. Wind whined through the cracks in the grime-covered window.

Her mind struggled to understand what was going on.

It all started when they came to Widow Lake three days ago. She'd been so excited at the prospect of swimming in the lake. Canoeing. Hiking in the woods. Seeing the waterfalls.

And making friends.

But then everything went wrong...

TWO

HOOTERVILLE, GEORGIA

Three days ago

DAY 1

All she ever wanted was to have a normal family. To live in a house where she could have friends, a yard, a dog—and not to keep moving around. But she'd been doing it for years now and didn't think her father ever intended to settle down.

His footsteps echoed on the rotting wood floor as he came into her room. Frowning, he shoved an empty box in front of her. "Pack up. Time to go again."

Frustration mounted inside her. She lived her whole life in boxes. "But Daddy—"

"No buts, Lorna Bea," her father said in his don't-argue-with-me tone.

"Lorna Bea?"

"Yes, that's your name now. Lorna Bea Jones. Memorize it and don't slip up this time."

She silently repeated the name in her head.

"Remember, just take your clothes, nothing else."

And her books. She'd never leave those behind. Reading was her passion. Her escape. The characters in the stories were the only friends she had.

"Lorna Bea?"

She gritted her teeth. "I know, I know." She'd learned the hard way. They took only the essentials with them. Nothing that would give away where they'd been or where they were going.

Or what they were running from.

And they *were* running. She'd figured that out by her tenth birthday when some man had followed them and her daddy had gone ape-crazy. He always said people were dangerous and you couldn't trust anyone.

She'd asked why but he never said.

Now, he cleared his throat from where he stood towering over her, then extended his hand, jaw hard. "Where's that notebook you're always writing in?"

Lorna Bea slid the small spiral notebook from her desk drawer and handed it to him. He didn't bother to read it, just tossed it in the trashcan, lit a match and set fire to it. Smoke curled upward as the pages began to crinkle and burn. Flames caught and jumped, the heat warming her.

The first time he'd burned the pages of her notebook she'd cried and cried. She wanted to be a writer one day so everywhere they went, she wrote down the names of streets, towns, businesses, people's names, even things they said, then used them to make up stories. But her dad had seen it and ripped it to shreds.

Now she kept two notebooks—one that he saw her writing in, and another, a notebook he knew nothing about. She wrote in it at night when he was fast asleep. It held all her secrets. Just like she thought the locked box in his closet held his secrets.

"Where are we going this time?" she asked.

He shrugged. "Wherever the car takes us." Then he stalked out.

She stared at the empty box. When she was little, her father called their moves adventures. Once they went out west, another time to the beach. Then they'd ended up here in this little dumpy town with nothing to do. Not that they got out and did anything anyway.

We have to keep a low profile, Daddy said.

Did that mean they had to live in Deadsville? That's what she called this place in the middle of nowhere.

She heard him whistling in the kitchen and knew she had to get busy. When he said pack, it usually meant they were leaving in a hurry.

Maybe they'd go some place fun this time. Some place with other kids.

She just hoped if there were, he'd let her talk to them.

THREE

WIDOW LAKE

The sign for Widow Lake taunted him with memories of his first kill. Some said the first was the most special. Most satisfying.

But with each one, he grew bolder and more confident.

Sunshine blared down on the asphalt as he drove past the Cabins for Rent sign and his truck was suffocatingly hot. The heat made him feel itchy like he had bugs under his skin. He flipped on the radio for the weather report, wondering how long this damn drought would last.

"Angelica Gomez, Channel Five news, reporting to you live from Widow Peak Mountain where Widow Peak College is hosting its annual tenth year class reunion for graduates. The dog days of summer have begun with a vengeance with temperatures soaring to one hundred degrees by noon and no relief in sight." She paused for a second, then zipped on, "The water level is at an all-time low on Widow Lake, creating problems for wildlife and stirring more stories about the lost city buried beneath the water."

His pulse clamored. It had been hot ten years ago, too. Had made him feel crazy.

"Widow Lake is widely considered by locals to be haunted by victims killed in the flooding that occurred when the dam was first built decades ago," the reporter continued. "This summer, two swimmers have already reported feeling body parts brushing against them. Some fear the receding water may expose other unmarked graves. Concerns abound that the heat and stories will deter alumni from returning, although judging from the full-to-capacity hotels and inn, it doesn't appear that way."

Excitement bled through him. The reunion. They'd planned it for years. He'd gotten the call. The brothers would be there.

It was the first homecoming of the resurrection of the darkness.

And they intended to celebrate.

Memories swirled around him, transporting him back to his first kill. *He raised the knife as he'd imagined so many times in his fantasies and with one quick motion slashed her throat. Her body jerked. Her breath panted out. Coppery red blood flowed down her milky white neck. Then her eyes widened in the shock of death.*

A boat puttered somewhere in the distance, dragging him back to the present. His breathing was choppy and erratic, his palms clammy.

He glanced at the murky water with a slow smile.

Widow Lake already held so many dead bodies.

It was the perfect place to leave another.

He had one in mind already.

FOUR

CROOKED CREEK

A scream pierced the air as Detective Ellie Reeves parked at the rustic cabin deep in the woods where the Rogers lived. She'd been here once before and knew the husband was a mean drunk.

Instincts on full alert, she eased from her vehicle, scanning the overgrown yard and front of the clapboard house.

The dog days of summer had brought scorching temperatures, drought and madness. Deputy Eastwood was working a domestic at the moment and Deputy Landrum had been called to shut down an out-of-control party of a group of inebriated coeds.

Suddenly two mixed pit bulls raced around the corner of the house, barking and snapping, a heavy-set man in overalls chasing them with a shotgun. A woman in a flowered house-dress followed, screaming and slapping a dishcloth at the man.

"Don't you dare shoot my boys!" she shouted.

"They got into my corn liquor again!" the man bellowed.

Ellie flipped on her siren to snag their attention and ducked behind her open door for cover. The woman skidded to a stop on the graveled drive. The man fired a bullet into the air.

The dogs raced around the side of the Jeep, barking and clawing at the ground, sending dust flying.

Ellie waited until they were behind her, put one hand on her weapon then eased her other hand up in the air. "Police," she called out. "Put the gun down, sir. Now."

He froze, chest heaving up and down. "I want them mad dogs gone."

"They wouldn't be mad if you wasn't so damn mean to 'em," the woman cried.

"Sir, the gun," Ellie repeated firmly.

Another heartbeat passed before he slowly lowered it. The dogs crept nearer Ellie, and she slowly offered her hand, speaking softly, "Hey, guys, I'm not here to hurt you." Though they looked fierce, they calmed as she soothed them. Their breed had gotten a bad rap. "It's okay now, guys, it's okay."

She glanced at the woman. "What are their names, ma'am?"

"Dante and Roscoe." She pushed her frizzy hair from her face and tilted her head toward her husband. "They ain't bad dogs. He just got a temper."

"Where do you keep them?" Ellie asked.

"We got a pen out back. But they must've got out."

"Damn right they did," the man snarled. "They need a good beating."

The dogs bared their teeth at him, and he stiffened, jowls red with anger.

Ellie eased to a standing position, barely holding her temper. "Listen to me, Mr. Rogers, you are not going to beat these dogs. If I find out you've laid one hand on them, I'll lock you up for animal cruelty." She folded her arms. "Do you understand?"

He cursed and spat tobacco on the ground near her feet. "You can't tell me what to do on my property. They're my damn dogs and I'll do what I want."

Ellie was so mad she saw red. "Mrs. Rogers, please put the dogs away for now."

The woman called them and they ran to her, nuzzling her legs.

Ellie strode toward the brute in the overalls. The stench of moonshine on his breath nearly knocked her over. "I am the police, sir, and where the law is concerned, I most certainly can tell you what to do. I meant what I said. If you touch them or your wife, I'll be back to lock you up." She hardened her voice. "And just so we're clear, I will send someone regularly to check on your wife and the animals." She'd take the dogs home herself if she had a fenced yard and didn't work such crazy long hours.

The man kicked the dirt then cursed again and stomped back to the house. She heard the screen door slam shut and hoped she wouldn't have to come back.

But she had a feeling she would.

Her phone rang as she climbed in her Jeep and started the engine. She connected.

"Detective Reeves," her boss, Captain Hale, said. "Four-year-old little girl has gone missing at Widow Lake."

Ellie pressed the accelerator. "I'm on my way."

FIVE

HAYES STATE PRISON

Special Agent Derrick Fox stared at Dominique Radcliff as he sat across the metal table in the prison interrogation room. The press had given Radcliff the title the Southside Slasher because he'd slashed his victims' throats, then left them naked and exposed to the elements near Springer Mountain, the southernmost terminus of the Appalachian Trail.

Radcliff had been arrested in early 2013 and was currently on death row for three heinous murders and was scheduled for lethal injection in four weeks.

The balding man was short and beefy, with ham-hock-sized muscles. Even in solitary, he must have been working out. His dark-brown eyes were set close together with an intensity that held a menacing evil.

Derrick pushed a can of soda and a candy bar toward him. "How's solitary?" Derrick asked. Some prisoners went insane in isolation, confined with only a mattress on the floor and an hour out of the hole daily.

"Suits me," Radcliff said, his voice cool. "Gives me time to think. To remember."

Derrick struggled not to react. Radcliff was baiting him. He enjoyed reliving the sadistic murders he'd committed.

Another minute stretched between them, then Radcliff finally opened the soda, ripped the wrapper off the candy bar and took a bite. Then he had the audacity to smile. "If you think candy and a Coke will sway me into telling you what you want to know, you're dumber than I thought. I'm not five years old."

No, he was thirty and a sociopath who'd exhibited no remorse over his crimes and zero empathy for his victims.

"You admitted to murdering three women in court," Derrick said, his tone neutral as he spread photographs on the table. "The first 2008, the second 2009, the third 2010. In early 2013, two more coeds, who fit the profile of your victims, were reported missing, Haley Worth and Judy Zane. Did you kill them?"

Radcliff cut his eyes toward the pictures, a twinkle in his icy eyes. "Pretty, aren't they?"

Derrick breathed slowly to keep his emotions in check. "Your victims were found with their throats slashed, their hair hacked off and their lips painted in a ghoulish smile with their own blood." Derrick folded his arms. "That's your MO. Though we haven't found Haley or Judy's bodies, a ghoulish smile was painted on their bedroom walls."

Radcliff crushed the candy wrapper then took a long sip of his soda. "What can I say? I'm famous."

"Police withheld the detail about the bloody lips from the press so how would a copycat know?"

"Maybe someone from the police leaked the information."

Derrick had considered that but they hadn't found evidence to substantiate it. "You're going to die, Radcliff, that's a given. So why not put the families at peace and tell us where you left their bodies so they can give the girls a proper burial?"

"Those two bitches got what they deserved," he said calmly. "But I didn't kill them."

Derrick's jaw hardened. Radcliff had insisted the same ever since his arrest. But why confess to three murders and not these two?

Was he playing a cat and mouse game, reveling in taking his secrets with him to his grave? Or was it possible he hadn't killed these two, that he had a conspirator?

If that was the case, that monster was still on the loose...

SIX

SOMEWHERE ON THE AT

Demons dogged Cord McClain every day. As hard as he tried to forget, he couldn't.

He *had* to remember.

Tormented by memories, he'd been hiking for days, losing himself in the wilderness and reminding himself where he'd come from.

From nothing.

As a kid, he'd been tossed from one foster home to another. The last one, he'd lived above a mortuary. That animal had been psychotic. Escaping had meant living on his own and had made him the man he was.

But it had come at a cost.

The sharp ridges and steep drop-offs of the mountains were home to both his past mistakes and his salvation. As a teen, he'd encountered dangers on the trail and managed to survive on his own instincts. Eventually he'd joined Search and Rescue for FEMA. It was the one good thing he'd done in his life.

Weeds and briars had overtaken the land here in the ravine where he'd buried his secrets.

Dead wildflowers, branches and brittle leaves lay in layers

from the years that had passed. Trees had been ripped from the ground during last year's tornado and rattlesnakes had infested the area, keeping everyone away. Their hiss punctuated the air as they coiled to strike.

The hot air barely stirred around him, mosquitos buzzing around his face, memories circling his mind in a blinding fog. His lungs strained for air, the stench of death and rotten moss hanging heavy.

His SAR dog, Benji, rubbed up against his leg and Cord patted his back. "Thanks for coming with me, boy. I know I can always depend on you."

Benji looked up at him with trusting eyes, ears perked as if he sensed something was wrong.

Cord's phone buzzed. Ellie.

His gut tightened. Ever since he'd parted ways with Lola Parks a few weeks ago, he'd dived into work and practically avoided Ellie. He knew she'd ask questions, questions he didn't know how to answer. Another reason he'd come back here: to remind himself why a flawed man like him had no business wanting her.

But she could be calling about work. Ellie and Special Agent Derrick Fox had asked him to join the task force they'd formed to investigate crimes in the area. He braced himself and answered.

"Cord, I just got a call," said Ellie. "Little girl is missing at Widow Lake. I'm on my way there now."

Cord stood, pulse hammering. "Do you know the location?"

"Striped Bass Cove," Ellie said.

"I'm not far from the lake now. I'll get over there and help coordinate search efforts."

He said goodbye to his past for now, then jogged up the hill and through the woods. His mind ticked off possible dire scenarios. Not only was Widow Lake supposedly haunted, but it sat at the edge of the Appalachian Trail. Miles and miles of untamed forest, wild animals, uneven grounds, drop offs and woods created their own set of dangers. Worse, every year there were drownings and accidents on the lake which became over-populated with boaters and partiers.

He hoped this child wouldn't be one of them.

SEVEN

WIDOW LAKE

As soon as her daddy went to his truck, Lorna Bea climbed through the window onto the tree outside her bedroom window.

"Stay in here while I go to the store," he'd ordered. "Do you understand me?"

She'd nodded, biting her tongue to keep from arguing. Why bring her to this beautiful place and lock her in the house?

Downstairs, Nana sat in the rocker working her knitting needles, humming some gospel song about gathering at the river.

According to Nana, who'd lived with her and her father as long as she remembered, ghosts roamed the lake. A bridge called the Lady in Blue Bridge had been named after a widow who threw herself off it out of grief. "They say you can see her ghost on a foggy night rising from the water and walking the bridge," Nana said.

Lorna Bea rubbed her hands together excitedly. She wanted to know more about the ghosts, wanted to see one for herself.

"Don't feed her imagination with gossip of ghosts," her father had snapped at Nana. "She makes up enough silly stories in that notebook of hers."

Lorna Bea's cheeks burned. One day she'd show him. She'd write stories that would be published. Then who would be laughing?

On the way here, she'd studied the scenery and jotted down names of the country roads and towns. From the window now she had the perfect view of the Appalachian Mountains. Her heart thudded at the sight of the jagged ridges rising like stacked stones in front of her. Gray clouds reached for the peaks, the two almost touching. The fading sunlight shimmered off the surface of the water, which was so still the silence was eerie. A pungent odor wafted in the air, one that held the scent of evil.

She searched the horizon for the bridge Nana talked about. Shadows from the pines and aspens darkened the bank.

Suddenly she thought she saw movement. It was a man, she was sure of it.

Tall. Creepy-looking. He wore a black hoodie. Black pants. And a mask.

Fear clutched her chest. What was he doing?

EIGHT

Ellie threw the Jeep into Park and spotted Cord. With his shaggy unkempt hair, beard stubble and broad shoulders, he was a sight for sore eyes. Handsome in a rugged way, a man of the land, a man with secrets in his smoky amber eyes.

And the best tracker she'd ever known.

As she climbed out, she noticed he was organizing search teams to look for the child. A squad car from Widow Peak Police Department was already on the scene. One uniform stood with Cord, another by the family. The auburn-haired woman, a dark-haired man and a brown-haired boy who looked to be about twelve or thirteen hovered by an outdoor fire pit. The kid wore a Braves T-shirt with shorts and kept shifting like he had the jitters.

Missing children cases were always the most upsetting, but Ellie banked her emotions. She had to in order to do her job. Too many scary possibilities. If she dwelled on them, she might crumble.

The legends and folklore about the lake echoed in her head. While the Corp of Engineers had paid for some property when they decided to build the lake to generate power, many folks were run off and the water overflowed, burying homes, businesses and causing deaths. Some said when they dove deep, they heard screams of the deceased under the water.

Deputy Landrum pulled up, and he and Shondra got out and walked toward her. The atmosphere hung as thick with fear and worry as the air was stagnant and hot.

Members of the County Boat Rescue Team joined Cord's team. Cord gave them directions then headed over to her.

"What's your take on the situation?" Ellie asked as he approached.

"Parents say the kid wandered off. They're frantic with worry. I alerted boat patrol to comb the lake," Cord said. "Officer Timmons and Officer Rodriquez from the local police department are here to help. Timmons was first to arrive."

"Thanks." She turned to Landrum and Shondra. "Canvass cabin guests and campers. Maybe someone saw something," Ellie said hopefully. "Or someone found her."

Concern filled Shondra's brown eyes. "On it."

The two of them discussed a plan, then headed in different directions.

Ellie joined the family who looked as if they were falling apart. Officer Timmons gave a nod of recognition. "Detective Ellie Reeves," Ellie said. "You've met Ranger Cord McClain. And my deputies are here to help."

"This is Gina and Ken Hammerstein," Officer Timmons said.

The woman wiped her swollen tear-stained eyes and clung to her husband who looked equally terrified. The boy looked down at his hands, twisting them together.

"Please help us," Ken said. "Little Betsy might be out there in the woods and it's getting dark."

Ellie fought her own disturbing memories as the sun dipped lower into the tall pines and thick oaks. As a child, she'd been terrified when she'd been trapped in the woods. After a while, every tree looked the same. "How long has she been gone?"

"About half an hour," Ken said, panicked.

So she couldn't have gone too far, at least not on her own. "How old is she?"

Gina hugged her arms around her waist as if to hold herself upright while Ken pulled a photo from his phone. "Four."

"I need a description, please. Hair color, eyes, what she was wearing."

Gina's lip quivered. "She has brown hair in a ponytail, green eyes." The woman clenched her hands. "Oh, goodness, what was she wearing?" She tapped her fingers on her temple, thinking.

"I know you're scared," Ellie said softly. "Just close your eyes for a minute. It'll come to you."

Gina did as she said. "Oh, yeah, a pink T-shirt with a rainbow on it and denim shorts. And pink tennis shoes."

"Good," Ellie said. "That will help."

Cord cleared his throat. "Can I share that photo with the search team?"

"Of course." Ken passed the phone.

"Do you have a blanket or stuffed animal belonging to Betsy, something my dog can sniff to track her?" Cord asked.

Gina turned to her son. "Cade, go get Betsy's stuffed kitty." She glanced at Ellie. "She's obsessed with cats."

Ellie offered an understanding smile.

The boy ran inside the cabin, then returned a minute later carrying a white stuffed cat. His hand trembled as he handed it to Cord.

"Thanks, man," Cord said. "Don't worry. We'll find her."

The boy shifted onto the balls of his feet. Cord gave him an encouraging pat then strode over to the search team. A minute later they fanned out in different directions, Cord and Benji leading the way.

Ellie addressed the family again. "Tell me exactly what happened. When did you last see your daughter?"

Gina cleared her throat. "We spent the day playing in the lake and had dinner out here, then I was cleaning up in the kitchen."

Ken pinched the bridge of his nose. "Cade and I went down to the cove to fish."

"I thought Betsy was with them," Gina said miserably.

"And I thought she was inside with my wife," Ken said. "The fish weren't biting so half an hour later, we gave it up and came back," Ken said. "The minute we realized Betsy was gone, we started looking."

"What if she fell in the water?" Gina cried.

"Would she go swimming without one of you?" Ellie asked.

"She knows not to." The father stood. "It's our number one rule. No one swims alone."

The boy looked away for a minute and Ellie's skin prickled. "Cade? Do you know where your sister is?"

He shook his head. "Betsy likes to wander off," he said, eyes fearful as he gazed over the murky water. Dried leaves and twigs bobbed in a ripple created by a passing boat. The water was unusually low, the grass on the bank dying. Brown leaves and twigs floated on the surface.

"Ranger McClain is the best tracker I know," Ellie assured him. "We'll find her."

Although, even as she said it, doubts crept in. Betsy could have fallen into the lake. Drownings happened here every summer. There was also another possibility...

"Did you see anyone else around here today?" she asked.

Gina's face grew pinched. "Another family was here picnicking," she said.

"But they left before we had dinner," Ken added.

"Anyone who looked suspicious?" Ellie asked. "Someone who showed a special interest in Betsy?"

Fear flashed across both the couple's faces. Cade sidled up to his father, his face paling.

A sob escaped Gina and her legs buckled. Her husband helped her to one of the folding lounge chairs by the firepit. "Oh, my God," she wailed, "do you think someone took our little girl?"

Ellie couldn't answer that. If she was lost, they would find her.

But if she'd been abducted, she could be long gone by now.

NINE

Lorna Bea couldn't tear her eyes away from the commotion at the lake. Something was wrong. She could feel it in the air. Hear a note of fear in the voices. The woman had been crying. She and a man shouting.

Then other people had showed up and everyone started yelling and moving along the edge of the dark lake as if searching for someone.

The man in the hoodie darted between the trees. She tried to follow his movements but lost him in the patches of overgrown weeds and bushes.

The voices came again. More movement. This time frantic. "Betsy? Where are you, honey?"

"Betsy!"

Lorna Bea glanced to the neighboring cabin. The little girl next door was named Betsy. She'd heard her brother teasing her.

Flashlights bobbed up and down as people combed the woods.

The air was hot, the reds, yellows and oranges of the sun disappearing over the lake. Lorna Bea imagined ghosts tiptoeing across the surface, hollow eyes staring back at her as if begging to be free.

"Betsy! Betsy, where are you?" a man called.

Lorna Bea craned her neck to see across the property. Flashlights waved through the darkness, bushes parting. The voices sounded more anxious by the minute.

"Betsy, if you can hear me, call out!"

"Betsy! Where are you?"

A dog barked in the distance, and Lorna Bea scanned the land to the right of the cabin, then climbed higher in the tree so she could see over a thick patch of briars. She spotted a boat dock and a small shed, then thought she saw the little girl ducking inside it.

The man in dark clothes was skulking through the brush toward the shed.

Her father's warning about bad people made her breath catch. What if he was after the little girl?

Heart hammering, she swung herself from one branch to another until she reached the lowest branch. Then she dropped to the ground. She quickly checked the driveway for her father's black Pathfinder but he wasn't back yet, so she snuck into the garage and found a flashlight. Gripping it tightly, she hurried toward the woods.

She used a stick to mark her path as she went. Bugs swarmed her face, and weeds made her legs itchy. She might be on a wild goose chase, but what if that man was after Betsy?

Sweat trickled down her the side of her face. The sound of a boat rumbling mingled with the croaks of the tree frogs and chirping crickets.

She didn't have a watch but she knew the minutes were ticking by. The shouting grew louder, more intense.

Night closed in, blurring her footpath. The sound of water lapping against the dock told her she was on the right path. Brush rustled to the right and she saw the man again. Cold fear licked her belly and she ducked behind some bushes so he wouldn't see her.

"Betsy?" she whispered. "Betsy, are you here?"

A light breeze rustled the leaves as she crept closer. When she finally reached the shed, she peered inside, but it was so dark she couldn't see anything. "Betsy?"

A tiny noise broke the silence. Maybe it was an animal?

Her heart raced. But she shined her light inside the shed, and saw it held a few ropes and paddles.

A second later, she spotted blood on the floor.

TEN

Ellie followed protocol for a possible child abduction and issued an Amber Alert, then called Sheriff Bryce Waters and explained the situation.

"Circulate her photo and description across the state and alert train stations, bus stations and airports," Ellie said.

"Copy that. What's your gut telling you about the parents?" the sheriff asked.

"They're distraught," Ellie said. "Each thought the other was watching her."

"Heard that story before," Bryce said. "Same thing happened at a pool party a couple of weeks ago. Kid drowned."

"I know." Worry churned in Ellie as she remembered the gut-wrenching faces of the parents on the news. All it took was a minute to lose a child—turn your head away for a second, and something bad could happen. "Cord has boat patrol scouring the lake. If we don't find her soon, we'll get them to drag it."

God, she hoped it didn't come to that.

A minute later, the local news van rolled up. Journalist Angelica Gomez—Ellie's half-sister—stepped from the van, looking impeccable in a black pant suit and heels, the streaks of red in her dark hair shimmering against her caramel skin. Her cameraman Tom unloaded his equipment from the van while Angelica walked toward Ellie with a sympathetic gaze.

"Little girl still missing?" Angelica asked.

Ellie nodded. "She's four. Parents think she just wandered off."

"You ready to go live?" Angelica asked.

"Yes. But for now, I've held off mentioning the possibility of a kidnapping to the parents."

"Got it."

Ellie led her over to the couple, who looked despondent. The boy sat slumped with his hands on his knees, tapping them up and down.

Ellie quickly made the introductions. "Ms. Gomez is going to post Betsy's picture on the news in hopes someone has seen her."

"Of course," Mr. Hammerstein said. "We'll offer a reward if that would help."

"Let's hold off on that for now." She didn't want to attract the greedy who might call with false leads and divide police manpower.

Betsy's mother dabbed at her damp cheeks with a tissue then clasped her husband's hand and faced the camera.

ELEVEN

Fear cinched Lorna Bea's stomach as she studied the shed floor. Yes, that was blood.

Wood boards creaked as she stepped inside the dark space. Bugs crawled across the floor. A rancid odor clogged the air. There were black widow spiders around her. Nana had said to watch out for them when they went inside the cabin.

A whimpering sound came from the corner, where wooden shelves had crashed down. Behind the mess, a hand peeked through, clawing at the floor.

Lorna Bea's heart stuttered, and she stooped down see who it was. Brown hair, a pink T-shirt.

"Help," a tiny voice cried. "Help."

Lorna Bea sucked in a breath. "Betsy?"

"Uh-huh," the little girl said.

"I'm Lorna Bea," she replied. "I'll go get help."

"Don't go. I'm scared."

For a minute, she just stood there, not knowing what to do. But she couldn't leave Betsy alone. And that man in the dark hoodie might still be out there.

She studied the small room then heard a tiny meow. "Is that a cat?" she asked.

"Uh-huh. I chased him in here," Betsy whispered.

Lorna Bea smiled as a yellow ball of fur popped its head up from where Betsy held it.

"Just stay still and I'll get you out."

Dust swirled around her as she pitched the shelves to the side. Then she saw a hole in the floor. The wood was splintered where Betsy had fallen through.

For a second, she froze again. On a TV show she'd seen, hadn't they said not to move someone if they were injured? That you might make them worse? She licked her suddenly dry lips. "Are you hurt, Betsy?"

"I dunno," Betsy whimpered. "My leg's stuck."

What if she had a broken leg? Lorna Bea would have to go for help. "Just be still. Let me see what we're dealing with." She shined the light around the hole edges then searched the shed for a tool to help her. Fishing lures were scattered on the floor. That wouldn't work. Neither would the fishing wire. There were clippers. No good.

Then a hammer.

Pulse racing, she carried it over to where the little girl was, then used it to loosen one of the boards. The wood was so rotten it easily came loose, and she pried another and then one more, making the hole bigger.

"Can you move your legs?" Lorna Bea asked.

Betsy whimpered again and the kitten meowed wildly, paws scratching at the floor.

"Come on, I'll lift you out." Lorna Bea perched behind Betsy then tugged beneath her arms and dragged her from the hole. She fell backward on her butt and Betsy fell on top of her, the kitten screeching.

"I want Mommy," Betsy cried.

"I know, I'll take you back," Lorna Bea said. "See if you can stand up."

The little girl managed to stand, although she winced in pain. "It hurts."

Lorna Bea gave her a hug. "It's okay, I'll carry you." She turned her back to Betsy and bent her knees. "Climb on and I'll give you a piggyback ride."

Betsy did as she said, wrapping one arm around Lorna Bea's neck and tucking the little kitten under her other. Using the flashlight to guide them, Lorna Bea followed the trail markings she'd left behind as she hiked back through the woods.

Bushes parted ahead, and for a second she went still. It was the man with the hoodie.

"Who's that man in the black?" Betsy whispered.

"I don't know, but he's scary. Let's hurry. Hang on." Lorna Bea took off running.

As she neared the cabins, she heard the shouts again. "Betsy!"

"Betsy, where are you?"

Betsy wiggled and called out for her parents. "Here, Mommy!"

Lorna Bea jogged toward the voices. Sweat beaded her skin as she reached the edge of the woods.

"Mommy! Daddy!" Betsy shrieked.

Lorna Bea set Betsy and the kitten on the ground. "Go to them, Betsy. Go."

The little girl hobbled away and her parents ran down the hill to scoop her up.

Lorna Bea's daddy's Pathfinder rumbled up the graveled road. No telling what he'd do if he found out she'd disobeyed him. He'd probably punish her.

She raced back to the cabin.

She didn't like his punishments.

TWELVE

There were too many damn people combing the woods around Widow Lake. It was dangerous to be here.

But it was the tenth anniversary of when it all began and he had to come. Had to honor the pact.

His pulse quickened. On second thought, having the police around would raise the stakes in the game.

Still, he had to be smart. Couldn't get caught. Besides, he'd seen an older girl—she was maybe twelve or thirteen—in the woods. She intrigued him. He'd never taken one that young but the thought of it sent his blood buzzing.

Ducking in the shadows, he moved stealthily through the woods away from where the girl had spotted him. Cops and rescue workers were everywhere. He had to stay out of sight.

He darted past tall pines and patches of poison ivy, making his way back to the deserted cabin. He kept the lights off as he entered and closed the blinds, taking solace in the dark.

Still, he saw the flashlight beams through the slats. They were getting close to the cabin. Might want to ask questions. Irritated, he slipped out back, then climbed into the crawl space beneath the house. They'd never look here.

It was dark, hot as hell and filled with spiderwebs. Black widows and brown recluses were the most dangerous.

Snakes were common in the area, and he held his breath, listening for the hiss of a rattler. He'd be ready to jump out of hiding if he felt the slimy, scaly creatures slithering across his body.

He closed his eyes and listened but a rancid odor swirled in the air. An odor that reminded him of death.

A smile tugged at his mouth.

Inflicting pain was an aphrodisiac. He kept a running video in his mind of each victim's screams. Although lately he'd grown bored. With his methods. With his choices. They were all starting to bleed together.

He needed to expand his thinking.

Murder, after all, was just a game. After ten years of playing, he needed to up the ante.

THIRTEEN

Gina, Ken and Cade started running and shouting with relief, and Ellie realized Betsy had been found. Her heart warmed as the family engulfed the child in hugs and kisses.

Thank God. Not every case wound up with a happy ending.

"Betsy, sweetheart, we were so scared," Gina cried.

"Honey, are you okay?" Ken pulled back to examine his daughter. "Are you hurt anywhere?"

"My foot hurts." She stroked the kitten's head. "I found Kitty. Can we keep him?"

Gina rubbed the animal's back, hesitating for only a second. "Sure, sweetie. I'm just glad you're okay."

Relief flooded Cade's face, although he kept looking up the hill at something.

"We're glad you're safe," Ellie said as she smiled at the child. "What happened?"

"I chased Kitty then I got losted and I found a shed and went inside and fell." Betsy sucked back tears. "Then that girl came and she gotted me out of the shed. And we saw a man in black in the woods and she got scared and started running."

The couple looked puzzled and Ellie waited; the little girl was more likely to tell her mother what happened than a detective.

"What girl?" Gina asked softly.

"The girl," Betsy said as if they should know. "She gots a hammer and banged up the floor where I fell and pulled me out and gave me a piggyback ride."

Gina hugged Betsy again. "Was she alone?"

"Uh-huh. Her name's Lorna Bea," Betsy said, then looked around. "Where'd she go?"

Cade pointed to the neighboring cabin. "I saw a girl running up there."

The couple exchanged a look and the mother tweaked Betsy's ponytail. "Next time, don't run off chasing an animal without us."

The couple thanked Ellie and she stepped aside to call Cord and an ambulance. But Ellie still had an uneasy feeling.

Had the man in the woods been a hiker or... was he up to no good?

FOURTEEN

THE LADY IN BLUE BRIDGE

Cord and the team had searched a two-mile radius when he spotted what he thought might be a car in the lake. With the water at an all-time low due to the drought, he remembered the stories about bodies buried below the surface. Marked graves had been moved during the damming and creation of the lake, yet many unmarked graves had not been relocated.

He aimed his flashlight across the lake's surface, hiking closer and climbing over a fallen tree for a closer look. His phone dinged on his hip and he glanced at the number.

Ellie. He swatted flies away as he quickly connected.

"She's been found, Cord," Ellie said. "She's okay."

"Good news. What happened?"

He gripped his phone as he looked up at the legendary bridge above, half expecting to see the spirit of a woman in a blue dress wandering aimlessly across it.

"She was chasing a kitten," Ellie said. "According to Betsy, the neighbor's daughter rescued her, but there was a man in black in the woods that scared her. Be on the alert for him."

"Understood." He reached the clearing at the edge of the

lake, directly in front of what he'd seen, and realized it was the rear bumper of a car.

"Cord?"

He cleared his throat. "El, we have a problem."

"What's wrong?"

"A car is submerged in the lake about two miles from where you are. Could have gone off the Lady in Blue bridge. Can't tell how long it's been here until I get a closer look. I'll dive in and see if anyone's inside."

"I'll be there ASAP."

Cord updated the search teams and requested his coworker Milo join him. He yanked off his T-shirt, belt and boots, then stuck his phone inside his shoes and set them beneath a tree. Gripping his flashlight, he dove into the lake. The water felt slimy and hot. Debris, mud and weeds sucked at him. Algae floated around him and fish nibbled at him.

He guessed the distance to the vehicle to be three-quarters of a mile. At its high, the lake was one-hundred-and-fifty-six feet deep and stretched over thirty-seven acres. If not for the drought, the car would have been completely submerged.

Mosquitos buzzed, the sound of frogs croaking blending with the soft lapping of the water as he pushed through. As he neared the vehicle, he noted mud, leaves and rust covering the bumper. This car had been here a while.

He took a deep breath, dove deeper and swam toward the driver's side. Squinting through the fog, he peered inside the car and silently cursed.

A skeletal body was inside.

FIFTEEN

WIDOW LAKE

Lorna Bea watched her father head to the house. She had to hurry. Get inside.

She jumped to reach the lowest tree branch, then swung her body to gain enough momentum to thrust herself up to the next one. The bark scraped her leg, but she ignored the sting.

Standing on tiptoe, she strained to reach the next limb and caught hold. Like a monkey, she propelled herself from one to the next until she landed on the branch outside her window. By then she was out of breath and sweating like a pig, so she straddled the widest part and leaned against the massive tree trunk to catch her breath.

A siren wailed in the distance. An ambulance pulled up. Two medics got out, walking over to the little girl and her parents.

Then she spotted the boy—he had to be Betsy's brother—staring up the hill as if he was looking for her. She ducked behind the leafy part of the tree branch so he couldn't see her.

SIXTEEN

After notifying all the parties that Betsy had been found, Ellie drove to the bridge.

It was a well-known landmark and only two miles away. She parked at the overhang, then hiked down the hill.

Cord stood on the bank, dripping wet and soaked in grime.

"You okay?" she asked.

He gave a quick nod and aimed his flashlight at the rear bumper of the car.

"There's a body inside, driver's seat," Cord said. "There are no fresh tire marks down here. Looks like it's been there a while."

Ellie glanced back up at the overhang. "Must have gone off up there and nose-dived in. I'll call the ME and a team to pull it out." Then they could find out who was inside.

SEVENTEEN

WIDOW PEAK COLLEGE

Professor Roland Pockley sat beneath the live oak in the quadrangle at Widow Peak College, his reward for finishing his paper on medicolegal forensic anthropology, which would be in print next month. He was not only a professor of zoology but had been published in numerous professional journals, and police had consulted him as an expert in three cases over the last five years.

The sound of cars and voices filled the evening air, coeds pulling up to unload suitcases as they moved into the dorms. They'd been doing so all day.

Each year he watched the ritual between parents and children, as the new flock arrived, eager for their foray into their new adventure.

Some were teary as they said goodbye to their mamas and daddies while others obviously couldn't wait to escape their parents' watchful eyes. Starved for independence, they were excited to dive into the party scene, shredding their mother's apron strings as they indulged in alcohol, drugs and sex.

He had been one of them once. Had attended this same school. Had imagined finding a different life for himself, one where his classmates didn't call him names like Pockface and the girls didn't laugh at his coke-bottle glasses or run and scream when they realized he was infatuated with insects and kept a collection of live ones in his bedroom.

College had disappointed at first. A place of fraternities and sororities. A place he didn't belong.

Until he'd enrolled in Dr. Dansen's criminology class on true crime. One entire semester was focused on the most famous serial killers in history.

Ted Bundy, Daumer, Dennis Radar the BTK, Ed Gein who inspired Leatherface in *The Texas Chain Saw Massacre*, Harold Shipman AKA Dr. Death, Edmund Kemper the Coed Killer, Gary Ridgway the Green River Killer... The list went on and on. Each with their own MO, depravities, needs and perverted desires.

Each famous.

He smiled at what he'd learned in that class then glanced at a cute brunette who passed by. She rolled her eyes at him then dashed to a blond who embraced her into a hug. The two of them whispered, then threw another eye roll his way and started giggling.

He curled his hands into fists, digging his nails into his palms. She might be laughing now. Might be innocent.

But now she'd come to Widow Lake, she wouldn't be laughing for long. And she certainly wouldn't be innocent.

EIGHTEEN

WIDOW LAKE

Lorna Bea heard her father's voice and crawled through the window into the bedroom. Quickly, to cover for being gone, she found her bag of books and stacked them on the bookshelf. The room was small and had a little dresser and plain white comforter. She'd dreamed of choosing her own bedding and paint for her room one day. And they'd stay in it like a real home.

She ran her fingers lovingly over the spine of her favorite mystery book, daydreaming. Maybe she'd take it down by the water under a shade tree and read it again this summer. Or maybe she'd be too busy exploring!

"You've always got your nose buried in a book," her dad grumbled constantly.

So? Moving around so much made it hard to make friends. Besides, her daddy didn't like her to get too close to people 'cause they asked questions. He didn't have friends either but didn't seem to mind. Said people were too nosy and got all up in your business.

The door was open but he rapped on it anyway. "Hey, girl. I got pizza for dinner."

"Sounds good, Dad. I'm starving."

She left her books on the floor, then followed him down the steps. The wood creaked, the air conditioner whirring. The living room and kitchen were one big room with a large round wood table separating them. The walls were dark paneling and a wild boar's head hung in the living room over the stone fireplace. Creepy.

Nana's messy gray hair was falling from her bun where she'd slept in the chair. She was setting out paper plates, and cups of water were already on the pine table. A knock sounded at the door and her father went very still, his big shoulders stiffening. Lorna Bea's stomach did a flip flop at the sudden tapping of her father's fingers along his leg. It was what he did when he didn't like something or was on the verge of losing his temper.

Nana wrinkled her nose. "Wonder who that is."

"I'll see. You two stay here."

Lorna Bea inched close to Nana who patted her shoulder while her father tugged at his Braves cap then opened the door. Betsy's mama and daddy stood on the other side. Betsy and her brother hovered beside them. Betsy, with her big green eyes, looked past them at the boar's head with fear, as if she thought it might come alive any second and eat her.

Lorna Bea knew how she felt. She'd hated the thing at first sight. Had wondered if someone who'd stayed in the cabin had shot it. Couldn't imagine someone killing an innocent animal just for fun.

"We're the Hammersteins," the man said. "This is our little girl Betsy and boy Cade."

"Dwight Jones," Lorna Bea's father said stiffly.

"Is your daughter here?" the mother asked.

Betsy piped up. "Her name's Lorna Bea."

Her father's fingers drummed faster. "What do you want with her?"

Lorna's stomach flip flopped again. She wanted to play with

the kids next door. Cade was about her age and she'd always
wanted a little sister.

But her dad would probably scare them off like he did other
kids she'd met. And if they told him what she'd done, she'd be in
trouble.

"Actually, we wanted to thank her," Betsy's mama said.
"Betsy wandered off earlier and your daughter found her and
brought her back."

"Is that so?" her father asked.

"Yeah, I felled in the shed and she got me out and gave me a
piggyback ride," Betsy said.

"We had search teams out looking," Betsy's father said. "We
owe her a big thanks."

Lorna Bea wanted to run over and say hey, but Nana kept
her arm tightly around Lorna Bea's shoulders like she did when
she meant business.

Her father's jaw hardened as he looked at her. "Lorna Bea,
these people want to thank you."

Nana gave her an encouraging little push and Lorna Bea
walked over, although judging from her father's look she knew
not to say too much.

"We are so grateful to you, sweetie," the woman said, with
tears in her eyes. "Thank you so much for rescuing Betsy."

"Yes, thank you," the father said. "We'd like to do something
to repay you."

Lorna Bea smiled up at them, especially the mother. She
had a sweet-sounding voice and kind eyes and made her wonder
what it would be like to have a mother who hugged her like
Betsy's mama had hugged Betsy when they'd played outside
earlier.

"My daughter doesn't need payment," Lorna Bea's daddy
said. "But thank you for offering."

The couple stood there for another minute as if waiting to
be invited inside. The clock ticked in the background. Lorna

Bea watched as one minute passed, then another. The room's air conditioner whirred noisily.

But her daddy said nothing.

"Can she come over and play with us?" Betsy finally asked.

Her father folded his jittery fingers into his fists. "Not now, honey. We're about to have dinner. But thanks for stopping by." Then he closed the door in their faces.

Lorna Bea bit down her lip as her father snatched her arm and yanked her toward the table. "I told you to stay inside," he said sharply.

"But, Daddy, I saw people looking for Betsy, then I spotted her. She was lost," Lorna Bea said, her voice almost as tiny as Betsy's now. "It was getting dark and I couldn't just leave her out there. Could I?"

Especially with that strange man in black in the woods. Although, she didn't dare mention him or her father would go ape-crazy.

An awkward second rattled between them. An odd look flashed in his eyes, then he heaved a breath. "No, I guess you couldn't. But you are not to go to their house, do you hear me?"

Lorna Bea nodded and blinked back tears. She wanted a friend so bad she almost let loose and screamed at him, asking why she couldn't go next door and play with them like normal kids did.

But Nana looked worried and gave a tiny shake of her head in a warning, so she clamped her teeth over her lip and said nothing.

NINETEEN

Derrick had had a killer of a day. He'd gotten nothing out of Radcliff.

It seemed the Southside Slasher preferred to go down in history in a blaze of glory, as he called it, because he'd outsmarted the cops.

But Derrick wasn't throwing in the towel yet. The tearful pleas of the victims in his head made him determined to get them home to their families.

As he neared Crooked Creek, he pressed the number for Dr. Leon Morehead, a forensic psychiatrist the FBI had consulted before. Morehead's receptionist answered then patched him through.

"This is Special Agent Derrick Fox with the FBI. We need your assistance on a case."

"Which one is that?" Dr. Morehead asked.

"Dominique Radcliff's execution is set for three weeks. We need you to persuade him to admit he killed two others and show us where he disposed of them."

Dr. Morehead cleared his throat. "I thought police found all of his victims."

"They found three, but there are at least two more who disappeared that may be connected. Radcliff is denying that he killed them. But those families want closure."

"I understand. I'll set it up ASAP and send you my report."

"Thank you, Doctor."

Derrick sped up, eager to see Ellie. Farmland passed by. Heat had dried the fields and pastures, his tires kicking up dust as he maneuvered a graveled strip where construction had torn up the asphalt.

The mountains with their natural beauty were an escape from the city, although they had their own share of dangers and crime. Still, he had family in Atlanta. His mother. And now his godchildren, nine-year-old Evan and Evan's little sister Maddie. He'd served in the military with their father Rick, who'd committed suicide after the guilt of a mission gone awry had overwhelmed him. Derrick understood all about guilt. He'd lived with it all his life.

He rubbed the back of his neck. In his will, Rick had asked Derrick to watch over the kids, although his widow Lindsey harbored animosity toward Derrick, making the task more difficult.

At least today, he'd played ball with Evan and Maddie had laughed when he pushed her in the swing on the playground at the park. Baby steps, he reminded himself. He wasn't their father and couldn't replace him.

Being around Rick's family made him feel even more inept. He didn't know how to be a father figure to those kids but he'd damn well try.

His phone rang, Ellie's ring tone. His pulse quickened the way it always did at the thought of seeing her again. Tough and tenacious, the damn woman drove him crazy, both with want and fear. He kept telling himself not to get too attached to her. He'd lost loved ones before and he wasn't sure the pain was worth it. Seeing Rick's wife's grief was a perfect reminder of that.

Ellie was a go-getter and a hothead. She'd literally run into a snake pit to save someone else with no regard to her own life. It was bound to catch up with her sometime.

Could he deal with it if or when it did?

Still, they were working a task force the governor had asked him to spearhead, to combat the ever-growing number of crimes in the Appalachian Mountains, so he connected.

"Derrick, are you back in Crooked Creek?"

"Almost. Why? Something going on?"

"We found a body in a car in Widow Lake. We're waiting on the medical examiner to get here before we remove it. Looks like it's been there a while. There was a car seat inside but no child," Ellie said. "Divers are searching the surrounding area in case a child was in the car and somehow got out."

Considering the body had been there a while, if the child had gotten out and was alone, they were probably looking for a body. "Was the door shut?" Derrick asked.

"Yes, Cord pried it open."

"If it was submerged, and the door still closed, the child couldn't have gotten out on his or her own. The water pressure would have sealed it."

"True. Which means if a child was inside, the only way he or she could have escaped was if someone helped him, perhaps before the car went in the water."

"That's possible, I guess," Derrick said.

Ellie's voice thickened. "Which means the child might not have been in the car or if so, was either rescued or... possibly taken."

TWENTY

THE LADY IN BLUE BRIDGE

After the team had pulled the vehicle from the lake, Ellie snapped pictures of the debris-coated car and the human remains inside before the medical examiner arrived. Divers were searching the lake and an investigative crime team was scouring for forensics although night would hinder that.

Dr. Laney Whitefeather, the ME, and Derrick arrived at the same time. Laney's long auburn braid hung over one shoulder, her dark eyes immediately going to the car, an old VW. At one time it must have been a nice shade of green but now what was visible beneath the layers of mud, leaves and sticks was rusted, the paint chipped and faded to a dull pea color.

Derrick looked tired, his brown hair ruffled as if he'd run his hands through it a dozen times. He was lacking a suit today but wore a black T-shirt that stretched across his muscular chest. Ellie wondered how his visit with his godchildren had gone this time, but that conversation had to wait.

Derrick whistled when he saw the state of the vehicle. "You're right. It's been here a long time."

"What do we have?" Dr. Whitefeather asked.

"Not sure yet," Ellie said. "Body's decomposed."

Laney lifted her medical kit. "Let's open the door so I can take a closer look."

Cord gave a nod. "Stand back. Water'll gush out when we do."

She, Laney and Derrick stepped onto rocks to the right, and Cord used a crowbar to open the car door which was rusted shut. A huge surge of muddy water poured out, debris floating with it. She waited until most of it drained then stepped closer to look inside. Derrick walked around to the rear where the car seat was and looked inside.

Laney shined a light across the remains which had decayed to the point of fossilizing. Brittle slivers of bones were scattered on the seat and floor, now floating in the slush.

"Water and temperature affect decomp," Laney said. "Hot water speeds up the process but cold water slows it down, so we'll run tests to determine estimated time and date of death. Closed doors help protect the body from fish and underwater creatures, although smaller ones could have seeped inside," Laney said.

"Do you think the impact of the crash caused the death?" Ellie asked.

"Won't know for sure until I get the body on my autopsy table." The ME examined the back of the skull with narrowed eyes, then slowly lifted the head and studied the front. "Skull looks fractured. Could have been the accident or blunt force trauma."

Ellie raised a brow. "As in he might have been dead before going into the water?"

"It's possible but I can't really say yet. Too many variables."

With gloved hands, Ellie opened the passenger door, checking the interior hoping to find a wallet. Nothing. She looked inside the dash next. More water spilled out along with something that looked like it might have been paper once. No driver's license there either.

"See a wallet beneath the body or seat on that side?" Ellie asked.

Laney took a minute to search, then shook her head.

"Odd," Ellie said beneath her breath. "Derrick?"

"Nothing back here either." He leaned over, checking the floor. "Wait, there's a child's book. Pages are disintegrated but the cover's intact."

"Maybe we'll get prints from it," Ellie said.

"Not likely," Derrick muttered. "It's probably been in the water too long."

Ellie nodded. "Then let's get the remains to the morgue so Laney can work her magic. We need an ID."

"I'll do my best," Laney said.

"I'll run the license plate of the car and see who owned it," Derrick said. "That'll give us a place to start."

TWENTY-ONE
ATLANTA

Forensic psychiatrist Dr. Leon Morehead smiled at the thought of interviewing the Southside Slasher.

Radcliff had owned up to three kills. But he wasn't spilling his guts on two others that the FBI wanted to connect him to.

His office door opened and his receptionist showed Odessa Muldane inside. He placed his mini recorder on the desk in his office and studied her. Although it was late in the day for an appointment, he'd made an exception. His coworker had recently retired and passed on his caseload, stating that this one was interesting.

Like most patients on their first visit, she was twitchy. The Exit sign was the first thing patients looked for when they sat down.

Although this was not the first time he'd met her, it was her first visit as his patient. The other time, in passing years ago at Widow Peak College... well, he didn't know if she even remembered it.

Odd that she would be nervous around him when she spent her life writing love letters to serial killers. He wondered if she had some kind of secret agenda in coming here today. He also wondered if she'd driven his colleague into an early retirement.

He adopted his calming, professional monotone to soothe her nerves, lulling her into pouring out her twisted heart. Oh, how he was fascinated by tortured souls, the challenge of unraveling their secrets and the innerworkings of their demented minds.

Underneath the surface, he understood her fascination.

"Odessa," he said, "tell me what's on your mind today."

She examined her nails, which were chewed down to the nubs.

"I... think Dom's seeing another woman."

He simply waited, knowing his silence would open the floodgates of her obvious distress until it poured out.

"I mean, he can't be since he has limited visitation at Hayes Prison. But I think someone else is writing to him, too."

He simply nodded. According to his former colleague's notes, Odessa suffered from hybristophilia, a condition where sexual arousal was linked to people who'd committed extraordinary crimes. An interesting paraphilia, which astounded some. Adventure-seekers felt a similar adrenaline when they skydived out of a plane or skied down a mountain. Her rush came from living vicariously through the stories of a man's power and the way he fed on inflicting pain.

"Serial killers often do have followers," he said. "But there's nothing you can do to stop him from receiving mail." Or other visitors, for that matter.

A sinister look streaked her eyes. "But he said he loved me. That I was special."

"You are special to him," he said. "He enjoys the attention you give him." He probably had dozens or more other women he fed the same line.

Her ruby-red lips formed a pout. "Maybe."

"What is it about this man that attracts you?" he asked, although he already knew the answer.

She closed her eyes, her breasts rising and falling as she appeared to be lost in her fantasy. "It was love at first sight. The moment I saw his picture in the news I had to get to know him."

Radcliff would also kill her if given the chance.

Leaning forward, she placed her hand over his. She thought she could use her sexuality to convince him to do whatever she had planned. Others had tried, too.

"Please, Doctor. All I need are some conjugal visits," she said. "If you write a letter of recommendation for me, say I won't try and sneak a weapon or contraband in again, maybe the warden would listen."

Leon eased his hand from beneath hers. "*Are* you going to try something again?"

Her lips curled into a wicked smile. "Of course not. All I want is to give my man some love. Doesn't he deserve that?"

"Everyone deserves love," he said matter-of-factly. "Although you know Dominique—"

"Dom," she interrupted. "He likes it when I call him Dom."

Leon gave an understanding nod. "Radcliff literally butchered several women, hacked off their hair and painted their lips with their own blood."

"I know. But he has another side to him." A dazed look lit her eyes. "When I'm with him, he's not like that. He's loving and tender. And there's the rush of danger. The closeness to death makes me feel alive."

He could warn her that Radcliff was using her and would discard her when she served no purpose anymore. But he'd be wasting his time.

She craved that rush.

He glanced at the clock on the wall.

The minutes were ticking away.

His phone signaled a text and he took a quick glance.

Widow Lake. The reunion.

He sucked in a breath.
He had to get on the road.
His pulse jumped at the thought.

TWENTY-TWO

SMOKY JOE'S

Beverly Hooper slipped into a booth at Smoky Joe's, where she and her friends had once gathered in college to party. The clock on the wall was layered with dust and the floor littered with peanut shells where everyone tossed them.

The place hadn't changed at all, as if it was lost in a time warp. Same cheap brown vinyl stools and benches, same tables with names of lovers etched into the wood by the students, same smells of burgers, greasy fries and onion rings.

Same jukebox with the familiar country tunes they used to listen to, with the exception of rap and rock that had been added to the menu.

A string of coeds' bras dangled from the ceiling with dollar bills taped to the wall, dollars earned by the girls shedding their underwear during a drunken dare.

Just like back then, kids hung in corners chugging beer, playing darts and making out in the hallway that led to the rear exit. Only now they'd added an area for ax throwing.

She rolled her eyes. Just the kind of recreation drunk kids needed.

Some of the creepy guys used to congregate here, too. One

had scars and tats all over his arms. Another claimed he wanted to be a director and convinced students to act out murder scenes while he filmed them.

A cold chill engulfed her. She wondered if they'd show up for the reunion.

The floor creaked as students piled onto the dance floor. The sea of people blurred her vision, but suddenly Janie appeared, the past decade falling away as if it was just yesterday. Although Janie had wanted to be a famous designer, she'd married a tax accountant, had climbed the social ladder and now had two kids. Still, she constantly complained about her boring life and craved excitement to break the doldrums.

"Did you hear they found a body in the lake?" Beverly said as Janie scooted into the booth. "I wonder how long it's been there."

Janie worried her bottom lip with her teeth, her eyes darting around. "I've been thinking about that. About Amy suddenly being gone back then."

They sat in silence for a minute, both reliving that night. There were things they hadn't told the police. Things that might have helped them find her.

TWENTY-THREE

He tugged his ball cap lower over his forehead and adjusted his dark glasses to shield his face as he watched from the corner of the bar. The cap would help him fit in. The glasses would offer a disguise. Not that anyone ever really looked at him or would recognize him if they did. He was *that* kind of guy.

He'd known this place well back in the day. It was where the pretty girls hung out. The sorority chicks and frat boys who partied like there was no tomorrow. Ones whose parents bought their admittance into schools instead of forcing their kids to earn it like he'd had to do.

Resentment bled through him.

He hadn't fit in. He'd thought no one was like him. But then he'd met the others and they'd created their own frat. Laughter burst inside him—their group wasn't recognized by the college, but it bore its own set of rules.

The brothers would be here soon. But tonight, he wanted to watch the crowd. He'd known some of the snots would show up. He recognized Beverly and Janie. They'd snubbed him like he was a pesty ant that needed stomping on.

They'd also reported Amy Dean missing which had triggered police to comb the campus and forced the Brotherhood to stay under the radar.

After that night, he'd had to find another hunting ground so he'd spread his wings.

Beverly stood, checking her phone then scanning the bar with a jittery look. Janie lurched up and the two of them wove through the crowd, eying everyone they passed as if they sensed something bad was going to happen this reunion.

He tried to recall which one of them had been the nastiest to him. He curled his hands into fists. Didn't matter. He'd make them both suffer.

TWENTY-FOUR

BUZZARD TRAIL

Odessa Muldane flipped on the news and poured herself a stiff whiskey.

"Angelica Gomez coming to you from Widow Lake where a body has just been found in a car submerged in the lake. Police have transported the vehicle and remains to the morgue for an autopsy and identification." Angelica angled her mic toward a female detective, Ellie Reeves, who Odessa had been following for nearly two years. She was known to track down the worst of the worst.

She'd have her hands full with this case. Laughter bubbled in Odessa's throat at the thought.

"At this point, all we know is that a car was submerged in the lake and appears to have been here for some time," Detective Reeves said. "We are treating the area as a crime scene and will be investigating the situation further. If anyone has any information regarding the unidentified remains in the vehicle, please call the local police. We'll update you as more information becomes available."

The police number flashed on the screen, then the reporter

continued, "All this at the beginning of the tenth-year reunion of the graduating class of 2013 at Widow Peak College."

Odessa flipped off the television, which was triggering memories of her senior year.

Nervous energy thrummed through her and she carried her drink down the steps to the basement of the Victorian house she'd inherited from her dead aunt. She kept a private office tucked behind a locked door. Hand shaking, she opened the door and went inside. Shelves housing her collections, all items she'd talked her lovers into sending her, lined the far wall. Trinkets from their victims. Her very own prizes so she could relive the thrill of their kills.

Souvenirs that forever linked them.

A locked cabinet held the photographs she'd taken during her senior year. She studied one pic of her and the brothers with a twinge of nostalgia for days gone by.

It had been initiation night and she'd wanted to be among them so badly, she would have done anything they said.

She *had* done everything they'd said.

Now she followed the notorious and most violent killers across the States, writing them letters and listening to tales of their heinous kills.

Dominique, AKA the Southside Slasher, was her current favorite. She sat down at her writing desk with stationery and put pen to paper.

Dearest Darling,

My heart is with you every minute. I talked to Dr. Morehead today and I'm hoping he'll write me a recommendation so I can visit.

Meanwhile, I'm headed to the college reunion at Widow Lake.

Hopefully the others will be there. I can't wait to see if they continued their obsessions.

TWENTY-FIVE

WIDOW LAKE

DAY 2

Lorna Bea woke to the sun painting rays of light across the wooden floor. The air conditioner whined like an old man snoring, but even it couldn't keep up with the heat.

She ran to the window and looked outside with a smile. Yesterday had been the most interesting day she'd ever had. She liked Widow Lake. Maybe she could convince her father to stay here for a while. Maybe forever.

The police had found a dead body. She'd heard Nana talking to her daddy about it in hushed voices last night when she'd hovered at the door after her daddy had sent her to bed. She wondered who it was and how it had gotten there.

This morning the lake was quiet and still, and she spotted a canoe moving steadily across the water. Curious, she opened the window and climbed onto the tree branch to watch.

Betsy and her mother were singing as they picked wildflowers by the lake. The little kitty ran and leaped through the blades of grass. Looking closer, she realized it was Cade and his father in the canoe.

Her heart raced and she hurriedly threw on clothes and ran down the stairs.

Nana was stirring oatmeal on the stove. Dried mud dotted the floor in a path from the front door to the sliders. Through the glass, she saw her father on the phone pacing outside, kicking dirt with the toe of his boot.

He'd mentioned swimming on the drive here. Today would be a perfect day for that!

"Breakfast will be ready in a sec," Nana said.

Lorna Bea brushed past her with an "okay" and burst through the screened door.

Her father was talking in a low voice, "Yes, it's the exact one he used—"

Lorna Bea was so excited she couldn't help herself. "Daddy, can we go swimming today? Or rent a canoe like Cade and his father?"

He pivoted, covering the phone with his hand as his eyes pinned her with an angry look. "No, get back in the house. Now."

"But, Daddy—"

His jaw tightened, that vein pulsing in his neck the way it did when he was angry. He ended the call then stalked toward her. "I said go," he snarled. "And don't even think about coming back outside today."

TWENTY-SIX

CROOKED CREEK

Plagued by the sight of that empty car seat, Ellie tossed and turned all night. In her mind, she saw a small child somehow managing to escape, then being sucked down into the mud, the child's little body lying among the unmarked graves thought to be at the bottom of the lake.

She jerked awake, heart hammering, and pushed her tangled hair from her face. Bright morning sunlight poured through the room, shimmering off the wood floor in orange and yellow lines.

The child couldn't have been inside, she told herself. She'd just had a nightmare.

Rubbing at her bleary eyes, she sorted through her thoughts, searching for logical alternatives. Judging from the car seat, the child could have been anywhere from age one to four. Hopefully the child had not been in the car when it went over. The driver could have stolen the vehicle.

That was the best-case scenario. But a hazard of the job triggered the dark thoughts.

If the child had been taken, had there been a missing child report?

She needed a time frame to know where to start searching.

Mind spinning with questions, she checked her phone for messages but had none. Antsy, she shoved the sheets aside then checked the weather on her phone.

Another scorcher today. High nineties. Humid. No chance of rain. Wind non-existent.

Perspiration trickled down the side of her face. Even with her air conditioner, it had been too damn hot last night to sleep under her comforter. She threw her legs over the side of the bed, padded to the bathroom and turned on the shower water.

Stripping her pajamas, she climbed inside and scrubbed her body. Hopefully, today they'd learn the identity of the remains in the car.

At least you aren't dealing with another serial killer.

Drawing some measure of relief from that, she dried off and dressed, then swept her sandy blond hair into a ponytail and headed to the kitchen for coffee. Minutes later, a steaming pot of dark pecan roast coffee scented the kitchen. The delicious aroma was like a shot of adrenaline and instantly buzzed her back to life.

A text dinged on her phone.

Derrick: *Meet me at the station. Have information on the car.*

TWENTY-SEVEN

On the way to the station, Ellie stopped by the Corner Café which offered the best breakfast in town. The place was humming with the morning crowd, and the gossipy old biddies led by Maude Hazelnut, AKA Meddlin' Maude, who grated on Ellie's last nerve with her judgmental attitude. Carol Sue, the owner of the Beauty Barn, was second in line for the title of gossip queen. No telling what they were blathering on about now.

Families filled booths, the diner décor creating a homey feel. Lola had built a thriving business with her friendly smile, her delicious pastries, homemade buttermilk biscuits and Southern specials like chicken and waffles and blueberry pancakes. Lola's country ham and red-eyed gravy could beat any chef who wanted to take her on.

Lola and Cord had been an item for a while, but lately Ellie hadn't seen them together. At her friend's wedding in May, she'd expected to see them together but Lola had come with Bryce instead. And Deputy Shondra Eastwood had come with her girlfriend Julie.

A fleeting memory teased her mind, a moment during the

ceremony when she'd actually seen herself as a bride. Marriage was not in her plans so that was unsettling.

She and Derrick had developed a closeness over the last few cases and had crossed the line into a personal relationship. But the face in her dream was blurry. She had an odd feeling that it wasn't Derrick. Though she didn't know what that meant.

Coffee cups clanged and voices echoed around her, jarring her from her thoughts. Lola stood chatting with Sheriff Waters. Ellie slid onto a barstool beside Bryce. He stiffened as if she was invading his morning with her presence. They'd butted heads before but lately they'd been on more of an even keel, working together.

Lola crossed her arms. "Sausage and cheese biscuit?" Lola asked.

Ellie nodded. "Add a ham and cheese biscuit with a fried egg for Special Agent Fox. And two coffees to go."

"Be right up." Lola disappeared into the kitchen.

The sheriff angled his head toward Ellie. "Any word on the body you found at Widow Lake?"

"Not yet. Derrick and I are meeting at the station. He has something on the car."

Lola returned with Ellie's order, and she paid and stood to leave.

"Keep me posted," Bryce said.

Ellie nodded, then bypassed Maude and her brood on the way to the door.

"Did you hear about that body they found in the lake?" Maude said in a hushed voice.

"Was it an accident or a murder?" Carol Sue whispered.

"My God, I hope we don't have more crime around here," Edwina, the mayor's wife, mumbled.

"This town used to be safe." Maude shot a pointed look at Ellie. "Detective, should we be worried about our families again?"

Ellie didn't think so. But she'd been wrong before. She cleared her throat. "If I learn that families are in danger, I'll report that. For now, I think this is an old case." She hoped she wasn't mistaken this time. "Good day, ladies."

Maude's look of distrust made doubts creep in, but Ellie ignored it and hurried to the exit. The best way to keep the town safe was to do her job.

Outside it was so hot she could hardly breathe. The sun was already beating down as if the sky was on fire, flowers literally wilting in front of her eyes.

She phoned Laney on the way to the police station. "Any info on the remains?"

Dr. Whitefeather cleared her throat. "No ID yet. But I have determined the remains belong to a man, early twenties at the time of death." Laney hesitated. "As for cause of death, I found signs of blunt force trauma that suggests he may have been struck on the head from behind."

Not a simple accident, then, Ellie thought. She was dealing with a murder.

Five minutes later, Ellie parked at her office. She spotted Deputy Shondra Eastwood giving her girlfriend Julie a big hug, then Julie drove off with a wave.

"You look happy," Ellie said as Shondra walked toward her.

Shondra blushed. "I feel like I should pinch myself."

"Just enjoy it," Ellie said, grateful Shondra had found someone special.

"Got another call from the Rogers woman early this morning," Shondra said, her smile fading.

"Did that bastard hurt those dogs?" Ellie asked as they walked up to the station entrance.

"He threatened to hit her. She sent him packing. Told him she'd rather sleep with the dogs than him."

"Good for her," Ellie said with a smile. "Do you think he'll stay away?"

"He will if he knows what's good for him," Shondra said. "I warned him if he touched her or those dogs again, I'd show him what a fist in the face felt like."

Ellie laughed softly. She loved Shondra's spunk.

The two of them parted as they entered, and she found

Derrick hovering over his laptop at the table in the corner of her office. She dropped the food and coffee on the table.

"I talked to Laney on the way over," Ellie said. "No ID yet, but the remains in the car are male and injuries are consistent with foul play."

Derrick looked up, eyes widening in surprise. "Interesting. The car was registered to a female, not a male." He opened the wrapper on his sandwich and thanked her.

"What do you know about her?" Ellie asked as she bit into her own breakfast.

"Name's Amy Dean," Derrick said. "Twenty-two years old when she disappeared. Light-brown hair, hazel eyes, attended Widow Peak College. Last seen ten years ago."

"Ten years," Ellie murmured.

"Yeah. She was reported missing. Police investigated but never found her." He wiped his mouth with a napkin. "No information on her since. But I'll dig deeper in case there's a paper trail I haven't found."

An image of the empty car seat flashed behind Ellie's eyes. "Did she have a child?"

Derrick looked back at his computer. "A two-year-old little girl named Paisley."

Ellie's breath stalled. "Where's the little girl now?"

"No information on her." He paused, jaw tightening. "And Amy Dean was never found."

Ellie rocked back in her chair. "So whether the dead man in the car is related to Amy and the child, we don't know. But it's possible Amy and her daughter disappeared the same night he died." That gave her a general time frame to begin with. "If she ran with the child, she might have been afraid of something and gone into hiding."

"Or she had something to do with the accident," Derrick said.

Ellie wadded up her sandwich wrapper. "I say we go to

Widow Lake and talk to the officer who investigated her disappearance."

First, she sent Cord a text:

Owner of the car in the lake was a woman named Amy Dean. She and her two-year-old little girl disappeared ten years ago.

Have search teams look for their bodies or a grave near the bridge where the car was found.

TWENTY-NINE

WIDOW LAKE

A feeling of trepidation plagued Cord, just as it had when he was a kid and knew bad things were about to happen. And now Ellie's text.

What if a child *had* been in the car before the crash? What if the child was taken... or worse? Murdered and thrown into the lake. Or buried somewhere on the trail.

He hated that his mind jumped to the worst, but it was a product of his past. Ellie must be thinking along similar lines or she wouldn't have requested he look for graves.

He texted his coworker Milo and explained their task. Milo agreed to meet him so Cord got on the road. A few minutes later, he met Milo and another SAR team member and they fanned out in different directions.

Heat blazed down, parching the weeds and leaves and turning the once-green grass into a dull brown that crackled as he plowed through the trees and bushes. He kept an eye out for snakes and spiders, remembering all the times he'd slept on the ground when he was a teen and had encountered the deadly creatures.

He searched the wooded area near the cabins, then veered

toward the shed where Betsy had been found. The dilapidated building was rotting, covered in moss and lichen, and had been abandoned for years. Normally, water would probably reach just below the rotting wooden dock but now it was so low you could practically see the muddy ground beneath.

Brush had been pushed aside and smashed. Footprints marred the soil near the opening of the shed. Footprints that would have been too large for the twelve-year-old girl who'd found Betsy.

Footprints that looked as if they were made by a man's boot.

Possibly from the search teams who'd been hunting for Betsy. Or maybe the crime team looking for forensics after they'd found the car in the lake.

He scratched his head. Although, his grid hadn't included the shed specifically so they might not have searched it, especially after Betsy was rescued.

Curious, he inched closer, shining his flashlight into the dark interior. The small structure smelled of rot, dampness and a fishy odor. Wet prints, recent ones, smeared the floor, indicating someone had been inside.

He crossed to the hole in the floor where Betsy had fallen. Dark stains that looked like blood—old blood—discolored the walls and floor.

Those stains could have been here for years, could have come from a hunter or fisherman or someone seeking shelter after being injured or lost on the trail. Even a homeless person, a recluse or... someone on the run.

The hair on the back of his neck stood on end.

He moved closer, studying the hole, and noticed dirt had been freshly turned, creating a deep hole.

He leaned over, peering closer.

A sharp sliver of something was protruding through the loose soil. A sliver that looked like bone.

THIRTY

WIDOW LAKE

The stifling August heat roused his thirst for blood.

He hadn't slept last night because the craving almost over-powered him. He'd watched the videos of the first four kills, the ones that had started his journey from the madness of depriving his needs into the euphoria of finally taking a life.

The time in between kills was a struggle. He took it one day at a time, fighting the urges, ignoring the opportunities...

It was important to time the kills just right. Too close together and too many victims would draw attention. Yet it was attention he craved, like Daumer and Bundy and the Boston Strangler had garnered. He wondered what they would call him.

But taking a victim today would be risky. Especially since those cops had been all over Widow Lake the night before, scouring the woods and diving into the water in search of that stupid little girl.

The older one's face taunted him. Something about her drew him.

But the woods were crawling again this morning. Inter-fering with his fun.

If they got in the way too much, he'd have to do something about that.

The old crowd was starting to roll in for the reunion, too. Girls who'd looked at him like he was a piece of gum on their shoe.

With so many returning, he had a whole pool of women to pick from.

THIRTY-ONE

WIDOW LAKE

The window was Lorna Bea's favorite thing about her room at the cabin. She could see the mountains and trees and lake and watch the birds flit from one tree to another. It was almost like being outside.

She'd tried to read but she couldn't keep her mind on the story. Books were fun, but now there was a real mystery here at Widow Lake!

Last night, she'd watched the little girl and her mother next door through the window. Betsy's mother sat beside her on the bed with a silver brush and combed through Betsy's hair. Although she couldn't hear them, she'd counted the strokes. A hundred.

Tears blurred her eyes. She wished she'd had a mommy to brush her hair.

Sniffling, she wiped her nose, blinking at the morning sun as she studied the woods. She'd stayed up half the night looking out the window and wondering what the police had found out there. From her vantage point in the tree outside, she'd watched workers drag an old muddy car from the lake.

She'd searched for the man in the black hoodie, too, but hadn't seen him again. Maybe he was just a hiker or jogger.

There were more people in the woods today, combing for something. Or someone.

She heard her father's footsteps pound the floor downstairs. Then the door slammed shut and his truck started up.

She bit her tongue to keep from shouting, *It's not fair!* Why did he go places all the time when she was locked inside? She waited until the truck kicked up dust as it disappeared down the road, then she tiptoed down the stairs.

Nana was scrubbing the pan where she'd made scrambled eggs for breakfast. "I'm going outside to play," she said as she rushed by.

Nana tskked. "No, girl. Your daddy said to stay inside."

She halted and gritted her teeth. "But why? The neighbor kids are out playing."

"Your father said it's dangerous and he's right. Last night they dragged a car from the lake. And there was a body inside."

Lorna Bea knew that. But she wanted details. "Who was it? What happened?"

"I don't know," Nana said with a yawn. "But your daddy will have my head on a platter if I let you go out."

Lorna Bea tapped her foot. She didn't want to get Nana in trouble. So, she slumped down in the chair and looked at the books on the shelf. She snagged the one about Widow Lake to take upstairs and thumbed through it as Nana finished cleaning the kitchen. When the dishes were done, Nana rubbed her temple with another yawn. Her naps were coming more and more often these days. And sometimes she didn't remember things.

"Lie down, Nana," Lorna Bea said. "I'll read for a while."

"Thanks, sugar," Nana said. "I'll just grab a cat nap."

Lorna Bea waited until Nana fell asleep in the rocker then tiptoed upstairs with the book. She tossed it on the bed, then threw open the bedroom window, climbed out onto the tree limb and studied the lake. Sunlight bounced off the pockets of moss and murky water. The air was so still, she smelled honey-suckle mingling with the cloying scent of dead flowers. Weeds drooped and birds foraged for food on the dry ground.

A steady stream of cars trailed toward the cabin rentals. She spotted Cade and Betsy outside playing at the edge of the woods by the water.

Quickly, she scrambled down the tree. Reaching the bottom limb, she swung herself down to the ground.

After a glance around, she jogged toward Betsy and Cade.

Betsy was chasing the kitten and Cade had binoculars, scan-ning the lake.

His curly brown hair was scattered all over his head. "Why was your daddy mad when we came over last night?" Cade asked, as soon as he saw her.

Lorna Bea bit her quivering lip. She didn't know how to answer something she didn't understand herself. Maybe it had been a mistake to come out here.

Betsy hummed as she chased the kitty. It ran toward the boat dock, and Cade called out, "Don't run off again, Betsy!"

She scooped up the furball and danced along the bank with the animal.

Cade's freckles bunched as he looked at Lorna Bea. "Is your dad always like that?"

Her cheeks burned. "He's just scared something bad will happen to me."

"Why does he think that?" He raked a stick across the dirt.

"I don't know. He's just always telling me to stay away from strangers."

Cade sighed. "Yeah, I guess I get it. My folks always warn us not to go too far and not to swim alone or get in the car with strangers."

Lorna Bea nodded, although she thought there was more to

her daddy. That he was upset about something. But she was too afraid to ask.

Lorna Bea sat down on the log beside him. "Nana said they found a body in the lake last night. Who was it? What happened?"

"I don't know," Cade said. "But Dad said he heard someone at the marina say they're looking for more bodies today."

THIRTY-TWO

As soon as Ellie saw Cord's name on her phone screen, she feared he'd discovered the little girl's body.

"Found something in the shed at Widow Lake," Cord said when she answered. "Looks like a bone, maybe a grave."

"Dammit," Ellie muttered. "Could belong to our missing woman or child."

"The dirt was recently turned. Might be more bones but I haven't disturbed it. I saw fresh prints outside and inside the shed, too."

"We'll be right there." She and Derrick hurried to her Jeep and got in. She started the engine, punched the accelerator, flipped on her siren and wove around traffic. Minutes later, she parked near the Hammersteins' rental cabin, then she and Derrick hiked to the shed. Dried weeds and brush swayed as they pushed through, the sun beating down onto the wilting greenery as they broke the clearing to the dock. The wood was weathered and broken with rotting boards, forcing them to watch their step.

Cord stood outside the building, a frown tightening the lines around his troubled eyes.

He pointed to the footprints as they approached, and Ellie and Derrick stopped to examine them.

"Definitely a male," Derrick said.

"Work boots, a man's," Ellie added, judging from the size. "Let's look inside and then see if we can track them."

They pulled on gloves and followed Cord, carefully dodging the streaks of mud inside. Ellie photographed the dark stains on the wall while Derrick examined the hole.

"You're right, McClain," Derrick said. "Looks like a possible grave."

Ellie's stomach knotted as she looked into the hole. Although it was scorching hot and bright outside, the shed had only a tiny window and with the trees shrouding it, the interior was dark. A cold clamminess hovered in the air, beads of perspiration dotting her neck and slipping down into her T-shirt.

"Looks deep enough and wide enough for a body." Ellie waved gnats away from her eyes. "The question is, who put it there? And who did the body belong to?"

"Let's see where those footprints outside lead," Derrick said.

Ellie pulled her phone. "I'll call a crime team."

She made the call then snapped pictures of the interior. Then Cord led the way outside, pointing out broken brush and trampled weeds where a person could have walked.

Peering closer, Ellie stooped down to examine a patch of briars. "There are fibers caught in the thorns. Looks like burlap."

Derrick pulled a hand down his chin. "You're right. Some of these prints look fresh. Our perp could have dug up the remains, put them in a sack and hauled them away last night."

Ellie glanced at the lake. "Then escaped via boat right under our noses."

THIRTY-THREE

A half hour later, Ellie rubbed the back of her neck as she watched the ERT sift through the dirt for more bones. So far, they'd found four fingers.

The photographer/videographer Dale Harvey was thirty-ish, thin with wiry brown hair, and was meticulously documenting each detail. Unlike some newbies, he seemed to be handling the gruesome job well. ERT was also searching the area, and Cord and Derrick tracked the boot prints they'd seen outside the shed.

"There are trowel marks," Ellie said, pointing out indentations in the soil. "Those are fresh, too."

"Someone was definitely digging around," Laney agreed. "Be careful as you rake away the dirt," she told the team. "We need to preserve whatever we find."

"How long would you estimate the bones have been here?" Ellie asked.

"Judging from the decomp level of those phalanges, I'd say for years, maybe a decade. Any remains we find may be fossilized."

"Which would fit with the timeline of Amy Dean's disappearance." Ellie worried her bottom lip with her teeth. "Did you find any clothing or a blanket indicating the body was wrapped up?" Ellie asked.

The head of the team, Sergeant Abraham Williams, shook his head. "So far, no. But we'll collect soil samples for analysis. Could be disintegrated fibers in there."

"If not, whoever buried the body callously dumped it," Ellie said. A blanket could have indicated the killer cared about the dead person, that the death could have been accidental. And that they were experiencing guilt or remorse.

Another tech stepped inside. "We found a button to a work shirt in the weeds out here and a trowel with fresh dirt on it in a briar patch."

Ellie considered that information, the proximity of the remains in the car and the fact that the owner of the car and her daughter had gone missing. "Culprit could have used it to dig up the bones," Ellie said. "What if this body is Amy Dean?"

Laney frowned. "You said she had a child?"

A tense second passed, then Ellie shuddered. "Dammit, both the mother and little girl could have been buried here in the shed."

THIRTY-FOUR

Derrick and Cord examined the footprints closest to the shed. "Looks like a man's boot," Cord said. "But they're muddy. With the drought, he may have come in from the lake or a marshy section where the soil was still damp. But if a body's been here for a while, why come back to it now?"

"Maybe he got spooked when cops were up here and decided to move the bones." Derrick glanced to the right at the flattened brush. It looked as if someone had plowed through them recently. "Those prints lead toward the lake."

Cord veered to the left. "There's more over here," he shouted to Derrick. "Looks like they come from the south and go toward the shed."

"Then he leaves the other way," Derrick said. He followed the trail of crushed weeds but the footprints became blurred, losing their shape. Several more feet and they stopped at the edge of the lake, disappearing.

"He went in the lake here," Derrick said. "Probably had a boat waiting." Derrick sighed. "Of course, this is all speculation. We need hard evidence."

Derrick photographed the footprints as they retraced their

way back to the shed. Ellie and Dr. Whitefeather stood in somber conversation.

"We followed the footprints to the lake," Derrick said. "Whoever was here left via boat. What did you find?"

Ellie's mouth thinned into a frown. "Bones of four fingers," she said grimly. "Forensics is collecting soil samples now to analyze for human decomp."

Cord shifted. "No evidence of a wheelbarrow or other device used to transport a body."

A heartbeat of silence passed, then Ellie made a sound of disgust. "If the body was severely decomposed, he could have dug up the remains and hauled them away in some kind of a sack or even a backpack."

And walked around the lake as if he was simply hiking on vacation.

THIRTY-FIVE

Dwight Jones lurked in the shadows of the thick oaks, the still water of the lake so eerie that he half expected bodies to rise to the surface just like his memories were.

It was a damn mistake to return to Widow Lake. He shouldn't have come, much less brought Lorna Bea. It was too dangerous.

Sweat rolled down the side of his face and off his chin, gnats swarming his eyes. Images of that night ten years ago shot through his mind, stirring his infatuation with death, and his shared obsession with the others. That obsession had made them blood brothers.

But that one night had changed everything for him. The things he'd done. The things he hadn't done. The panic and the decision that had come with it.

A crow soared overhead, perching on the branch above him, a sign of death and evil. There had been dozens of crows that night. Sometimes he woke up hearing their caw, their beaks pecking at the glass windowpanes to get in. Glass shattering. The black crows circling his bed as if they'd come for him.

He'd told so many lies over the years he didn't know if he even remembered the truth. Lies to his daughter. To his mother.

To himself.

Lies that kept him running. Lies Lorna Bea must never know about.

THIRTY-SIX

WIDOW PEAK POLICE STATION

A half dozen scenarios played through Ellie's mind, none of them good, as she parked at the police station nearest Widow Lake. She and Derrick had left the forensics team processing the shed and Cord searching in case there was more than one grave. She'd texted Laney and asked her to request medical and DNA records for Amy Dean to compare to the bones discovered at the shed.

Hopefully, Sergeant Benton, the officer in charge of investigating Amy's disappearance, could add insight.

Derrick had called ahead to verify he was at work.

The police station was tiny and set in the neighboring little community called Widow's Peak. A receptionist with teased platinum hair greeted them. "Hey there, I'm Luna," she said, her eyes twinkling as she raked them over Derrick.

Ellie and Derrick flashed their credentials. "I called ahead," Derrick said.

"Oh, yeah. You the ones that found that car in the lake."

Derrick nodded. "We'd like to speak to Sergeant Benton."

"Sure thang, honey."

Ellie ignored the way the woman jutted out her breasts as she stood. Derrick showed no reaction.

A minute later, a tall black man with a broad face appeared, his expression grim. "Sergeant Benton."

Derrick introduced them and then Benton led them to his office.

"I figured you two would be here today," he said in a baritone voice that fit with his broad body. He probably played football in high school, Ellie thought. Maybe a tight end.

"Sorry I wasn't out there myself last night. Found a phrogger hiding out in one of the cabins and had to handle that. Owners were freaked."

"That a problem around here?" Ellie asked.

"Not much, more drifters than anything. And not usually during the summer but the winter, when business slows down and there's empty cabins, we find people holed up." His chair creaked as he leaned his bulk back in it. "But that's not the reason y'all are here. I know you transported the remains you found in the lake to the county morgue. IDed the vic yet?"

"No," Ellie replied. "All we know at the moment is that the body in the car was male."

Sergeant Benton made a clicking sound with his teeth.

"We did track down who the car belonged to," Derrick said. "A young coed named Amy Dean. Apparently, she was reported missing ten years ago."

The sergeant's eyes sparked with recognition. "It was hers? You're sure?"

Derrick nodded. "We know you investigated her disappearance. And that she had a little girl."

The man exhaled. "Yeah, but never found out their whereabouts. Finally concluded she took the child and just left the area." He stood, walked over to a metal filing cabinet and removed a file. With it in hand, he sat down again. Papers rustled as he looked through it. "Talked to a couple of college girls who lived in her apartment building, the ones who reported her gone. Beverly Hooper and Janie Huggins. Both were concerned something bad happened to Amy, but I didn't find evidence to support that."

"Did she live alone?" Ellie asked.

"No roommate or boyfriend, if that's what you mean. Just her and her little girl." He pulled a photo of Amy and her daughter. "Pretty little thing," the sergeant said. "Everyone said the mother doted on her."

With her light brown hair and hazel eyes, Amy was pretty as well, almost hauntingly so. "Did those girls have any idea why she might have run off?"

"No," he said. "Apparently, she didn't date because of the kid. She did some cleaning for the ladies on the lake to help with money but took the kid with her. She never left her alone."

Ellie and Derrick exchanged a look. "So she wasn't involved with anyone?"

"Nope," he said. "I talked to other residents in the apartment complex and they confirmed the other girls' stories."

"She never used a babysitter or left the little girl with a neighbor?" Ellie pressed.

"Not according to them. Girls said she grew up in the system and didn't trust anyone."

"Do you know the name of the child's father?" Ellie asked.

He shook his head. "Beverly and Janie were under the impression he was dead."

Ellie rubbed her temple in thought. That could be true or there could be more to the story.

"What about her phone or computer?" Ellie asked.

"Never found either one," Sergeant Benton said.

"How about siblings or other foster relatives?" Derrick asked.

"Like I said, her friends said she was a loner." He worked

his mouth from side to side. "So you only found a man's body inside the car. No Amy and no child?"

"That's right," Ellie said. "But the man was driving Amy's car so he may have known her or had something to do with her disappearance."

THIRTY-SEVEN

"Do you have the names of the ladies she cleaned for?" Ellie asked.

Sergeant Benton shuffled the papers again. "Four of them. Susie White, Ina Dickerson and Gayle Farley still live around here. Hilary Hagan was another but she passed about a year ago."

"We'll need their addresses," Ellie said. "And if you have contact information for the ones who reported Amy missing, I'd appreciate it."

"We'd also like a copy of your notes," Derrick added.

"Sure. Be right back." He stood and walked from the room to make the copy. A few minutes later, he returned and handed it to Derrick. "When you ID the man in the car, let me know." He checked his watch. "The women Amy cleaned for call their group the Ladies of the Lake. I think they meet every week about this time at the Sip and Paint. You might catch them there."

"Thank you. We'll do that," Ellie said.

As Derrick took the report, they left the office. "What's the Sip and Paint?" he asked.

"A shop where you drink wine and paint. Apparently, they're going to open one in Crooked Creek."

Derrick frowned. "I can't imagine a bunch of drunk women painting my house."

Ellie laughed. "They aren't painting houses. The shop has ceramics, pottery, figurines and canvases to choose from. It's a popular bridal and baby shower activity. They even host birthday parties for kids, although they're served lemonade instead of wine."

Derrick chuckled.

Outside, the heat had already climbed to the high nineties with no relief in sight. White puffy clouds hung in the sky as if they were stagnant in the dead humid air. A few cars passed, many loaded down with canoes, a truck pulling a fishing boat, RVs and vans and SUVs filled with families.

Her phone rang. Ellie answered as they walked across the street. "Deputy Landrum?"

"Yeah, lab results came in for that car in the lake. Water destroyed any prints inside along with the pages in that children's book. Found pieces of a small child's blanket, pink fibers."

Probably belonged to Amy's daughter... "What about the car seat?"

"Nothing. Sorry. Divers did collect a pocketknife about two hundred feet from the car, covered in mud. They're working on it now."

She thanked him and hung up, then noticed a sign for the upcoming class reunion boasting, *Welcome Class of 2013!*

2013 was the year Amy disappeared. Some of her classmates would probably be here this week. Although Sergeant Benton had learned nothing concrete from them, after all this time one of them might have remembered something.

"While you talk to the ladies, I'll wait in the diner next door and research Amy. Maybe the Bureau's database will turn up a paper trail on her."

Derrick ducked into the diner next to the art shop and Ellie glanced through the hand-painted glass door. Three women sat around a circular table, sipping wine and laughing as they painted clay flowerpots. The ladies ranged in age between forty and fifty and were dressed for a country club luncheon.

Colorful pieces of art adorned the wall, and shelves held assorted paints and projects to select from along with jars of sequins and ribbons, beads and glitter.

A young woman with a bright red braid and feather earrings dangling to her shoulders roamed among the group, assisting. She fluttered a hand in greeting then introduced herself as Ruby, the owner.

Ellie identified herself and suddenly the women's conversation died, brushes paused mid-air.

"You're here about that body they found in the lake, aren't you?" a perky brunette asked.

"I'm sorry to say but yes," Ellie said. "The car the body was found in belonged to Amy Dean. Sergeant Benton, the officer who investigated her disappearance, suggested I speak with you." An awkward silence followed.

"Amy Dean worked for you?" Ellie continued.

The women exchanged a look. "Yes, I'm Gayle Farley," the brunette said.

The woman with wavy brown hair and pensive eyes laid her brush down. "Ina Dickenson."

A platinum-blond looked at her, wide-eyed. "Susie White. Was Amy in that car?"

"No, the body belonged to a male. But Amy's disappearance may be connected to his death somehow. Sergeant Benton said she cleaned houses for y'all." Ellie decided to omit information about the bones in the shed until they knew more and released that news to the press.

Susie nodded. "She cleaned for me for a while. Then just left without saying goodbye."

"She was a sweet, quiet young woman," Ina said. "I was a chef back then and needed help with the house. She came once a week and worked hard. She always brought her little girl with her."

"She told me she couldn't afford a babysitter," Gayle said. "My goodness, I thought she just moved away. I hope nothing bad happened to her."

Susie leaned forward. "She was kind of fidgety. Like she was nervous about something. When I asked her if something was wrong, she clammed up."

"She did seem paranoid about something," Ina whispered. "Figured she'd had a bad experience with a guy or something."

"Why would you say that?" Ellie asked.

"Well," Ina said. "She said she never dated. *Never.*"

"When I asked about Paisley's daddy, she looked panicky," Susie added.

"Did she mention his name?" Ellie asked.

The women shook their heads in unison.

Gayle's eyes widened in horror. "Oh, my word, that precious little girl wasn't in the car, was she?"

"So far, we haven't found any signs of her. What else can you tell me about Amy?"

"She seemed lonely," Gayle added. "And really protective of Paisley. Told me she didn't date because she didn't trust anyone with her child."

"Was there anyone in particular she was concerned about? Maybe another student or a guy in her apartment complex?"

Ina took a sip of her white wine. "She didn't say."

"But one day, shortly before she disappeared, she was really flustered," Susie chimed in. "Admitted some guy got mad when she turned him down for a date. That after that, she felt like someone was watching her."

Ellie's pulse jumped. "Did she tell you his name?"

Gayle shook her head. "No, but she said she might move so it could have been someone from the complex where she lived."

Ina made a low sound in her throat. "You know, that year some weird stuff was happening at the college. There was talk about some cult."

Ellie went still. "What kind of cult?"

"All I heard was there were some guys into death rituals," Gayle said. "About the same time, the news reported that a girl named Darla Loben was attacked by spiders in the apartment building where Amy lived."

"Does Darla still live in the area?" Ellie asked.

Ina nodded. "Yeah, heard she lives with her mama, Monica, in the cove at Robin's Nest."

"I heard Darla had a breakdown," Gayle murmured. "That she had to go away for a while and never finished college."

Ellie wondered exactly what had happened to Darla.

THIRTY-NINE

ROBIN'S NEST

Ellie filled Derrick in on what she'd heard from the ladies as she parked at Robin's Nest, a cove a few miles north of Widow Lake.

"Amy did not formally withdraw from the college or terminate her lease," Derrick said.

"No renewal of her driver's license, record of her buying or renting property since, no job history, hospital visits, insurance claims or social media."

"Let's talk to the apartment manager and get a list of other tenants at the time Amy was there. Maybe someone else can fill in the blanks."

"We definitely need to look into the cult angle."

Ellie nodded and pulled into the driveway of Monica Loben's house. "Maybe Darla can tell us about them."

As they got out of the Jeep, she heard the faint ripple of the lake water and a motorboat's hum somewhere in the distance. Monica lived in a small white clapboard house, on a hill in the cove, with a swing and rockers on the front porch. The cove was named for the beautiful robins that flocked there in the spring. A blue bird feeder sat in the front yard, and a welcome wreath crafted from vines and flowers hung on the front door.

Ellie rang the doorbell and waited, then knocked. "Mrs. Loben, it's the police. We need to talk."

A second later, a curtain was pushed to the side and she saw the shadow of a woman peering at them.

"Please, Mrs. Loben, it's important," Ellie said.

The sound of multiple locks unclicking echoed from the other side.

Finally, a thin woman with dark circles beneath her eyes and her silver-streaked hair twisted into a knot at the base of her neck answered. She glanced between the two of them with a wrinkled brow.

"Monica Loben?" Ellie asked.

The woman nodded, her fingers digging into the door as Ellie made the introductions.

Monica's eyes looked panicked. "You're here about that body they found in the lake, aren't you?"

"Yes," Ellie said. "May we come in please?"

"I don't know anything about it," Monica said, her voice quivering.

"Please," Ellie said. "We won't take up much of your time."

Monica threw a nervous look over her shoulder. "Look, my daughter's here and she's not well. She gets upset easily by strangers."

"I'm sorry but it's important, and we think she can help us," Ellie said quietly. "The car belonged to a young woman named Amy Dean who disappeared ten years ago. We're looking for her and her daughter."

"I don't understand," Monica said. "Was Amy in the car?"

"No. The body was a male, but that leaves us wondering why he was driving Amy's car and where Amy is."

Monica tugged the collar of her shirt. "I'm sorry but I can't help."

Derrick cleared his throat. "Amy attended college with your daughter Darla and lived in the same apartment complex."

Monica shifted, her breathing unsteady. "I told you my daughter isn't well. She especially doesn't like to talk about that time in her life."

Ellie gave her an imploring look. "Please, Mrs. Loben, we think something happened to Amy and her daughter."

Monica sighed warily but stepped aside and allowed them to enter. The house was decorated in neutral shades with lake décor. Ellie glanced around for the daughter but didn't see her.

"You said Darla is here?" Ellie asked.

Again, pain flashed across Monica's face. "In her room. That's where she stays most of the time. She feels safer in there."

"Safe from what?" Ellie asked.

"From the world," Monica said. "She has so many phobias that she's practically paralyzed with fear."

Her comment explained the multiple locks on the door. Sympathy for the mother and daughter swelled inside Ellie. "I'm sorry to hear that. Has she always suffered from phobias?"

Monica shook her head sadly. "Not when she was little. But that year at college did something to her. I don't know everything that happened but... she was traumatized. The doctors say she had a psychotic break."

"Were drugs involved?" Derrick asked.

"My daughter didn't do drugs," Monica said emphatically. "But you're right. She did live in that apartment building. One night, she woke up and there were spiders in her bedroom. She was bitten by several black widows."

"How scary. They're poisonous but not always deadly," Ellie said.

Monica nodded. "I know, but she was sick for weeks and after that, had nightmares of spiders and woke up screaming all the time."

Derrick pulled a hand down his chin. "How did the spiders get in her room?"

Monica shrugged. "She thought one of the creeps that lived in the building put them there."

Ellie's mind raced with more questions. "Did the police investigate?"

"They talked to one kid but he swore he didn't do it, insisted that someone stole the three black widows he kept. Police had no proof he put the spiders in Darla's bedroom. His father paid for a lawyer and that was the end of it." Her voice cracked. "But my daughter has never been the same."

"Do you remember the boy's name?" Ellie asked.

Monica pinched the bridge of her nose as if battling her emotions. "I'll never forget it. Vincent Billings."

A shrill scream erupted from the bedroom and Monica ran toward the closed door. Ellie followed. When Monica jerked open the door, Ellie saw a rail-thin skeleton of a girl in full-fledged panic.

"Get them off me!" She slapped her hands across her body as if she was on fire. "The spiders are all over me! Get them off!"

FORTY

Poisonous spiders crawled up and down Darla's arms, their tiny legs traipsing over her skin as if they planned to feast on her. Their pinprick bites were like needles jabbing into her, a thousand at a time. Their eyes piercing her.

She slapped at them, beating them away, but dozens more flew at her and fell from the tangled web they'd spun above her bed.

"Darla, honey, there are no spiders in here," her mother said in a soothing voice. "Wake up and you'll see they're all gone, honey."

Her mother's voice barely registered through the fear pulsing through her. Her mom was wrong.

The spiders were very real. They came at her when she closed her eyes and especially when she was alone. No one seemed to be able to see them except her.

Everyone thought she was crazy.

But she wasn't. Her body stung as if it was on fire. Her throat was starting to get thick and close up. Her vocal cords twisted together like intertwining ropes cutting off the sound of her cries. Nausea built in her chest, trapped inside as the spiders crawled in her ears and made their way through her ear canal. Her muscles started to spasm and sweat streamed down her face.

She slapped at them again, raking her hands across her body, sending some of them scurrying.

Blood rushed to her head and the world tilted.

"Darla, honey, it's okay now," her mother pleaded. "The police are here. They want to talk to you about a girl you knew in college."

"Her name was Amy," another female's voice broke through the fog. "We think you knew her from your apartment complex ten years ago."

Darla didn't remember an Amy or any other friends. Only the shock of that night when her life had come to an end.

FORTY-ONE

LAKE HAVEN APARTMENTS

Ellie couldn't erase the image of Monica's distraught daughter from her mind as she parked at the apartment complex where Darla and Amy had rented units. How awful to live in a never-ending nightmare where spiders were attacking you.

Derrick looked up from his phone. "Manager ten years ago was a guy named Omar Coolidge. He's still there."

"Let's see what he recalls about Darla, Vincent Billings and Amy."

The sun was blistering the grass, blinding their way as they walked to the door. Ellie's scalp tingled with a burning sensation.

Derrick knocked and Ellie stood back as the door opened and Derrick introduced them.

The skinny man in jeans and a T-shirt looked scruffy and unkept, a throwback to the hippie days with low hanging jeans and shaggy shoulder length hair. A single earring glittered on his left lobe. His eyes were glassy and he reeked of pot.

"Mr. Coolidge," Derrick began then introduced them. "May we come in?"

Coolidge fidgeted, one hand on the door jamb as if preparing to slam the door—or run.

"Please," Ellie said. "We just need to talk to you for a minute. It's important."

"What's this about?" Coolidge said, his voice edgy.

"We need information on a couple of young women who rented apartments from you ten years ago," Derrick said. "The first, a woman named Amy Dean who went missing."

His eyes shifted past them. "That was a long time ago. These apartments had a lot of renters since. I can't remember them all."

"But you might recall her because she had a little girl," Ellie said diplomatically. "And the police questioned you when she was reported missing."

He shrugged. "Yeah, so?"

Derrick elbowed his way in. "There was also trouble with another young girl, Darla Loben, who claims she was attacked by spiders in her apartment."

Coolidge's breath rattled out.

Ellie studied the place as she entered. The apartment was small, a combination living area/kitchen that was stuck in time with a dingy mustard-color paint, cheap furnishings, and a hall that probably led to the bed and bathroom. Ellie couldn't tell if it was a one-bedroom or two.

Worn furniture, faded builder's grade carpet, sports posters of the college's football team and PBR cans gave the impression the guy was repeatedly reliving his college days.

His body language was defensive, raising suspicions. He knew something but didn't want to get involved.

"Did you attend Widow Peak College?" Ellie asked.

His beady eyes turned wary. "For a semester but got bored," he muttered. "Got the job managing the complex here and it worked out."

"And you're happy as a manager?" Ellie asked.

The guy lifted a wheat-colored brow. "Pays the bills."

"Do you handle maintenance as well?" Derrick asked.

Coolidge twisted his mouth sideways as if that was a trick question. "Yeah. My dad was a handyman. I learned from him."

"I'm sure the young girls in the complex appreciate having a smart guy like you here to help them when things go wrong in their units," Ellie said.

A small smile tilted the corner of his mouth. "I guess so."

Derrick cleared his throat. "Now, tell us what you remember about Amy?"

Coolidge picked at a crumb on his shirt. "Not much. Like I said a lot of girls have come and gone since then."

Ellie's tone grew sharper, more to the point. "The police questioned you and the residents about her. What did you tell them?"

The man's eyes twitched slightly. "That students drop out all the time. Go home to Mama or run off with a boyfriend."

Ellie and Derrick exchanged a look. He had a point. But his I-don't-care attitude bothered Ellie.

"Did you notice someone watching Amy? Anyone skulking around the complex?" Ellie crossed her arms.

"Hey, it's a college town. Guys and girls party and hang out. I keep to myself and don't bother them."

Derrick crossed to the kitchen window. Ellie realized he was probably checking Omar's view of the parking lot.

"All right. Then let's talk about Darla Loben," Ellie pressed. "We just came from her house and she still has nightmares about those spiders."

"That girl was a drama queen," he muttered. "Another student, Vincent Billings, kept spiders in his apartment for a biology experiment."

"Is that legal?" Ellie asked.

"Not like he asked permission," Coolidge said. "But word got around and some of the girls were freaked out, so I gave him a warning to get rid of them. He got pissed and moved out." He pulled a cigarette from his pocket and tapped it on his hand. "Besides, he only had three. There were a dozen in Darla's."

Maybe he bought more? Or he lied and put them in Darla's apartment as revenge? If they'd just gotten loose, surely they'd have scattered in different directions.

"Where did he go?"

"Hell if I know," Omar said. "I don't keep up with students after they move out."

"Don't your tenants leave a forwarding address?" Ellie asked.

"With the post office, not me," he replied.

"What about deposit refunds?" Derrick asked.

Coolidge made a low sound in his throat. "Not many get anything back. Students are rough on the apartments."

Derrick turned from the window. "Did you have security cameras in the parking lot?" Derrick asked.

Coolidge cut his eyes toward the bookcase in the corner, then down the hall and back to them. "Not back then. We put some in about two years ago."

Derrick returned to stand beside her, and Ellie pulled a card from her pocket. "If you think of anything else that would be helpful, please give us a call."

Coolidge walked them to the door, locking it behind them. Ellie paused to scan the parking lot for the cameras and spotted two attached to the streetlights. Although they faced the parking lot, not the units themselves.

Ellie had a bad vibe about Coolidge. He was hiding something. And she would find out what.

FORTY-TWO
ROCKY LANE

He fought his need to fidget as he watched Beverly Hooper jump from her Honda and race into her house. She looked anxious and kept looking over her shoulder as if she knew she was being followed.

He hadn't exactly been discreet. He *wanted* her to know she was being watched. Wanted her to sweat. To anticipate what was to come.

Her door closed swiftly and he saw lights flipping on as if she thought that could save her.

But nothing would stop him from executing his plans. He'd dreamed of her blood on his hands for years. Dreamed of watching the light fade from her eyes as she struggled for another breath and realized fighting him was futile.

Maybe he'd follow the footsteps of Gary Ridgway, the Green Mile Killer, and kill her then dump her in the river. No... he didn't want to be a copycat.

Sure, in their kills, the brothers had imitated Radcliff's MO. But they had their reasons for that.

Creativity was the component that made the famous killers'

MOs stand out. He was starting a new decade of killing. It was time to make his own name and stand out from the pack.

Widow Lake would be the perfect place to leave the body. She'd be buried underneath the water, covered in sludge and sticks and scum.

Then she could float among the ghosts already living below and no one would ever find her.

FORTY-THREE

BLUFF COUNTY MORGUE

While Ellie drove toward the morgue, Derrick ran a background check on Vincent Billings. "Billings was cleared by the police regarding the Darla Loben incident. After that, he moved across the country and has been working at a reptile house in California."

"Was he questioned in the disappearance of Amy Dean?"

"Let me pull the police report."

Ellie focused on the winding road as he did so.

"Looks like police questioned everyone in the complex," Derrick said. "But Billings had already left town, before Amy's disappearance."

"So he's not our perp," Ellie said, glad to strike him off the list. Methodical policework involved eliminating persons of interest to narrow down the suspect field.

The sun was fading, although the heat was still oppressive as Ellie parked, and she and Derrick entered the morgue. After all the cases she'd worked, she should have grown immune to the acrid scents of death and formaldehyde, along with the tools Laney used. Scalpels, a measuring scale, bins for organs, test tubes and the drain pan. But even with the ventilation, the smells turned her stomach and a chill swept over her.

Derrick was a rock and seemed unfazed by this part of the job. "What do we have, Dr. Whitefeather?"

Laney adjusted her safety glasses. "Definitely a male. Guess his age to be around twenty- to twenty-two at the time of death. Scarring on the skull indicates he died from blunt force trauma to the back of the head."

Laney pointed to an X-ray she'd clipped on her board. "There are also striations on his arms indicating he may have fought with someone before his death."

"Which means this man was most likely murdered," Ellie said. Just as they'd speculated. "Either he fought with someone in the car or he was killed elsewhere, then the killer put him in the car and forced it over the bridge."

"Do you have an ID?" Derrick asked.

Laney nodded. "DNA and dental records confirm his name was Reuben Waycross."

Derrick stepped from the room, his phone in hand. "I'll see what I can find on him, if he was in the missing persons' database."

"Anything else you can tell us about him?" Ellie asked.

"Not at this stage of the game."

Moments later, Derrick returned. "I have an address for Reuben Waycross's father."

Ellie thanked Laney. "Let me know what else you find. We need to make the death notification."

Hot air blasted Ellie as they exited the morgue, and she dragged in deep breaths to erase the lingering odors of the autopsy.

"Where does Mr. Waycross live?" Ellie asked as they got in her Jeep.

"Dawsonville," Derrick said. "He's the mayor. The odd

thing is there was never a missing person's report filed on Reuben."

Ellie raised a brow. "You mean he's been dead ten years and no one has even been looking for him?"

FORTY-FOUR

ROCKY LANE

He waited long after the lights in Beverly Hooper's little house were turned off and the place was dark, then another hour to give her time to be fast asleep. Then he slipped around to the back door, hiding in the foliage as he checked each window. Living in the shadows, behind the scenes, was a way of life for him.

It served him well now as it had before.

The windows and door were secure, so he pulled his tool from his pocket and picked the lock on the door.

The place was quiet, the other houses in the neighborhood practically deserted as many folks were vacationing before school started.

It was a perfect time to go in and explore.

The scent of vanilla perfumed the air as he entered. But he didn't see any baked goodies, only a candle on the table. He sniffed it, realizing the candle was scented like vanilla pound cake. Judging from the pristine kitchen, he doubted Beverly ever cooked. She was probably too busy running to the spa and hair salon. Her life was as cushy as it was ten years ago when she thumbed her nose at him.

His mother's words rang in his ears: *Sticks and stones can break your bones but words can never harm you.*

That old saying was a big fat lie.

Just like the adage: *Laughter is the best medicine.*

It was if someone was laughing with you. Not so if someone was laughing *at* you.

He spotted Beverly's knife block on the counter and chose the butcher knife, gripping it in one hand as he tiptoed to the living room.

He ran his fingers over the photographs of her and Janie on the mantle, then Beverly and some guy in a fancy suit at a country club function. Bitterness toward her seized him and he turned the photos face down. Glamour and fashion magazines were stacked neatly on her coffee table. He scattered them on the floor, smiling as he imagined what she'd think of the clutter in her pristine house.

His hand closed more tightly on the knife handle as he inched down the dark hall. The air conditioner rumbled, camouflaging the sound of his footfalls, and as he reached her bedroom, he heard a noise maker playing ocean sounds.

"Thank you, Beverly," he mouthed.

She lay face down in the bed, head buried in the pillow, long hair spilling across the white sheets. He crept by her bed to her dresser, then eased open the drawer and found her underwear. His body hardened, and he picked up a pair of black lace panties and buried his face in it, his fantasies building with each one.

Bundy, the Lady Killer, liked coeds, especially brunettes. Four women in fifteen minutes when he snuck into a sorority house. Maybe he should wait until Beverly and Janie were together.

Beverly stirred, rustling the comforter, then rolled to her back and kicked off the covers. Moaning, she flung one arm over her head to rest on her pillow and the other to her chest. Her T-shirt rode up, revealing her belly button. She wore no PJ bottoms, just a red pair of lace panties.

His breath quickened.

The blade of his knife glinted in the dark as he used it to saw off strands of her long brown hair to replicate the first murder. He wanted whoever found her to see that she wasn't the beauty she pretended to be. This detail would confuse the cops, too.

He could always add his own personal touch later.

FORTY-FIVE

WIDOW LAKE

Night shadows plagued the area as Ellie and Derrick climbed in her Jeep. The humidity was suffocating, the temperature in the high nineties and making her clothes stick to her skin. Even her hair felt damp with sweat.

A sliver of moon light wormed through the clouds above. "It's been a long day. Let's notify Waycross's father tomorrow," Ellie said.

"Might as well. If he didn't report him missing in ten years, what's one more day?"

Her phone rang. Her boss.

"Detective Reeves," Captain Hale said as she answered. "Break-in at Widow Lake on Rocky Lane. Woman named Beverly Hooper called 9-1-1. Local officer responded, but due to the location, I thought you should go."

Ellie's mind raced. Beverly Hooper was one of the girls who'd reported Amy's disappearance. This had to be connected. "Send me the address. Agent Fox and I are on our way."

The text came through as she hung up. She started the

engine and headed back toward the lake. "Two bodies found there and now a break-in," Ellie said to Derrick. *Definitely dog days of summer.*

Could all three be connected?

They lapsed into silence as she drove, the Jeep eating the miles on the mountain road until they reached Widow Lake. She followed her GPS to a side street near the college then turned onto Rocky Lane, a narrow strip surrounded by boulders, giving the appearance that the road had been cut through the mountain. Finally, the stretch gave way to a country road lined with cabins and small bungalows and cottages.

Ellie swung the Jeep in beside the police car in the driveway.

Together, she and Derrick made their way to the front door, which stood ajar. A uniform from the local police department greeted them.

"What happened?" Ellie asked.

"Caller had an intruder. Officer Timmons is with her now trying to calm her."

"Is she hurt?" Ellie asked.

"Not physically, although she was hysterical when we got here."

Derrick's gaze swept the yard then the door. "Any sign of the intruder or another vehicle when you arrived?"

"No." The officer shook his head. "Ms. Hooper said he ran off when she screamed."

Ellie took a breath. "I'll talk to her, Derrick. Call a forensic team and take a look around yourself."

Derrick nodded and she went into the house. Officer Timmons was sitting on the couch beside the woman who wore a thin cotton robe. He looked flustered as if he had no idea how to calm her. Raggedy brown hair draped her shoulders, and her face was buried in her hands as she sobbed.

Ellie spoke to him quietly. "Let me talk to her. You can help search the perimeter with Agent Fox."

"Okay." Obviously relieved, he jumped up and practically ran toward the door.

Ellie slid onto the couch beside the young woman. "Hi, Beverly," Ellie said softly. "I'm Detective Reeves. I'm so sorry you had an intruder." Ellie handed her a tissue and Beverly twisted it in her hands. "I know you're upset and frightened, but I want to help," Ellie continued. "Now tell me exactly what happened."

Beverly sniffed, wiping at her nose with the tissue. Red swollen eyes turned toward Ellie. "I w... was sleeping," she said, choking out the words. "Then I heard a s... sound." She gulped back another sob. "I woke up and h... he was just th... there," she cried brokenly. "In my b... bedroom. Standing over me... watching." She raked a hand over her hair. "Oh, God, he cut off my hair. Why would he do that?"

"I don't know, but we'll find out." Ellie swallowed hard as she examined the jagged section where her hair had been chopped. The Southside Slasher had cut his victims' hair. But he was in prison. Maybe this man was a copycat?

"You said he? So it was a man?"

Beverly's brows rose and fell as she thought. "I... think so. I mean he was big... tall."

"Did you see his face?"

She swiped at more tears. "No. He wore a black hoodie with his face covered by a mask. All I saw were his eyes through the holes. They were so mean. Like sinister cat eyes staring at me."

Ellie rubbed Beverly's back to soothe her. "That must have been scary. Did he say anything?"

Beverly shook her head. "No. I heard him breathing. Real fast like. Then I screamed and... he ran."

Ellie surveyed the room and noted picture frames turned face down and magazines scattered on the floor. "Did you put those magazines there? And did you turn the pictures face down?"

Fear darkened Beverly's tone, "No, he must have. But why?"

"Maybe he just wanted to frighten you. Or maybe he was going to steal something and when you woke up, you scared him off."

"No... he was going to kill me," Beverly whispered. "He had a knife and he... dropped it in my bedroom."

"Did you touch it?"

"No," Beverly said shrilly. "I ran in here to get my phone and call the police."

"Good," Ellie said. "I need to look around in there now." She squeezed Beverly's arm. "Will you be all right here for a few minutes?"

Panic flashed on Beverly's face but she gave a little nod, then wrapped her arms around herself and backed into the corner of the couch.

Ellie gave her an encouraging smile, stood and walked down the hall. The space was dark except for the hall light, indicating either Beverly or the officer who first arrived on the scene had turned it on.

She pulled her flashlight from her pocket and shined it on the floor as she searched for evidence. The hall appeared clear. No footprints or signs of trouble. She moved onto the bedroom. The room was somewhat lit by the hall light. Just as Beverly said, the butcher knife lay on the floor.

Beverly was right. This guy was dangerous.

Careful not to touch anything, she scanned the room for blood or any signs of forensics but at first sight saw nothing. The bed covers were rustled, the comforter falling off the bed.

One of the dresser drawers was open and it looked as if the underwear had been rifled through. A black thong lay on the floor, a red lacy pair on the end table.

Her breath stalled as she glanced at the mirror above the dresser. A smiley face had been drawn on the glass in blood.

FORTY-SIX

Ellie clenched her teeth as she photographed the crime scene with her phone. A couple of strands of Beverly's hair lay on the floor but not as much as the perp had hacked off. He must have taken it as a souvenir. Another facet of the Southside Slasher's MO.

According to the profiler, Radcliff chopped off the woman's hair to deface her beauty and to point out her vulnerability, as a woman's sexuality often had a correlation to long hair.

Hopefully ERT could pull DNA or prints off the knife. Beverly had no visible injuries, so she wanted to know who the blood on the mirror belonged to.

Next, she studied Beverly's lavender sheets and bedding for biologicals, but saw nothing. Forensics would have to confirm.

Turning in a wide arc, she examined the entire room with the same results. Nothing on the surface so she did the same in the master bathroom. Coming up empty, she returned to the living room and found Beverly with her knees pulled up to her chest, arms wrapped around them, rocking herself back and forth as she repeatedly ran her fingers over her hair. A siren wailed, signaling an ambulance's arrival.

"Hang in there, Beverly," she said. "I'll be right back. I need to talk to the medics."

She wanted to ask about Amy Dean, but at the moment Beverly seemed lost in trauma. Ellie stepped outside and saw Derrick looking around the property.

"Female, terrified by an intruder," Ellie told the medics. "Physically, she appears fine, but she's shaken up."

The female medic nodded, then they went inside to Beverly and Ellie watched as they checked her vitals.

"Her blood pressure is high but that's normal under the circumstances," the medic said. "We can take her in for observation."

Ellie arched a brow toward Beverly in question. "Beverly?"

"I don't want to go to the hospital. But I can't stay here."

"Do you have a friend I can call?" Ellie asked. "Husband or boyfriend?"

"I'm divorced. No boyfriend." The young woman rubbed her hands together as if to warm them. "But I can call my friend Janie and stay with her."

Janie, the other girl who'd known Amy.

Beverly gave Ellie Janie's number, and she carried it to the officer at the door and asked him to make the call. Then she returned and seated herself beside the young woman again.

"Do you have any idea who'd break in?" Ellie asked. "Have you seen anyone lurking around? Someone casing your place?"

"No, and I don't have anything valuable to steal," Beverly said. "Other than a few pieces of jewelry that belonged to my grandmother. But it's old, not like I wear it or anyone knows about it." She swallowed hard. "All my other valuables are in a safe and in storage. I put them there when I divorced."

"It's possible your intruder knew you personally. Maybe someone you crossed. How about your ex? How are things between the two of you?"

"Trust me," she said shakily. "He's on a yacht with his new

girlfriend living the good life. He didn't do this. He wouldn't have the guts."

Ellie offered her an understanding smile. "Can you think of anyone else who'd want to hurt you or scare you? Maybe a coworker or neighbor?"

"No, I get along with all of them." Beverly pressed a fist against her mouth. A second later, her eyes widened.

"But ten years ago, there were a bunch of weird guys at the college. Everyone thought they were in a cult."

Had to be the same students the Ladies of the Lake mentioned.

"The past two days I thought someone was following me," Beverly said. "Oh, God, the reunion. I thought they might not come. But what if they're back?"

FORTY-SEVEN

Ellie tilted her head to the side considering Beverly's comment. A knock sounded at the door and a tall blond rushed in.

"Oh, my God, Bev, are you okay?"

Beverly's face crumpled as her friend drew her into a hug.

"No. Someone broke in and he had a knife." Beverly ran her hand over the jagged ends of her hair. "And he cut my hair."

"That's horrible," the other woman said with a gasp. "Who would do that?"

"I don't know," Beverly whispered. She glanced at Ellie. "Can I shower now?"

"I'm sorry," Ellie said. "But we don't want to disturb anything until after the crime team is finished."

"Pack some things and you can shower at my place," the woman offered.

Ellie introduced herself. "Are you Janie?"

The woman nodded. "Bev and I have been friends for years."

"Then maybe you can help," Ellie said. "Beverly mentioned she thought someone was following her. And that she thought it might be some weird guy she knew in college."

Janie's eyes widened. "There were some creeps who were kind of scary, but we had nothing to do with them," she said. "I think I saw one of them today in town when I went into the coffee shop."

"Tell me about them," Ellie said.

Beverly shivered. "One of them liked to organize mock murders and filmed them on campus. Another guy had creepy eyes, bad acne scars and wore T-shirts with emblems of heavy metal bands on them."

"Anything else?"

Janie rubbed her arms. "There was another one, too, a skinny geeky guy who liked to cut himself. Once I... saw him staring at a cut on his arm and watching it bleed."

Ellie had to admit that was disturbing. "Were they violent or did they hurt anyone?"

Beverly chewed the corner of her fingernail. "No, but the mock murders looked so realistic, it was unsettling."

"I thought they might have used real blood and the guy filming had a sinister smile when the victims were screaming," Janie added.

"They all took Dr. Dansen's criminology class together," Beverly said.

"Go on," Ellie encouraged.

Beverly continued, "She taught about serial killers and famous criminals."

"Thanks, ladies, that may be helpful." Ellie breathed out. "You both lived in Lake Haven Apartments at the time?"

Beverly jerked her head up, eyes startled. Both women quickly nodded.

"Did you know Darla Loben?"

Beverly's lower lip quivered. "Not well. Just that she found spiders in her apartment. And after that, she dropped out of school."

"The police's only suspect was a guy named Vincent

Billings," Ellie said. "Did he hang out with the other guys you mentioned?"

Janie shook her head. "No, but he was odd, too."

"He was," Beverly agreed.

"Around that same time, you reported Amy Dean missing?" Ellie said, switching gears.

Beverly and Janie traded nervous looks. "We did," Beverly said.

"How did you know that?" Janie asked warily.

"I spoke with the officer who investigated her disappearance. Were you friends?" Ellie asked.

"Not really," Janie admitted. "I saw her around with her little girl. But she didn't hang out with anyone, especially the sorority girls."

"Why did you think she was missing?" Ellie asked.

Beverly bit her nail again. "I... My apartment was near hers. I... thought I heard screaming in the night. The next morning, I went to check on her but the door to her apartment was wide open and she and her little girl were gone."

The hairs on Ellie's arms bristled. "Did you see signs of foul play?"

"I was too freaked to look," Beverly said. "I got the apartment manager to check on her, but he said I must have imagined the screaming."

Back to Coolidge.

"But I didn't imagine it," Beverly insisted.

Janie spoke up, "Amy was in my Psychology class and never showed that day. She was a straight A student. Never missed class. *Never.*"

"I assume you heard we found a body in a car in Widow Lake," Ellie continued.

Beverly gasped and clenched her friend's hand. "Was that Amy?"

"No, but the car belonged to her," Ellie answered.

"Good heavens," Janie murmured.

Ellie had a hunch. She grabbed her phone where she'd downloaded a photograph of Reuben Waycross. She hadn't yet notified Waycross's father so had to tread carefully. But so far Beverly and Janie had been a wealth of information.

"One more question," Ellie said as she showed them a photo of Waycross. "Do either of you recognize this guy?"

Beverly wrapped her arms around herself again and Janie inhaled sharply. "He was one of the creeps," Beverly said. "The one who liked to cut himself."

FORTY-EIGHT

Derrick left the ERT to do their jobs and addressed the local police officers, "Rope off the area as a crime scene. We'll need someone to surveil the property overnight in case this perpetrator returns." He doubted the guy was dumb enough to come back to Beverly's building, but sometimes criminals returned to the scene of the crime. Some even hid in the shadows to watch the police chase their tails.

Scanning the property, he found no doorbell camera or security system. He went inside and informed Ellie.

"Looks like the intruder picked the lock on the back door."

Fear flitted across Beverly's face.

"You should install a security system," Derrick advised.

"I will," Beverly said. "Although, I don't know when I'll be able to sleep in that house again."

"You can stay with me as long as you need to," her friend assured her.

"That's probably a good idea. Try to get some rest," Ellie told Beverly. "And if you think of anything else, maybe a detail about the intruder or Amy, please call me."

Beverly took Ellie's card.

"Before you leave, Beverly, we need to photograph your hair," Ellie said. "We have to document every detail. Then we'll have an officer make sure you and Janie get to her place safely."

Beverly reluctantly nodded. The ERT arrived so Ellie filled them in, then asked Dale Harvey, the photographer, to document Beverly's appearance along with the bedroom and dresser mirror.

Ellie led Derrick, Sergeant Williams and his team members into the bedroom. Before entering, they slipped on foot coverings and gloved up. "Butcher knife is on the floor. Must have dropped it when Beverly woke up and screamed."

"Did she pick it up?" Williams asked.

Ellie shook her head. "But the knife indicates criminal intent."

A frown darkened Derrick's face as he studied the mirror. "Now, this is interesting."

"He's making a statement," Ellie asked.

Derrick hesitated, his voice gravelly when he eventually spoke. "I've seen something similar before."

Ellie wracked her brain for a similar case. "Where?"

Derrick went very still, eyes intent on her and Williams. "The Southside Slasher drew his victims' lips into a smile with their own blood."

Ellie's heart thundered. "I don't remember that detail."

"Because it was never released to the public," Derrick said. "And this can't be either."

"You think we have a copycat?" Ellie asked.

"It's possible. Radcliff could have garnered followers in prison."

"And with his impending execution, one of them might have decided to mimic his crimes," Ellie suggested.

"I'll check into that angle." Something sparked in Derrick's eyes. "You know he only admitted to killing three women, but we suspect there were more."

Ellie's stomach clenched. "Maybe he had a partner." If so, that partner could be at Widow Lake now.

FORTY-NINE

WIDOW LAKE

DAY 3

Lorna Bea's daddy left early this morning, although he didn't say where he was going. He never did. But she was glad he was gone. He'd always been moody, but his mood swings had been worse lately. Escalating—she'd just added that word to her vocabulary list. Her dictionary and thesaurus were her favorite tools. Writers had to know a lot of words.

Before he left, she'd seen him talking on the phone. He looked upset about something. When she asked Nana, Nana told her not to ask questions. That it was grown-up business, not for kids.

Then he'd stowed something in the back of his vehicle, slammed the door and tore off, gravel slinging.

The urge to see what was inside that big, locked box in her daddy's room, the one he told her to stay away from, had been gnawing at her for a long time. "You'll be sorry if you touch that," he'd growled. That only made her want to see inside more. There had to be something important there.

Over the years, she'd made up dozens of stories about the

contents. When she was little, she thought it was a princess crown. Later, she imagined him hiding presents in there for her.

But at Christmas and on her birthdays, he never took anything out of it to give her.

Her imagination ran wild and last night she'd decided it was money. Maybe a lot of money he was saving for a special day. Or... maybe money he wasn't supposed to have.

She couldn't imagine her daddy as a thief but maybe someone paid him a bunch or he found some money, and the reason they moved all the time was because bad guys were after it.

Nerves tickled her tummy, and she tiptoed toward the closet. The wood floor creaked and she went still. Nana poked her head around the corner into the doorway.

"What in the world are you doing in your daddy's room, girl?" Nana glared at her with that *look* that said, *you're in big trouble.*

"Just looking for some scissors," Lorna Bea said.

Nana's wrinkled frown was followed by a disapproving shake of her head. "Don't lie to me, girl. And get out of there. If I find you in here again, I'll tell your daddy. And he won't be happy."

FIFTY

CROOKED CREEK

Ellie barely slept for nightmares of the murders at Widow Lake. One moment she saw Radcliff's victims, throats slashed, bloody bodies. Then she was in the lake. An arm floated up beside her, then the sightless eyes of the dead below stared at her as if they needed to be freed. Then there was Beverly... only this time Beverly had the bloody throat and the hair hacked off.

It was like a bad scary movie replaying in her head as she climbed from bed. Desperate to erase the images from her mind, she brewed coffee, texted Captain Hale to ask everyone to meet at eight in the conference room, then climbed in the shower.

Poor Beverly. Break-ins like the one at her house destroyed a person's peace of mind.

After scrubbing herself, she towel-dried off, dressed in a thin cotton T-shirt and jeans then headed to the kitchen. She poured a cup of coffee to go, then drove to the Corner Café to pick up donuts and a breakfast sandwich to eat on the way.

Cord was not at his usual bar stool, and Lola was talking to Bryce again, her smile flirty.

What was going on there? Not that she had time to dwell on it.

She paid for her food, grabbed it and headed back outside. Five minutes later, Ellie settled in the conference room at the police station, preparing for the briefing.

Derrick arrived first, looking fresh in a pale blue button-down shirt and slacks, his dark-brown hair still damp from a shower. He glanced at the donuts with a grin, snagged two and some coffee, and seated himself as Sheriff Waters, Captain Hale, and Deputies Shondra Eastwood and Heath Landrum filed in. Cord loped in too, looking rugged in jeans and a black T-shirt, with beard stubble still grazing his jaw. His gaze met hers, intensely dark and mysterious as always.

While everyone got refreshments and seated themselves, she divided the whiteboard into sections, labeling them with numbers and scribbling details below the photographs.

"Okay, let's start from the beginning," she began. "First, while we searched for a lost little girl who was found safe, Ranger McClain discovered a car submerged in Widow Lake. Remains of an unknown man were found inside." She pointed to a photo of Waycross. "We have now identified him as Reuben Waycross. Agent Fox and I are going to make the death notification to his father when we're finished here. That said, we also learned the car he was driving belonged to a young woman named Amy Dean."

Ellie moved to section two. "This is Amy Dean. Single mother to a little girl named Paisley. At this point they're both missing." She gestured to their photos from ten years ago. "In 2013, the year they disappeared, they lived in an apartment complex named Lake Haven Apartments. According to our interviews, Amy kept to herself and cleaned houses for several ladies, three of whom still live on the lake. They described her as nice, an adoring mother, who didn't date but seemed nervous."

Ellie moved to the third section. "Her employers mentioned strange things happening at the college that year which we've also heard from other sources. A student named Darla Loben who also lived in Lake Haven Apartments was traumatized when she woke to find poisonous spiders in her bedroom."

Shondra waved her hand. "How did the spiders get in there?"

"That was never determined. A man named Vincent Billings was questioned but never charged. He'd already moved out of state when Amy disappeared so we ruled him out as a suspect in Amy's disappearance and the Waycross man's murder."

"I checked and verified that he's still in California," Derrick added.

"Thanks." Ellie tapped the board where she'd written the name Omar Coolidge. "This man, Omar Coolidge, was the apartment manager at the time and still is. Some female residents claim he comes in their apartment while they're gone but police dismissed their allegations."

"Because he had legal access," Bryce supplied.

"Exactly," Ellie said. "Yes, he's in charge of maintenance." She gestured to Shondra and Landrum. "What did you learn when you canvassed the current residents at the apartment complex?"

Landrum spoke first. "Several females stated that the manager gave off a bad vibe. No specific evidence but they didn't like him."

Shondra adjusted her gold turban. "My skin crawled just being in the room with him. One girl said he seemed to know things about her that he shouldn't. It's possible he's some kind of peeping Tom."

"Shondra, ask those tenants for permission to search their units for cameras. If we find some, we can get a warrant to search Coolidge's."

"Copy that," Shondra agreed.

Ellie turned to Cord. "Ranger McClain, fill them in on what you found at the shed."

Cord's voice was gruff as he explained about discovering the bones in the shed.

"Hopefully Dr. Whitefeather can identify those bones soon. But..." Ellie paused. "Last night a break-in occurred at a house owned by a young woman named Beverly Hooper. Beverly also attended Widow Peak College ten years ago, lived in the same apartment complex as Amy and was one of the girls who reported Amy as missing. She did not see the intruder's face, but he had a butcher knife, cut off some of her hair and painted bloody lips on her dresser mirror."

The room went very quiet as she placed a photo of the bloody smiley face on the board.

Derrick cleared his throat. "This information stays inside the room. Under no circumstances should this be leaked to the public or the press."

Nods of understanding followed.

Derrick continued, "The smiling lips mimic the Southside Slasher's signature, although Radcliff painted his victims' lips instead of drawing the smile on a mirror. He's also currently in prison."

A restless energy flooded the room as the implications sank in.

"A copycat?" Shonda asked.

"Quite possible," Ellie said.

"Or Radcliff has a follower," Derrick said. "The details about the bloody lips were never released, so this perpetrator may know Radcliff. Using the mirror could be his way of either distinguishing himself or he got rushed."

"It was a warning," Ellie suggested.

"Or it was meant to throw us off," Derrick said.

"What if he worked on the case or was privy to the police reports?" Ellie pointed out. "That opens up a world of prospects, everything from crime scene clean-up crews to court reporters to inmates who've served with Radcliff."

"All avenues to pursue," Derrick agreed.

Ellie added Beverly's name and the incident to the board. "Beverly mentioned a group of guys at college who were into weird dark stuff. They attended a criminology class taught by a professor named Dansen that focused on the study of serial predators, famous killers and the psychology of deviant minds. Beverly suspects one of them might have been the intruder." She scribbled a big question mark on the board.

Derrick cut in, "Amy Dean's employers described it as a cult and so did Beverly and Janie. Although, I didn't find police reports of an investigation into a cult or cult-like activity."

Ellie sighed. "Our victim from the car, Reuben Waycross, belonged to this group. We'll talk to Waycross's father, then Dr. Dansen and see if she can give us the names of the other young men." She turned to Bryce. "Have your people look into renters from ten years ago. If one of these guys terrorized Darla Loben, stalked Amy Dean or broke into Beverly's house, maybe someone will recall helpful details."

"I'll get my deputies right on it," Bryce agreed.

Ellie had half expected a protest from him, but maybe the fact that Bryce had a daughter had mellowed him. Didn't matter what his reason for cooperating was. She'd take it.

Cord stood, glaring at Bryce, and Ellie wondered again what the hell was going on. But she had a case to work.

The bodies were getting colder by the minute. And they might have another serial killer on the loose.

FIFTY-ONE

DAWSONVILLE

Although the tall mountains looked ominous, the rays of sunlight shimmering off the peaks as Ellie drove through the mountains were stunning. Fall hadn't arrived yet, but the scorching heat had blistered the greenery and pockets of the landscape were turning brown, grass dying, wildflowers wilting.

The air conditioner worked overtime to cool the car as they passed signs for the tourist sights in Dawsonville, where Reuben Waycross's father lived.

Praying Paisley had survived, she had to cover all the bases. "Let's search for children placed in foster care or adopted around the time of Amy's disappearance."

Derrick pulled his laptop. "Good idea. I'm on it. Paisley was what—two?"

Ellie nodded.

"This will take time," he said. "Many adoptions are private and not in public records. The foster care system can be a mess, too." He made a phone call to his partner Bennett and explained what he needed regarding Radcliff's case, then about the missing child. "It would have been 2013. If someone found the little girl or took her from her mother, they may have dropped her at a church or hospital." He paused, listening to his partner. "Yes. Run it through police reports. Also look for adoption rings around that time involving stolen children and send me a list if you find anything."

That might be like finding a needle in a haystack. But it was worth it if Paisley turned up in the system. Derrick thanked Bennett, then hung up as Ellie maneuvered the road into town.

Dawsonville was home to the southern terminus of the Appalachian Trail, which started at Springer Mountain, and accessible to Amicalola Falls, one of the most popular tourist spots in North Georgia.

Ellie parked at The Pig, a barbecue place at the edge of the state park. The heavenly scent of smoked pulled pork, brisket and baked beans swirled around them as they entered. Outside picnic tables held diners, offering a view of the creek, but it was so damn hot today she craved the air conditioning.

The waitress kept the iced tea coming and they finished off with fried peach pies, then drove to City Hall.

"Why would a man not report his son missing all this time?" Ellie said as they parked.

"Guess we'll find out."

The office looked fairly new and modern, although paintings of Dawnsonville's history and the town as it looked in the era of horse-drawn carriages adorned the walls. A friendly middle-aged receptionist showed them into the mayor's office.

They exchanged introductions, then the mayor gestured for them to sit. Dennis Waycross looked to be in his fifties. He had salt and pepper hair, was neatly groomed and fit, and had teeth so white they must be veneers. His smile was friendly, his demeanor confident.

"What can I do for you?" Mayor Waycross asked.

Ellie clenched her hands. "Mr. Waycross, when did you last see your son Reuben?"

Shadows of sadness passed across his face. "My son and I

have been estranged for years," he said quietly. "What is this about?"

"What happened?" Ellie asked.

"I don't see how that's any of the police's business." His curt tone held an underlying layer of pain.

Ellie and Derrick traded looks, then Derrick spoke. "Just answer the question, please."

A muscle ticked in the man's jaw. "My son had issues in high school, and then in college." He leaned back, a defeated sigh escaping him. "Drugs. I forced him to go into rehab a couple of times but eventually he left. He couldn't seem to kick the addiction. Finally, I had to cut him off financially."

Could drugs have had something to do with his murder? "Mind sharing the details?"

"Started off with weed," the man replied. "Gradually moved on to coke. I caught him in the house with it and threw him out." He rubbed a hand over his chin. "It was unpleasant. My son was rebellious. He... got ugly when he was high. Did things that I couldn't tolerate."

Ellie folded her arms as she recalled that Reuben was a cutter. "What kinds of things?"

He leaned forward, hands steepled on his desk. "I really don't want to talk about this. Now, tell me what this is about. Is he in trouble or something?"

Ellie inhaled deeply. "Sir, I regret having to inform you but your son is dead."

Shock glazed the man's eyes and he rocked back in his chair. Seconds later, something akin to acceptance registered. "An overdose?"

Ellie shook her head. "No, sir. I'm sorry to say that he was murdered."

FIFTY-TWO

Silence lingered while Waycross processed the news. "When did he die? Who would kill Reuben?"

Perhaps a drug deal gone bad, Ellie thought. "That's what we're trying to determine. His body was found two days ago in Widow Lake."

"When was the last time you saw him?" Derrick asked.

"Ten years ago, the day I cut off his finances. He was furious with me." A weariness overcame him. "Hardest thing I've ever done."

Sympathy for the man welled in Ellie's chest. "Did you have contact with him during the time he attended Widow Peak College?"

Waycross's face looked tortured. "I visited once. I hoped he was getting his act together. But he seemed in an even darker place. Everything in his apartment was black and morbid. A couple of other guys were there. Then I saw odd things on the table."

"What kind of odd things?"

Waycross looked away, obviously debating how much to say.

"I understand this is difficult," Ellie said. "But we do want to find out what happened to him. Anything you can tell us about his friends could be helpful."

He hissed. "I don't know names, only that there were photographs of gruesome murders on the table. Bloody scenes, graphic sex scenes, mutilated bodies."

Ellie and Derrick traded a look. "Your son took a class on criminology," Ellie said. "That could explain the photos." Or he was obsessed with murder and enjoyed the gruesome images.

Mr. Waycross shook his head as if to erase the images from his mind. "How did he die?"

"Blunt force trauma to the back of the head," Derrick said.

"We believe his body has been in the lake for ten years," Ellie added.

"It was probably one of those weirdos at his apartment," Mr. Waycross muttered angrily.

"We're trying to locate them now," replied Derrick. "If you think of one of their names, please let us know."

Mr. Waycross nodded tightly.

"There's something else," Ellie said. "Your son was driving a car that belonged to a young woman named Amy Dean. She had a small child, a little girl, and both are missing."

Waycross jerked his head up, eyes alarmed. "What are you saying? That my son was involved with this woman? Was the child his?"

"At this point, we don't believe they were involved, not romantically anyway."

"Then why was he in her car?"

"I don't know yet." Ellie paused. "Mr. Waycross, we spoke to a couple of young women who knew your son. Were you aware he liked to cut himself and watch himself bleed?" Cutting and self-mutilation were ways of releasing pain that a person was experiencing. It gave them control.

"Jesus," Waycross muttered.

Ellie leaned forward, studying him intently. "Do you think Reuben was capable of hurting someone else?"

A helpless look flashed across his face. "I... honestly don't know. He wasn't violent when he was little, but the drugs... they changed him. It was like he became someone else."

Questions mounted in Ellie's head. Had Waycross been dangerous? Could he have hurt Amy and her daughter before he died? If so, who had killed him?

FIFTY-THREE

WIDOW PEAK COLLEGE

"Dr. Camilla Dansen earned a bachelor's degree in criminology twenty years ago and worked in local law enforcement for three years before returning to university to earn her doctorate," Derrick said thirty minutes later as Ellie parked in front of the Justice Hall at the college. "She's been employed at Widow Peak College for the last fifteen years and has been a guest speaker at conferences focusing on criminology and law enforcement along with a Writers' Police Academy for crime fiction writers."

"Interesting background," Ellie commented as she scanned the quadrangle. A few students had gathered on the lawn and two girls were posing for selfies by the arches. "Let's see if the professor remembers the group of guys Beverly and Janie mentioned."

Heat blazed the pavement and her skin, and the dry air made it hard to breathe. Ellie tugged at her clothes, which were damp, as they climbed the steps and entered the building. The air conditioner felt heavenly in the quiet halls, as they made their way to Dr. Dansen's office.

The door stood ajar and Ellie spotted a woman, mid-forties,

dressed in a black pant suit, her shiny black hair styled in a chin-length bob. Her skin was so pale Ellie wondered if she'd ever seen the light of day. Probably applied sunscreen before she even got out of bed.

Derrick knocked and Dr. Dansen glanced up, waving them in.

As she stood, she buttoned her suit jacket then extended her hand, but her demeanor seemed slightly austere. "Nice to meet you, Special Agent Fox, Detective Reeves. I've admired your work the last couple of years."

Ellie raised a brow, surprised she knew of her. "Thank you."

"Of course." She gestured for them to sit and they did, Ellie immediately profiling her as detail-oriented, business-focused, intelligent and a no-nonsense type of person. She was certain the professor had profiled her as well, which unnerved her slightly.

Dr. Dansen folded her slender, manicured hands on her desk, which was neat and organized. Books on criminals, personality disorders, crime scene investigations, blood spatter and various other related topics filled a bookcase behind her.

"What exactly can I do for you?" Dr. Dansen asked.

"I'm sure you've seen the news about the body we found in the lake," Ellie said.

The professor nodded.

"We identified him as a young man named Reuben Waycross, a former student at the college here." She paused, waiting to see if the name registered. When the woman didn't react, Ellie continued. "He died of blunt force trauma to the back of his head."

Dr. Dansen raised a brow. "He was murdered?"

"Yes," Ellie said. "He was also driving a car belonging to a female student at the time, a young single mother named Amy Dean. She disappeared about the same time Waycross died. At this point, we're concerned something happened to her and her two-year-old daughter."

"I'm sorry to hear that," Dr. Dansen said, "although I'm not certain how I can help you."

Derrick shifted. "Last night, a young woman named Beverly Hooper, who attended college at the same time as Waycross and Amy, called 9-1-1 because of an intruder."

Dr. Dansen straightened. "Is she all right?"

"She is, although shaken up. The intruder had a butcher knife but her scream scared him off." Ellie licked her dry lips. "Beverly, her friend Janie Huggins and some other ladies we spoke to who knew Amy, mentioned that some male classmates were into strange, disturbing things, cult-like behavior. One was a cutter, another filmed mock murders on campus."

"Beverly Hooper thinks one of them might have been her intruder," Derrick added.

Dr. Dansen drew a deep breath, a look of concern flickering in her eyes. "Hmm. Interesting."

"We understand it's been ten years," Ellie said. "But we believe Waycross was the cutter. And that he and this group of young men attended your class."

"I've had hundreds of students over the past decade. Give me a minute to look back at my records." She pivoted in her chair and clicked several keys on her computer. Seconds later, she turned back to them.

"Yes, Reuben Waycross took my class. Most students who do so are interested in pursuing jobs in police work, crime scene investigations, the FBI. More than one went on to be a medical examiner and another is a forensic psychiatrist. Some of those jobs require a certain amount of morbid curiosity."

"Did any of them ever concern you?"

"Occasionally, yes."

"Was Waycross one of those?"

She consulted her computer. "Yes, he was specifically inter-

ested in the more sadistic details and photographs of crimes."
She sighed, skimming her notes. "I did notice scars on his arms
and suspected he might be a cutter. When I asked him about it,
he got angry and stormed out. After that day, he stopped
attending class. I assumed it was because I confronted him."

Ellie crossed her legs. "Do you remember who his friends
were?"

She tapped a few more keys, then nodded. "He belonged to
a small group who met weekly to play chess. One student was
named Frank Wahlburg. He wrote a paper about collectors of
murderabilia." She tilted her head sideways as she read from her
files. "The second was a student named Roland Pockley. He's
actually a professor of zoology here at the college."

"How about a student who filmed mock murders?" Ellie
asked.

She tucked a strand of hair behind one ear. "I remember
hearing something about that, but he was studying film. Police
checked him out and decided he was harmless."

"Did he attend your class?"

"No. After the police shut him down, I heard he transferred
and attended film school."

"What was his name?" Ellie asked.

"I'm afraid I don't recall that either."

"Did either Pockley, Waycross or Wahlburg exhibit violent
tendencies?"

Dr. Dansen murmured a wry sound. "I really can't answer
that. Our only interactions were in the classroom. But as you
know, criminals, especially sociopaths, sometimes experiment
before they actually commit a crime. Some have elaborate
fantasies about killing and mutilating others. Some start by
killing an animal. Often, the first victim is someone personal
then they get the taste of blood and escalate from there, altering
their MO until they perfect it." She rubbed her temple. "If you
think they're suspects you should look at their backgrounds."

"I intend to do just that." Derrick studied her. "Did you happen to discuss the Southside Slasher case in your classroom?"

Ellie went still, waiting for her answer.

"Yes, of course," Dr. Dansen said, nonplussed by the question. "The story was just breaking and all over the news so it was a hot topic."

"Did Radcliff take your class, too?" Ellie asked.

"Yes, but not in the same year that the others you've asked me about did."

A frown darkened her eyes. "Maybe I should have seen something, but he seemed charming. And he was fairly quiet so didn't draw much attention."

"A lot of sociopaths are," Derrick said. Radcliff could have met the others somewhere else on campus.

She sat back in her chair, arms folded. "Why are you asking about him? He's still in prison, isn't he?"

"Yes," Derrick said.

Ellie's phone buzzed and she checked the number. "Excuse me. This is our medical examiner. I need to take this."

Ellie stepped outside for a moment and connected the call.

"Ellie, I have an ID on the bones found in the shed. They belong to the missing woman, Amy Dean."

Ellie's chest squeezed. So she was right. Amy was dead and had been buried beneath the shed. Had her daughter been buried with her?

Dr. Leon Morehead parked at Hayes State Prison, Georgia's maximum-security prison and home to many of the most violent inmates in the state. Typically he was enlisted to determine whether a defendant was mentally competent to stand trial. During the course of his questioning, he also solicitated facts about the crime and was surprised at how eager some inmates were to spill the details, some bragging about the depth of violence, their strategies to escape being caught, and specifics about the victims, their fantasies and their MOs.

Today his task centered on uncovering the whereabouts of two other women who may have been victims of the Southside Slayer.

Before entering the prison, he pulled up the video of the man's trial and watched it a second time in his car to ensure the details were fresh in his mind. Radcliff was first sworn in and asked to confirm his identity.

"I am the Southside Slasher," Radcliff admitted.

"Tell us about the murders," the attorney prompted.

"It was so easy," he said. "I watched them for several days on campus, then slashed their tires. When they left their apartment or school, I followed them onto the highway. By the time they were on the mountain road, the tire deflated and they had to pull over." His laughter erupted. "Then I came to the rescue and played the hero."

His victim type was always brunettes with long hair. "I love to run my fingers through their manes," he said. "Then I cut off that glorious hair and slashed their creamy white throats. They look exquisite with red blood streaming down their necks." His breath quickened. "I even timed how long it took for them to die..." A sinister laugh echoed from him.

"And you painted their lips in a smile with their own blood," the prosecutor said.

"Oh, yes, they weren't so pretty then."

The attorney waited calmly. "Why the smile, Radcliff?"

He leaned back in the chair, a picture of nonchalance. "Why do you think?"

"Because murdering them made you happy," the prosecutor suggested.

Radcliff's eyes flared with excitement, and he touched his own neck then looked down at his hands as if he was seeing the blood on his hands from the kill.

"Go on," the attorney coaxed. "Tell me about the victims."

"The first girl was Pamela Louis. I called her Perky Pam because her tits bounced all over the place when she talked." He licked his lips.

"Pamela was twenty years old, a former cheerleader and belonged to a sorority," the prosecutor stated. "You admitted to stalking her. Did you ever make contact or talk to her?"

He grunted. "Bitch was too stuck up to give me the time of day. Thought she was better than everybody. But I showed her. In the end, she knew my name and she used it. She begged me to stop." He flexed his hands. "And I did. I ended it for her." His breath quickened as if the memory was euphoric.

The prosecutor continued, "And you left her naked and exposed at Springer Mountain?"

"I did. She thought she was so uppity, but without her fancy clothes and that long hair, she was just ugly."

A brief pause on the part of the prosecutor to allow the jury to process Radcliff's statement before he continued, "What about victim number two, Kari Bernard? Did you know her?"

Radcliff tunneled his fingers through his wiry hair. "She was a little more interesting. It was raining the night I followed her and she eagerly got in my car to escape the downpour." His voice turned shrill. "Talked my head off. Said she was studying journalism. Wanted to be a crime reporter."

"Even though she talked to you, you still killed her?"

He shrugged. "I kept thinking about Pam and I wanted to feel that way again. Wanted to hear her scream. Watch as she struggled for another breath and another then... then the shock on her face when she realized she was dying."

"You left her the same way, naked and exposed. But you left Pam that way because she thought she was better than you. What about Kari? Did she think that?"

"They all think that," Radcliff said. "All the sorority types do."

"You had a vendetta against sorority girls?" the prosecutor pressed.

"They're all stuck up." He chuckled. "Besides she wanted to be a crime reporter. So I gave her that. Her dead body told the story."

Another pause before the prosecutor moved on. "Jordie Nixon was not in a sorority," the prosecutor pointed out.

Radcliff's body jiggled up and down, his eyes darting sideways. "Maybe not. But she was an actress, a liar." He leaned forward with a grin. "And she wanted it."

The prosecutor waited a beat. "Did she tell you she wanted to die?"

He gave the prosecutor a cold look. "I heard her talking to another girl, saying she was going to try out for a show being filmed in Atlanta. Some kind of paranormal suspense flick." Another shrug followed by a menacing laugh. "So I let her star in my thriller. I even set a mirror in front of her so she could watch herself perform the victim role as she died."

Nervous tension rattled in the air as the jury shifted and glanced at the photos of the victims on display.

The prosecutor gestured to the last two photographs. "We also found cars belonging to these two women abandoned with tires slashed. The first is Haley Worth, the second Judy Zane. Did you also murder them, Mr. Radcliff?"

The bastard simply shrugged. "No. But I think about them all the time."

Morehead's pulse pounded as the tape ended. Radcliff was toying with the police. And him. Enjoying the game.

Per prison rules, Morehead left his computer and phone in the car, although he'd gotten clearance to bring a mini recorder with him. He stepped from his vehicle, walked up to the guard gate and went through three checkpoints before being allowed inside. After another security screening, he was escorted to a private room for the interview. Seconds later, he was seated.

The door creaked open and a guard escorted Radcliff inside. The shackles and chains rattled as he shuffled to the chair which was bolted to the floor. His head was shaved, his body muscular, and a tribal tattoo trailed from the neck of his prison shirt up the side of his face.

Morehead gestured to the guard that he could step outside and the guard left the room. The metal door clanked, the clicking of the lock echoing in the hollow room.

"Hello," Morehead said quietly.

Radcliff dropped into the chair, a sinister smile tilting the corner of his mouth as their gazes met. "Hello, Leon," the inmate said quietly. "I've been expecting you."

FIFTY-FIVE

WIDOW LAKE INN

Odessa claimed a seat in one of the wing chairs in the lobby of the Widow Lake Inn, her gaze searching the faces of each guest as they arrived. Signs advertising the reunion detailed times and dates of organized events.

Tonight started with a cocktail party and appetizers. People milled around, dressed to party. No doubt, the frat boys hadn't changed, although they'd probably switched from hooch punch and cheap beer to bourbon and specialty beers. The women would come decked out in jewels and designer clothing, hair, nails and makeup as perfect as they were ten years ago with the addition of Botox to smooth the crows' feet that had already started around the eyes.

Deciding the brothers probably wouldn't check in early, or they might not even be staying at the inn, she walked across campus. She stopped and sat on the bench facing Justice Hall where Dr. Dansen had drawn her into the world of violent and abhorrent behavior.

She'd been mesmerized by the images of bloody murders and mutilations. The brothers had somehow found each other in that class and she'd trailed them around campus, eavesdropping on their conversations like a groupie following a rock star.

They *had* been her rockstars. Had introduced her to the cunning, methodical planning of a murderer's brilliant mind.

"Midnight meeting," Frank had said one day in a hushed tone.

Odessa had straightened. Where was the meeting?

Then came the interesting part. "I found a site on the dark web and managed to buy the knife used by the Mutilator in those Charleston killings."

"I fantasize about mutilation," Reuben Waycross said. "I've been practicing on myself. But when I make my first kill, I might completely dismember her. Like Dahmer, I'll keep some of her body parts. The rest, I'll scatter in the lake."

The air grew charged with anticipation as each of the brothers described dark fantasies.

"Ed Gein turned bones into lampshades and bowls. I might do something with skin."

"We can't simply copy the killers we've learned about," another one said. "We have to create our own signature."

That was the first time she'd heard them making plans. The day her infatuation started. The day she realized that she wanted to be part of it.

FIFTY-SIX

THE JAVA JUNKIE

Ellie ducked into the coffee shop at the college while Derrick returned Lindsey's call. She'd been falling apart more often now than ever and had his number on speed dial.

Ellie ordered a mocha coffee for herself and black coffee for Derrick, along with pastries, then claimed a booth in the back facing the door so they could view anyone who entered. Not that she expected to recognize Amy's killer.

A minute later, Derrick appeared, a look of frustration deepening his eyes.

"Everything okay?" she asked.

He sighed. "Lindsey and the kids are still struggling. I promised to come back and take Evan to ball practice soon."

"That's nice of you," Ellie said softly.

"I care about those kids. I know what it's like to grow up without a father," he replied, bitterness lacing his voice. He slid his laptop onto the table and seated himself across from her. "Thanks for the coffee."

"No problem." She finished off her cinnamon roll, unsettled by his comment. But she had to focus. "I've been contemplating whether Waycross killed Amy," Ellie said. "He was a cutter which is a form of self-mutilation. He could have graduated to murder, killed his first victim, Amy, and then tried to get away in her car." She sipped her coffee. "Then someone killed him. But who?"

"We need Amy's cause of death," Derrick said.

"Hard to do with what little of her remains were found," Ellie said, thoughts scattered. "What if Waycross didn't kill Amy? What if Waycross was trying to help her escape and her killer murdered him?"

"That sounds feasible," Derrick agreed. "Although, judging from his father's comments about the photos his son had at his apartment, Waycross doesn't sound like the hero type."

"True. So what was his involvement? Did he know someone intended to kill her?" She ran her fingers through her hair. "I'll look for other coed murders around that time frame across the States. Maybe we'll find a connection."

Derrick opened his laptop. "I'll work on addresses for Wahlburg and Pockley and run background checks on them." He checked his watch. "Our forensic psychiatrist is inter-viewing Dominique Radcliff today." Derrick scratched his head. "Maybe he'll get something."

Ellie twisted her mouth sideways in thought then pulled her own tablet from her bag, and they lapsed into silence as they got to work.

Paisley's precious little face haunted Ellie as she accessed police databases. *Where are you, sweet girl? Where are you?*

FIFTY-SEVEN

WIDOW LAKE

He hid in the foliage surrounding the shed where the kids had congregated. The little girl they called Betsy. And then the older one, she must be what—twelve, thirteen?

A teenager. That could be fun. Lately he'd been bored, almost complacent. Taking a teenager would up his game. Missing children always got more attention in the media.

He had to lure her away from the other kids. Formulate a plan. Choose the right moment.

He looked down at his fingers. In his mind, he could already see the blood dripping...

Their hushed voices echoed from the bushes, then the boy leaned closer to the older girl. Lorna Bea was what they called her.

"Dad said they found some bones under that shed where Betsy fell," the boy said.

Lorna Bea lifted her hand to the side of her mouth as if to whisper a secret. "First a man in the car. And now another body in that shed. Cade, maybe the lake is haunted like they say."

"Dad said they were murdered," Cade said. "I wonder if the killer's still around here."

Lorna Bea peered through the thick trees and bushes. He had the sudden urge to move but he didn't.

A man's shout suddenly burst through the woods. "Lorna Bea, where the hell are you?"

He balled his hands into fists, kneeling in the bushes as he watched a big man in a T-shirt and jeans stalk through the thicket of pines and oaks. Thick dirty brown hair. A craggy face. Scar on his chin and... yes, on his hand.

His heart thundered. It was *him*. The missing link.

The one who'd inspired them to make the pact. The one they thought had broken it.

The girl took off running toward the cabin, hair flying behind her as she darted through the bushes and weeds. When she reached the clearing, she stopped, breath panting out, fear in her eyes.

"I told you to stay inside," he barked.

She bit her lip. "Sorry, Daddy. I just wanted to play with the kids."

"You should have listened to me." He jerked her arm then dragged her toward the cabin.

"So you did come back to see us, Frank," he muttered. And he had a daughter. Was there a wife hiding somewhere in this picture? Had Frank actually *settled* down?

Laughter mushroomed in his chest at that thought.

No, the man he'd known would never settle into family life. And the kid... Wouldn't she be surprised to know why her father was here?

FIFTY-EIGHT

SOMEWHERE ON THE AT

Odessa drove to the gathering place for the brothers where they'd first carried out the initiation. She parked, studying the concrete structure. The building had been shut down twelve years ago, left abandoned and standing. The overgrown kudzu covering the outside of the building and the grimy mud-coated windows reminded her of the day she'd first met Dom.

Ever since she'd written him that last love letter, she'd hoped for a call from him but one hadn't come. Maybe he hadn't received the letter yet? Of if it got there, those uptight assholes might have confiscated it?

Dom had his own decree. Had built his reputation with his signature.

The brothers looked up to him. They'd met weekly behind closed doors in a secret location, had literally formed their own fraternity, modeled on things they'd learned in that criminology class. The things they'd discussed were private.

Their motto—*if you talk, you die.*

No one knew about their secret society.

Would they return here this weekend? Relive the initiation?

Would they remember her and what she'd done to help them?

Adrenaline pulsed through her. She slipped from her car and darted around the edge of the building to the private rear entrance. Vines and brush covered it, but she knew how to get in.

Smiling, she raked the weeds aside and unlocked the latch with the key she'd kept for a decade now. Then she crawled into the opening that led her into the dark where they'd all brought their fantasies to life.

FIFTY-NINE

THE JAVA JUNKIE

Working with the copycat theory, Derrick phoned the prison warden where Radcliff was incarcerated.

"Warden Brewer, this is Special Agent Fox. I arranged for Dr. Leon Morehead to interview Dominique Radcliff."

"Yes, he was here."

"Did he speak with you after the interview?"

"No, he said he would report directly to you."

"I'll give him a call next. Meanwhile, I need you to pull visitor and phone logs and compile a list of everyone in communication with Radcliff. Also, include his former prison cell mates."

"Of course," the warden said. "It may take a few minutes. Although, upfront, I can tell you that the only visitor he's had these last few months is a woman named Odessa Muldane. She's one of those groupies obsessed with violent criminals. We caught her trying to sneak him in a shank and blocked her from the visitor list. She's also been writing him love letters."

"Interesting. Do you have her address?"

"Yes, she had to supply that when she first applied to visit. I'll find it and send it with the other list."

"Thanks." Derrick hesitated, thinking. "Did Radcliff have computer privileges?"

"Not on death row, no."

"Did he make friends with anyone inside? Another inmate or guard?"

"I'll verify that, but I don't think so. He's been in solitary confinement for the last year and only allowed an hour outside his cell for exercise each day."

"He's been seeing the mental health counselor?"

"Yes. But as you know, she was unable to extract information from him about the victims."

That was what she'd reported to him. "Hopefully Dr. Morehead had better luck. Get that list to me ASAP," Derrick said. Meanwhile he'd look for Wahlburg, Pockley and Odessa Muldane.

Moments later, the warden texted him her contact information, and he called her cell number. The phone rang five times then went to voicemail. "Ms. Muldane, this is Special Agent Fox. Please call me back. It's urgent I speak with you."

If she wasn't a conspirator, perhaps she could get the information he wanted from Radcliff. Or... he had to consider another possibility. Perhaps she'd used his MO to murder in his honor.

SIXTY

Doing her due diligence, Ellie searched for coed murder victims across the States, starting three months prior to Amy Dean's disappearance and extending it to three months afterward. She checked the dates on Radcliff's cases and found he was in jail awaiting trial at the time of Amy's disappearance. Next, she began with each death marked suspicious.

A suicide popped up, a young coed who threw herself off the Lady in Blue bridge two weeks after Amy disappeared. According to the police report, suspicions surrounded her death, although drugs had been found in her system and her friends stated she'd been depressed for months. With no evidence of a homicide, they ruled it suicide and closed the case.

Two other drownings at the lake raised interest, although again, alcohol and drugs were involved, coloring the case. And they had no evidence of foul play.

Scratching her head, Ellie narrowed the search to focus on coeds who'd been stabbed.

Ten days after Amy disappeared, a girl named Zelda North had been found sixty miles away, disposed of in a ravine. Her throat had been slashed, knife marks marred her body, but no mention of bloody smiley lips or hair having been cut.

Still, there were similarities with Radcliff's victims.

The girl's boyfriend had been arrested. Although he pleaded innocent, the fact that he and Zelda had broken up the week before and that he had no alibi condemned him. Circumstantial evidence—her DNA in his apartment, his in her apartment, an eyewitness's testimony they'd had a bad fight the night Zelda died, and her blood in his car—had convinced a jury he was guilty. He was currently serving a life sentence in prison for pre-mediated murder. His case was awaiting appeal.

Digging deeper, she found that over the past ten years, two more girls had gone missing in a fifty-mile radius of Widow Peak College. Across the state of Georgia, there were at least five more that were unaccounted for.

Some had been dubbed as runaways but in three instances, family and friends insisted there was foul play. These girls were happy, well adjusted, belonged to sororities, were popular and were excited about their futures. Two had already been accepted into desirable master's programs and the third was transferring to a more prestigious college.

Digging deeper, she discovered another body was found outside Dawsonville almost a year to the date after Amy disappeared. Her name was Vanna Michaels. This time she was found, throat cut, naked, left in the woods on the AT. No bloody smiley lips or chopped-off hair mentioned in the report. Several persons of interest had been questioned but police decided Ms. Michaels had been murdered by a drifter, one that had never been found. That case was still open.

Another open case in South Georgia had a similar profile—Kitty Korley, her throat cut, body left on a park bench in front of the Coastal College of Georgia's campus.

"Listen to this," Ellie said to Derrick. "I found two cases of coeds from different colleges in Georgia murdered within months of Amy's death."

"No, at least not divulged in the reports. But I'll check with local law enforcement for details. Although Waycross was already dead at the time of those murders."

"And someone killed him." Derrick released a frustrated breath. "That leaves us with Pockley and Wahlburg as our two primary persons of interest."

The break-in at Beverly's taunted Ellie. A killer was still out there. One who'd been taking lives for ten years. And no one had even connected them.

SIXTY-ONE

WIDOW LAKE

Lorna Bea was so mad she could spit. Her daddy could be so mean sometimes.

"I told you to stay in your room and to not go outside," he shouted as he hauled her into the house.

Nana looked up from her knitting. "Son, what in the world's going on?"

"It's dangerous out there and I gave her orders to stay inside." He whirled toward Nana, his face ruddy.

That was another word she'd learned. Ruddy meant your skin turning red from being mad.

"When I'm not here," he barked, "I expect you to make sure she doesn't go out."

"I try," Nana said. "But it's a pretty day and I thought we came to the lake to enjoy it. Kids need fresh air."

"Not when a killer's on the loose," his voice boomed.

Nana dropped her knitting into her lap. "What do you mean? A killer's on the loose?" Nana whispered. "I thought the man they found in his car died years ago."

Lorna Bea's daddy paced across the kitchen floor, the wood floors creaking from his muddy boots. "He did. But someone found bones beneath that shed where Lorna Bea rescued the little girl next door. For all we know, whoever put them there is still around and might come back for the rest of the body."

"The rest of the body?" Nana gasped.

Lorna Bea stared, wide-eyed, at her father. "What do you mean?"

Her father's breath huffed out as he glared at her. She moved closer to Nana as if her grandma's scrawny little body could protect her.

"You're too young to hear about such things," her father said. "Now get to your room."

"But, Daddy," Lorna Bea said. "Cade was talking about it, too, and—"

"What did he say?" her father bellowed.

"His daddy thought the man in the car was murdered. And that the police were looking for more bodies."

"That's all you need to know," her daddy shouted. "So don't go nosing around asking questions. And you sure as hell aren't going into those woods where some maniac could be lurking."

She thought about the man in the black hoodie she'd seen. But she couldn't tell her daddy or he'd go crazy.

He slung his finger toward the staircase then dragged her up the stairs. "Now stay in there till I say you can come out."

Tears stung Lorna Bea's eyes as he shoved her in her room and locked the door. She pressed her ear to it and listened, hoping he'd come back and change his mind. But the clock on the wall ticked the minutes away, and ten minutes later, she gave up and ran to the window.

She pushed the curtain aside and peered through the branches of the tree. Cade and Betsy were next door in their yard, probably thinking her daddy was a big bad brute.

Night was setting in, the sun slipping behind the covering of the trees. Leafy shadows looked like hands reaching toward her. Outside, she heard the cicadas and tree frogs croaking and a flock of crows soared past the window.

She didn't care what her daddy said. She wanted to go outside so bad and listen to the water lap against the shore. She reached for the window to open it. She'd show him. She'd climb out and see Cade and Betsy and maybe she'd even wade in the shallow water. But just as she started to turn the latch, a movement caught her eye.

Her hands curled around the edge of the window, and she glanced across the woods near the shed. A dark figure moved toward it.

The man in the black hoodie again.

SIXTY-TWO

BLACK SNAKE COVE

Cord hadn't heard from Ellie all day and he didn't like it. He knew she was working the case and he needed to be working, too. SAR was his salvation. The only thing that kept his mind from his sins.

Some sins can't be undone.

He had to live with them. Trouble was, he didn't have one ounce of regret. That made him evil, didn't it?

"We're calling off the divers," the chief said. "After all this time, even if they found remains, it'd take weeks to analyze, especially with unmarked graves below. Some people think that it's sacrilege for us to disturb them."

He was right. It had been an impossible task but they'd had to try.

The teams packed up and headed out, tired and frustrated but telling themselves they'd given it their best shot.

"Go home and get some rest," the chief said. "You never know what trouble tomorrow will bring."

Didn't Cord know it? But he wasn't ready to go home. He'd seen the picture of that innocent little girl and her face was stamped in his mind, a reminder of other little ones who'd been lost.

Night was setting in with a vengeance, the last rays of sunshine shimmering off the lake. God knows he loved nature, but this place reminded him of growing up in that mortuary, of the vile things his foster father had done. Of the fact that death was always there, just waiting to grab you and drag you into the underground.

That evil was everywhere, like a fire-breathing dragon, as real as the unbearable heat killing off nature at that very moment.

He pulled his flashlight and decided to search a nearby secluded spot he'd found when he was hiking. Gnats and mosquitos swarmed like crazy, nipping at his face and arms as he hiked through the woods. He grabbed a stick and used it to part the foliage, checking as he went for the black snakes that lurked in the grasses.

Dry brush rattled, brittle limbs cracking and twigs snapping as his boots crushed them. A mile, then another and he wound up the mountain to a cove known for water moccasins and rattlers. A warning sign had been erected to deter campers and hikers. Even daredevil teens and drunks who congregated to party and dive into the lake from the ridges above avoided the area.

He shined his light across the mossy clearing near the cove, past a fallen log and thick brush. Suddenly he spotted a tiny handmade wooden cross stuck in the ground beneath a patch of honeysuckle.

Swallowing hard, he crossed the distance, pebbles tumbling down as he climbed a few feet to where the cross stood. He could hardly see it for the overgrown vines but as he got closer, he realized it looked like a grave.

His chest wrenched for a breath. A grave just the size for a small child.

SIXTY-THREE

THE JAVA JUNKIE

While Ellie compiled a spreadsheet of missing persons fitting the profile of the other victims, Derrick researched Pockley's background, then received a text from his partner at the Bureau.

He quickly skimmed it. "Bennett didn't find a record of any abandoned babies in this area around the time of Amy's disappearance. No local adoptions either that were accessible, although he's still searching across the States."

Ellie sighed. "She could be anywhere."

Derrick nodded grimly and phoned Dr. Morehead. The phone went straight to voicemail so he left a message asking him to return his call as soon as possible.

"I need to know if you learned anything from Radcliff. He might be connected to a series of other murders that we just become aware of."

He hung up, but something Dr. Dansen said about her former students and their careers niggled at him. He quickly checked Dr. Morehead's background and credentials.

"Dammit," he said to Ellie. "Looks like the forensic psychiatrist I asked to question Radcliff attended Widow Peak College for undergrad."

"Do you think he knew Radcliff or these other guys?" Ellie asked.

"I don't know, but when I talk to him, I'm going to find out."

Annoyed Dr. Morehead hadn't mentioned a connection, he called Radcliff's mental health counselor at the prison. Although it was after hours, she answered immediately.

"Reba Boles," she said. "The warden gave me a heads-up that you might want to talk to me."

"Thanks for taking my call," Derrick said. "It's about inmate Dominique Radcliff."

"Understood. I know he's only weeks away from execution and his lawyer is petitioning for a stay of execution order. I also know you enlisted Dr. Leon Morehead to interview him today."

"Yes. Did Radcliff ever mention knowing Dr. Morehead?"

Papers rattled in the background. "No. Never."

Maybe it was nothing and he was seeing connections that weren't there.

"I highly doubt the inmate will give up anything," Ms. Boles said. "He still insists you found all of his victims."

Derrick muttered a sarcastic sound. "I doubt that. Actually, we believe he's connected to several other murders." He quickly explained about Reuben Waycross's body, the discovery of Amy Dean's bones, and their theory about a possible connection with Radcliff to a follower, an accomplice or a copycat.

Silence vibrated between them for a long minute. "This is certainly all new information. He never talked about having an accomplice or conspiring with anyone."

"I understand that his sessions with you are confidential," Derrick said. "But there's a possibility he either acquired a follower or conspired with others, and that that person or persons continued after Radcliff was incarcerated."

"I'll review my notes from our sessions and get back to you if I find anything," Ms. Boles said. "Although, one thing that stuck out to me was his fantasies. He was consumed with them and mentioned that a college class on famous serial killers inspired him to take his first victim."

Damn that class and people's morbid curiosities. "We are looking at two persons of interest from that very class. Let me know if he mentioned names."

"I will."

"Tell me about his fantasies."

Derrick heard tapping on the other side of the line.

"They consisted of sadistic violence, murder, mutilations, and causing suffering indicative of a sociopath," she answered. "He was highly intelligent, detail-oriented, organized and meticulous."

Things Derrick already knew. "Did he explain why he hacked off the women's hair or painted their lips?"

"No, he just laughed when I asked him about it."

"Anything else?" Derrick asked.

"He was fascinated with science and medicine and once mentioned he'd considered pathology as a career."

"Interesting," Derrick murmured.

"Yes." She hesitated, her voice breaking slightly. "He also watched Alfred Hitchcock, *The Twilight Zone* and *Frankenstein* when he was a kid. He was fascinated with the possibility of taking severed body parts of different people and putting them together to create another human."

Derrick's blood chilled at the thought.

SIXTY-FOUR

WIDOW PEAK COLLEGE

As night set in, images of the man who'd broken into her house filled Beverly's head. This morning, she'd woken up screaming and had been too afraid to go back to sleep. Now, she had a raging headache and every nerve cell in her body was on edge.

"You didn't see his face?" Janie asked as they walked toward Memorial Hall where the cocktail reception was underway.

"No, I told you, he was wearing a black mask." Shivering, she searched the faces of the former students as they passed through the quadrangle then climbed the steps to the student center. Was her intruder here now? Could he be watching her?

As they entered, she recognized three girls from their sorority and two guys she'd once thought were hot. One of them was still attractive but the second had gained at least thirty pounds and had jowls the size of baseballs.

Beverly halted, a knot of fear in her stomach. "What if they're here?"

Janie licked her lips. "We'll keep an eye out for them. But the man who broke in could just be some other perv."

"I know," Beverly said although neither of them believed

that. The timing was too coincidental. She had seen too much that one night.

She'd looked over her shoulder ever since.

Ten years was a long time, she reminded herself. Maybe those freaks had moved on. Grown up. Forgotten about their college days.

Changed.

She might not even recognize them if she saw them.

A scraggly-haired thin guy in glasses caught her eye. Her eyes darted toward a shorter guy with wavy brown hair in black jeans and a black shirt. A shiver went through her. Something about his eyes seemed familiar.

Was he the one who'd filmed the mock murders on campus?

Suddenly, the air in the room grew hot.

Janie nudged her arm as they entered the room, which held tables laden with appetizers and drink stations. "Forget about last night and those creeps. Let's have fun like the old days."

Beverly heard laughter and saw people hugging as they greeted each other. College had been fun... until that one night.

The one night she wished she could forget. The one night that had introduced her to the fact that real monsters were hiding among them.

SIXTY-FIVE

THE JAVA JUNKIE

Ellie tapped her fingers on her notepad as she studied the names of murdered coeds during the past ten years. This case might be the biggest one she'd worked to date.

She started with the death of Zelda North, ten days after Amy Dean's. She pulled the police report and called Detective Brad Simmons, the lead investigator.

The desk sergeant plugged her through to him and Ellie explained the reason for her call. "There are similarities between Zelda's murder, the Southside Slasher's victims and other cases I've found. Did you make connections yourself?"

Detective Simmons made a clicking sound with his teeth. "No, I didn't find any similar cases."

"I understand Zelda's throat was slashed and you arrested her boyfriend."

"Yes. I pressured him for a confession but he insisted he was innocent. But we had enough circumstantial evidence to make the case."

"When you searched his place and car, did you find a souvenir? Piece of her jewelry or clothing?"

"We found her scarf in his closet."

They'd dated so that didn't prove anything. "What else can you tell me about the crime? Was there anything unique about it? A detail that was disturbing."

"It was a murder, so of course it was disturbing. A crime of passion," he muttered. "I don't get why you're calling about it now."

"As I said, I'm looking for a connection to a case on my desk," Ellie said, not wanting to give too much away. "The killer cut Zelda's throat. How about her hair?"

"What?" the man stuttered.

"Did he cut her hair? Maybe took a piece for himself?"

Papers rustled in the background. Then his voice cracked slightly. "As a matter of fact, her hair had been chopped."

Ellie sucked in a breath. "Anything else?"

"Listen to me, I got the right guy," he said, his defenses up. "I don't know why you're trying to stir up old wounds. The family is satisfied."

Ellie dug her nails into her palms. Because they thought their daughter's killer was behind bars. Which might not be the case.

Ellie filled him in on the deaths and timing of Vanna Michaels and Kitty Korley.

"Zelda's boyfriend Theo Morton was locked up at the time, so they can't be related," he argued.

Ellie rolled her eyes. "Unless you put the wrong man in prison."

His breathing grew heavy. "Listen, Detective, I did my job. The couple broke up the week before. Another student heard Theo say she'd be sorry. He was the only one with motive. And there was blood in his car."

"How about her mouth? Did he paint her lips with blood?"

"No," he said. "Why would you ask that?"

Maybe the case wasn't connected. Or maybe the boyfriend did kill her. Or... maybe the killer got interrupted before he could finish and the boyfriend made the perfect scapegoat. The killer could have even planted her blood in the boyfriend's car.

"Did it occur to you that a stranger might have killed her? Or that she had a stalker?"

A thick silence riddled with the man's labored breathing again. "There was no evidence of that. Besides, his DNA was all over her apartment and car. And hers was in his car."

"Because they dated," Ellie said through gritted teeth. "That DNA could have been there for days or weeks."

"I don't know what to tell you," he said. "Jury convicted him. I moved on. You find something says he's innocent, I'll take another look."

With that comment, he hung up.

SIXTY-SIX

Ellie scribbled a note about the detective's reaction regarding the Zelda North case, then moved to the next name on her list. Kitty Korley. She was killed on Halloween, only two months after Amy disappeared. She called the Brunswick Police Department in South Georgia and asked to speak to the lead investigator, Detective Geoffrey Lambert.

A quick introduction and she explained the reason for her call. "Tell me about Kitty."

The detective sighed. "Seemed like a nice girl. A real pretty one, although some kids at the school described her as aloof. Family had money, lived in a mansion on Sea Island."

Ellie had heard of it. The island was home to multi-millionaires and the famous and exclusive Cloister Hotel.

"Did you have any suspects in her murder?" Ellie asked.

"Afraid not. We canvassed faculty, students and her friends but got no leads. That area is a tourist draw. College kids gather on the beaches to party and sometimes things get out of hand. Lots of booze and weed, that kind of thing. Halloween brings out the crazies. But never anything like this." He drew a breath. "We figured whoever killed her left town fast. But that one won't leave me alone. I don't like knowing someone got away with murder in my town."

"Was there anything unique about the way the killer left the body?" Ellie asked.

The man muttered a sound of disgust. "He left her in front of the school. Students that found her were pretty upset."

"Understandable. Did the killer cut her hair or paint her lips with blood?"

Another beat that seemed to drag on. "How did you know that? In respect to the family, I never released those facts."

Ellie inhaled sharply. "Because there are other murders with a similar MO. I've been trying to connect them to a case I'm currently working."

"Geez," he hissed. "That means her killer may have murdered again."

"It's possible. Do you mind sending me photos of the way she was found?"

"I'll get right on it. I'd like to nail this guy. The family was devastated. They still call me monthly to ask if there are any new leads."

"Thanks, Detective. I'll be in touch." Ellie hung up, frustrated that he didn't have more. But at least he wanted to help.

One more call. Dawsonville, where Vanna Michaels' body was found. The detective in charge of that case was out of the office so she left a message.

She didn't like the way things were shaping up. If she kept looking, how many more victims would she find?

SIXTY-SEVEN
HALL OF ZOOLOGY

Ten minutes later, Ellie and Derrick parked in front of the university building that housed the biology, science and zoology departments. The sticky heat made sweat trickle down Ellie's neck. Blades of grass were turning brown, the flowers flanking the building drooping and begging for water. A jogger ran past, and a couple parked their bikes in the allotted slots and headed toward a shade tree. At least the students were heeding the heatwave warnings and carried water bottles and sports drinks to keep hydrated.

She and Derrick hurried into the building, then to Professor Pockley's office on the third floor, a fairly small one on the end with the door closed.

Derrick knocked and Ellie tapped her foot as they waited. Another knock finally brought the man to the door.

Clichéd as it sounded, he looked the part of the science nerd. Thin face, gangly body, eyes that bulged and looked almost buggy. His skin was rough with acne scars, his nose was crooked and he wore a lab coat as if he'd just been conducting research.

"Professor Pockley, I'm Detective Ellie Reeves and this is Special Agent Fox with the FBI. We'd like to talk to you."

He adjusted his glasses. "I'm kind of in a hurry. Can you come back later?"

"It won't take long. It's really important." Derrick elbowed his way into the office, which was crammed full of science books and charts depicting species of spiders and snakes. A glass case housed a yellow anaconda. Another case on the opposite corner was home to what looked like a tarantula.

Ellie shivered, remembering Darla Roben's traumatic experience.

Professor Pockley seated himself behind his desk as if he thought he needed a safety net between them. Ellie almost laughed at that. The man worked with poisonous animals.

"I'm sure you've heard that the remains of former students Reuben Waycross and Amy Dean have been found," Derrick said as they claimed chairs across from the man. "You probably also heard on the news that another former student, Beverly Hooper, was attacked in her home."

Pockley steepled his long bony fingers together, and Ellie noted scars on his hands and wrists.

"Of course. Everyone on campus is talking about it. The female students are really shaken up."

"Understandable," Ellie said.

"You attended college with Waycross, Amy Dean, and Beverly Hooper," Derrick said.

"The college has hundreds of students so yes, I did." Pockley cut his eyes toward the window, a tell-tale sign he was hiding something.

"But I didn't know Amy or Beverly very well."

Derrick arched a brow. "But you were friends with Reuben Waycross?"

His fingers twitched. "I believe we had a couple of classes together."

"The criminology class taught by Dr. Dansen," Derrick said bluntly.

Pockley rocked his head from side to side. "I do seem to recall that. It was a fascinating class."

"Yet you didn't pursue a career in police work or criminology yourself." Ellie gestured around the room at the posters and books. "You chose zoology."

"The class was an elective, that's all. I've been fascinated with reptiles and arachnids since I was young." He smiled as he looked at the spider in the glass case.

"I see," Ellie said, hoping the cage was secure. "Do you remember a student named Darla Roben who lived in Lake Haven Apartments?"

He shook his head. "No, why should I?"

"There was an incident where poisonous spiders were released into her apartment, traumatizing her."

Pockley snapped his fingers. "Oh, I do remember something about that. Thought they caught the guy who did it."

"Actually, he claimed innocence and there wasn't enough proof to make an arrest." She studied his body language. Tight shoulders. Fingers twitching. Eyes darting to his snake.

He blinked and angled his head toward her. "I still don't understand what any of this has to do with me. I told you I didn't really know any of those girls."

"But you knew Waycross and he's dead," Derrick cut in.

Lines fanned beside the man's eyes. "I only learned about his death from the news."

"We believe you were also friends with another student named Frank Wahlburg," Ellie continued. "We're looking for him to question. Do you know where he is?"

Pockley shifted some folders on his desk. "I haven't heard from Frank in years. He moved away after college and we didn't keep up."

"Where were you last night?" she asked.

Pockley stood, stacking the folders neatly. Signs he had OCD, Ellie thought. All the books on his shelf were evenly aligned as well. "Here, working on an article for publication. Now, I want you to leave. I don't like where this is going."

Derrick cleared his throat. "Were you also friends with Dominique Radcliff?"

The professor threw his shoulders back, his tone slightly shrill. "That serial killer?"

"Yes," Derrick said. "Did you know him?"

"No, but we studied his case in Dr. Dansen's class. He was arrested early 2013 so she added it to the spring semester syllabus."

"Tell us about your relationship with Wahlburg and Waycross," Ellie said. "We heard that you guys formed a cult."

Pockley went so still Ellie heard his breath wheezing out in tiny pants. His face reddened and his fingers went wild, twitching. He opened his mouth as if to argue, then seemed to catch himself and his lips thinned into a straight line. "It was not a cult. It was a chess club," he said, his tone calm but defensive. "Now, if you want to talk to me again, you can go through my attorney."

Ellie and Derrick both stood, presenting what she hoped was a formidable force.

"Don't leave town, Professor Pockley," Derrick said curtly.

Ellie cut him a warning look. "If you had anything to do with the deaths of Amy Dean or Reuben Waycross or the break-in at Beverly Hooper's or know who did, it would behoove you to speak up now." She gave a pointed look at his pets. "Or else you're going to end up caged just like them."

She spun on her heels and stalked out, Derrick following her.

"Do you believe him?" Ellie asked.

"Not for a minute. He's too jumpy and defensive."

"Agreed. I think he's lying through his teeth." Hot air

swirled around her like a slap in the face as they stepped outside. Her phone rang as they headed toward the Jeep, and she punched Connect. "Cord?"

"Ellie, I was hiking near Widow Lake." Cord's voice sounded gruff. "I found a small grave near Black Snake Cove.

Ellie's pulse clamored. *Please don't let it be Paisley.*

SIXTY-EIGHT

BLACK SNAKE COVE

"Cord, send me the coordinates. We're on our way," Ellie said as they headed to her Jeep.

Derrick grimaced at the ashen look on Ellie's face. Although she was tough and played it cool under pressure, he'd worked with her long enough to recognize fear in her eyes. "What's wrong?"

Ellie pocketed her phone. "We have to go. Cord found what he thinks is a small grave near Widow Lake."

Derrick's lungs tightened as the implications set in. "You want me to drive?"

She shook her head. "Driving is a stress release for me," she said in a raspy voice.

Derrick caught her hand as she reached for the door. "It might not be the missing little girl, Ellie. It might not."

She nodded, but he saw tears pooling in her eyes and her body trembled. A second later, the determined detective snapped back in place and she pulled away, yanked her keys from her pocket and he trailed her to the Jeep.

Outside, crickets chirped and fireflies flitted across the dusty sky, the night sound of the lake echoing in the still, humid air. Ellie called Dr. Whitefeather as she got in and started the engine.

"Cord found a grave at a place called Black Snake Cove near Widow Creek. I'll send you the coordinates so you can meet us there." She hesitated and he knew Laney would agree. She was always dependable and worked alongside Ellie and the team to see that justice was served for the dead.

Ellie ended the call as she peeled from the parking lot. The lights of the Java Junkie and parked cars at the college campus disappeared into a blur as she wound up the mountain road.

"Did Cord say anything else? Was there evidence of a child there?"

Ellie shook her head. "He wouldn't disturb the gravesite, especially if he thought a child was buried there. He'd preserve evidence so we could catch this animal."

As she sped along, she phoned Deputy Eastwood. "Shondra, I need you to question Professor Roland Pockley's colleagues and get their impression of him. He may be involved in all this."

"I'll get right on it," Shondra replied.

As she hung up, Derrick dialed the number for Dr. Morehead and put him on speaker.

"You interviewed Radcliff, didn't you?" Derrick said.

"I did," the forensic psychiatrist answered. "But he's not talking, Special Agent Fox. He insists he didn't kill the two women you're looking for."

"Do you believe him?" Derrick asked.

A hesitant pause. "I'm inclined to. Although he thrives on playing cat and mouse."

Derrick wondered the same thing about Pockley. "By the way, Dr. Morehead, I looked at your credentials. You failed to mention that you attended Widow Peak College around the time Radcliff did. Did you know him?"

A heartbeat passed. "Not personally. There were over two thousand students at that time."

Derrick's mind teetered on the edge of disbelief. "Considering your profession, I would have expected you to have followed his trial. And that might have sparked your memory of him but you failed to mention it when we asked you to interview him."

"I did not say I didn't know of his case. But I didn't know him personally. Radcliff is a psychopath, not exactly the type to be social or to make friends."

"True, but it's a small college. You may have heard things."

"I don't listen to gossip, Agent Fox. And for the record, that was my senior year. I was doing an internship at the time, buried with work, studying for the MCATS and applying to medical schools."

"You took Dr. Dansen's criminology class, didn't you?"

"Yes, my sophomore year. Her class inspired me to study forensic psychiatry."

"Did you know Frank Wahlburg or Roland Pockley?" Derrick asked.

"Not that I recall. Why?"

"We believe they formed a cult with Reuben Waycross, the man whose body we just found in Widow Lake. He was driving Amy Dean's car."

"You think Radcliff is connected to those three men?" Morehead asked.

"It's possible," Derrick said. "And that Amy Dean may have been the first victim in a long line of similar murders orchestrated by them."

"If that's the case, then I'll help you get to the truth," he offered. "As a matter of fact, I just arrived at Memorial Hall for the class reunion. I'll keep you abreast if I glean any information."

SIXTY-NINE

"Do you believe he didn't know them?" Ellie asked as Derrick ended the call.

Derrick shrugged. "I don't know. I remember some of the trainees I worked with at the Bureau and ones I served with in the military. But not all."

"I don't buy it," Ellie admitted. "Dr. Dansen did mention one of her students was a psychiatrist." She couldn't help where her mind took her these days, not after all she'd seen on past cases. "What if psychiatry is a channel for his own criminal mind?"

"It's possible, I suppose," Derrick said. "But the Bureau has used him on numerous cases and no one has ever considered him suspicious. Just brilliant."

The sky grew darker as they dove into the higher part of the mountains, the tips of the trees shrouded in black clouds. Dried up crops and wilting grass definitely in need of rain stretched before them, an outbreaking of brush fires a real threat.

They fell silent as she maneuvered the switchbacks and veered onto a narrow mountain road leading past the main body of the lake toward the cove. Wide leafless branches hung low, creating a canopy-like tunnel across the thin ribbon of dark road before she reached a clearing and parked.

She and Derrick grabbed flashlights and head lamps then pulled on boots to wade through the mud and snake-infested grass. Ellie used her compass to lead the way, illuminating the ground and checking for poisonous creatures as they hiked. Brush crackled and twigs splintered.

The water was still and quiet, the occasional sound of a frog erupting. Worry clogged Ellie's throat. She tripped over a broken branch and lost her footing but Derrick caught her arm before she went down. For a second their gazes locked. She squeezed his hand, grateful he was there.

They continued on another half mile, then she spotted Cord's flashlight and headed toward him. She struggled to steady her breathing in the dank air as she reached the peak.

His grim expression made her stomach twist.

"I don't know what we're looking at, El, but there are dozens of these small mounds scattered across the area."

Ellie thought she might be sick as Cord's flashlight beam highlighted the mountain of tiny graves on the hill.

SEVENTY

WIDOW PEAK COLLEGE MEMORIAL HALL

Three martinis in and Beverly had almost forgotten about the break-in at her house. This morning she'd visited a salon and had the hairdresser shape up her raggedy hair. Still, she was self-conscious and anxious as she searched the faces of the male attendees for the man who'd been in her house.

Three guys had hit on her, but after her disaster of a marriage she wasn't interested. She didn't trust a man as far as she could throw him. However, Janie seemed to be flirting as if she'd forgotten her husband was waiting at home with her kids.

She was a bored housewife now. That mindset and the alcohol were a dangerous combination. Beverly nudged her and whispered, "Take it easy, Janie. Don't do something you'll regret in the morning."

Janie shot her an irritated look. "Who are you, my mother?"

Beverly stiffened at the venom in her tone. "Just trying to be a friend," she murmured.

"Then don't be a spoilsport." Janie ordered a shot of vodka. "Besides we haven't seen these people in ten years and probably won't for another ten so who cares what anyone thinks?" She tucked a dollar in the tip glass and knocked back the shot. "You know what they say? What happens on vacation stays on vacation."

Maybe she was being a prude, but the break-in at her house had Beverly on edge and tonight every man here looked ominous. Any one of them could be the man behind the mask.

She left Janie flirting and joined a group of women from their class who were talking about old times, sorority dances and parties that seemed like a lifetime ago. She desperately wanted to call it a night. But she and Janie had a code—they'd promised years ago they'd never leave the other alone.

Nothing about that had changed for her.

For a second, her gaze latched onto another bartender with coal-colored eyes and square framed glasses who seemed to be watching her.

Unease skated up her spine and she nestled in the circle of girls and listened to them chatter about their jobs and husbands and kids. Diamonds and jewels glittered on their hands, the designer clothing and makeup indicating they hadn't changed since college. When she'd married David nine years ago, she'd imagined a life of shopping, traveling and the country club herself.

So shallow, she realized, now she'd learned her husband was a thief, a liar and a cheat.

"How about you, Bev?" one of her former sorority sisters asked. "Heard you married some hotshot entrepreneur. Where is he tonight?"

The *couples* conversation always made her uneasy, as if being single or divorced was a cardinal sin. Maybe she should just wear a big fat D for Divorced on her forehead like the scarlet letter.

She lifted her chin, shoving the hurt and shame deep down inside where her heart lay in shambles and her pride was tattered. "Actually, I'm single and loving it," she said with a fake smile. "I have full control of the remote."

Amelia gave a nervous little laugh and the others sipped their drinks, ice clinking in glasses as they imbibed.

"Time for a refill," Beverly said and raised her empty glass. Smiling as if they hadn't just opened up an unhealed wound and poured salt into it, she headed toward the bar, scanning the room for Janie. She didn't spot her at the bar or the food tables. A quick glance at the dance floor told her she wasn't there either.

Her cell phone buzzed in her clutch and she checked the number. Seeing it was a spam call, she ignored it and stepped into the ladies' room. "Janie? Are you in here?"

Two women were fluffing their hair and touching up their lipstick but the stalls were empty.

Surely Janie hadn't left without her.

She pushed open the door and searched the room again, then thought she spotted her friend by the rear entrance. Ready to give Janie a piece of her mind then call an Uber, she hurried outside.

Suddenly she thought she heard a shout. Janie's voice.

"Bev! Help!"

Panic shot through her and she raced down the steps. But just as she reached the landing, someone jumped from the shadows and grabbed her. She tried to scream but she felt a sharp jab to her neck, then the world blurred. Seconds later, she fell into nothing.

SEVENTY-ONE

BLACK SNAKE COVE

Ellie's lungs strained for air as she stared at the small graves scattered among the rough terrain. She counted at least half a dozen, maybe eight. While they waited on the ERT, medical examiner and recovery team, she captured pictures of the small mounds and surrounding area. Derrick and Cord broadened the search to look for other graves.

The scene reminded her of another case where they'd located the bones of several children, a gut-wrenching, horrifying crime that that occurred over a twenty-year period.

Paisley had been missing for ten.

You don't know it's her, she told herself.

Ten minutes later, Laney had arrived, along with a recovery team to excavate the remains. Derrick returned, his jaw clenched as his gaze fell on the graves. He was probably thinking about his own little sister's death, one that still haunted him with guilt because he was supposed to be watching her the day she disappeared.

She wanted to reach out and hug him, to console him. But he blamed her father for negligence in that investigation and that hung between them.

Laney halted, her breathing uneven as Ellie pointed out the number of graves.

The ME approached the first one, then stooped and carefully raked away dirt with her gloved fingers. Ellie's pulse throbbed. This was going to take some time.

An ERT team arrived, a different crew than last. They'd all been working overtime and had to take a break at some point. They fanned out to document the findings as the remains of each grave were revealed.

Derrick stepped away for a second, then stood ramrod-straight as he looked up at the stars glittering above the cove. Night sounds echoed around them, vultures soaring in the sky as if waiting to dive down and feast.

Ten years faded in a flash, memories bombarding Odessa as she slipped down the steps to the room where she'd watched the initiations.

The cameras still hung on the wall, and a camera stood on a tripod in the center of the room, once used to film the depraved acts. The walls were soundproofed to camouflage the sound of the victims' screams.

Ropes, chains and harnesses attached to the ceilings occupied another section. A drab tiny room to the right had been used to isolate the target for hours or days at a time to incite fear.

She wondered how many times the brothers had met here during the last decade. How many victims they'd taken.

The police had now found Amy Dean. How many were there that they knew nothing about?

Suddenly the sound of a scream jarred her eyes open. At first, she thought it was just her memory coming alive. Then another shrill cry pierced the air.

"Please let us go!" a woman's voice begged.

"Don't hurt us," a second voice pleaded. "We'll do whatever you want."

"I have kids. They need me," came the first voice again, this time weak and shaky.

A gruff, menacing laugh echoed through the chamber. She peeked through the glass and saw both women on the floor on their hands and knees.

Odessa ducked low in the shadows as a man in all black shoved each of them forward. Then he used the rope attached to the ceiling to tie their arms above their heads.

"Please, stop," one of the women pleaded.

"Why are you doing this?" the other cried.

Another laugh, then he took a scalpel from the metal table in the corner. The cold metal glinted in the dark as he waved it in front of their faces.

SEVENTY-THREE
BLACK SNAKE COVE

A fine sheen of sweat coated Ellie's forehead as she watched the team carefully recover the remains buried in the small graves. Fear vibrated in the sweltering air, the vultures' hissing and grunting setting her on edge. Although typically vultures ate fresh carrion, not bones, they often circled if they sensed death.

She tried to shake off her unease as the team laid bones from each grave onto the collection pans. The forensic analyst photographed each one and Laney moved closer to study the first set.

"We'll need to use anthropometers to measure and establish what we're dealing with here." With gloved hands, she examined what looked like a skull.

Ellie held her breath. "Is it a child's?"

Laney shook her head. "I can't say for certain that there aren't human bones mixed in here, but the skull belongs to an animal." She held up the skeleton. "Animal bones don't have a clavicle. Some have a useless ossified structure but it doesn't provide support or scaffolding for other bones as the human does." She angled it sideways. "Animal bones are also more porous and are thinner in the cross section than human bones."

Relief whooshed through Ellie. "Thank God."

Derrick squeezed her arm and Cord rocked back on his heels, wiping his forehead with the back of his arm.

"Check the other graves," Ellie said. "Just because this one is an animal doesn't mean the others aren't." Or hell, some sadistic killer could have mixed them to throw off the police.

"Will do," Laney said. "I'll be thorough. We'll also determine the type of animal they came from."

Laney headed to the next gravesite and Derrick grew grim-faced.

Realizing the small graves were getting to him, Ellie gave his hand a small squeeze and felt his fingers tighten around hers for a brief second before he let go.

But the air was filled with tension as they watched the recovery team work for the next hour.

"There are no human skulls here," Laney said an hour later after she'd analyzed the bones that were uncovered. "In each grave, we found four legs indicating they all belong to animals. The bones are different sizes though, so could be different species ranging from rabbits to deer, maybe coyotes. I'll have a team work on that."

Ellie's thoughts raced. If these animals were killed by hunters, why bury them? That didn't fit with a hunter's lifestyle. But... serial killers often practiced on animals before they worked up the nerve to take a human.

By the time the teams had excavated each grave, stored the remains for transportation to the morgue and marked the area as a crime scene to keep the situation contained, it was nearly midnight. A few stars fought through dark clouds rolling in, a quarter moon distant and shadowy.

"Why did you come to this specific place?" Derrick asked Cord as they hiked down a steep hill through thick brush that opened to a clearing. The clouds had stirred a slight wind that rustled the dead leaves, and the lake water in the distance lapped against the bank.

Cord's gaze darkened as they reached their vehicles. "The idea that the little girl had never been found bugged me," he said gruffly. "I just figured I'd widen the search grid."

"Your instincts are good, McClain," Derrick said.

Cord looked away with a small shrug, although from the way his jaw tightened, Ellie wondered if there was something else going on with him. Something he didn't want to talk about. It wouldn't be the first time.

SEVENTY-FOUR

WIDOW LAKE

Lorna Bea slid from bed and pushed the curtain aside to see out. Moonlight skidded off the dark lake and for a moment, she imagined ghosts rising from the inky black, humming as they tried to find their way to the light.

Through the window, she'd watched Betsy's mother read her stories and tuck her into bed. Her heart ached. She wished she had a mama like that.

Or that her daddy would at least spend some time with her. But he was not the affectionate kind. She froze at the sound of footsteps downstairs. She'd eaten her dinner alone locked in here tonight while she listened to Nana's creaking rocker and her father banging things around.

She had no idea what had put him in such a foul mood, although he'd been acting strangely ever since they came to Widow Lake. His moods were like the wind. Sometimes calm and quiet. Other times brooding as if building into a storm. Then tumultuous—another word she'd found in her thesaurus—and raging like a tornado.

Usually after one of those storms, he stalked into her room, handed her a box and said it was time to hit the road again.

Wind whistled through the eaves, drawing her back to the gloomy sky and surrounding woods. The lonely spirits of the lake called to her as if they understood, and she took solace in the fact that the dead cared about her when her father could hardly stand to look at her.

A sob welled in her throat, but she swallowed it back, pushing her fist against her mouth. She used to think he blew up because he was afraid someone would hurt her. That he did it out of love.

But sometimes she wondered...

One night she'd heard him talking in a hushed voice on the phone, "Don't call me again," her father had growled. "If you do, you'll be sorry."

A noise startled her and she jerked her attention back outside. In the shadow of the moon, she saw a figure skulking along. Her breath tightened. Was it the man in the black hoodie she'd seen, watching her window again?

Downstairs, she heard the door screeching as her daddy left. A tiny voice inside her head whispered for her not to look. That whatever her father was doing was his business.

But she couldn't drag herself away from the window. Her heart racing, she watched her father meet up with the other man. Then they disappeared into the woods together.

Dog-tired, Ellie and Derrick left the ERT and Laney at Black Snake Cove to do their jobs and got in her Jeep to drive back toward town. But her phone buzzed before she started the engine.

Her pulse jumped when she saw it was her captain and she answered. "It's Ellie."

"Detective, just got a 9-1-1 call from a woman at Widow Peak College Memorial Hall. She claims two classmates, Beverly Hooper and Janie Huggins, were abducted."

Ellie's gaze latched with Derrick's. "Agent Fox and I are on our way. Send back-up." She turned to Derrick as she ended the call. "I should have assigned someone to guard Beverly Hooper. She and her friend Janie have been taken." Self-blame pummeled her as she started the engine.

"Don't go there, Ellie. You can't predict this perp's every move." Derrick pressed his warm hand over hers. "We're a team. All we can do is follow the clues."

Ellie heard him but silently chastised herself as she sped toward the college. Halfway there an idea struck her. "That's it... We're a team. These crimes aren't being committed by just one person. There have to be at least two perps working together."

"That's possible," Derrick agreed.

Ellie digested that, her mind shifting pieces of the puzzle into one that made sense. According to what they knew, there had been three guys in what some claimed to have been a cult. Dr. Dansen had provided names and claimed the young men were possibly dangerous. Frank Wahlburg, whereabouts unknown. Professor Roland Pockley, who worked at the college. Reuben Waycross, dead and a suspect in Amy Dean's murder.

Then there was Dominique Radcliff who may have been part of it or an inspiration to the others because they'd studied his case.

"You know Coolidge could have been part of the group," Ellie said. "If not, and he's just some pervy peeping Tom, his cameras might have caught something that could help us."

"Excellent idea," Derrick said. "I'll call Bennett and have him collect all the footage from Coolidge's cameras over the years and review it."

For the first time in days, hope sparked that they might have just caught a lead.

He made the call as she drove through campus. Decorations and twinkling lights adorned Memorial Hall where a sign out front announced a cocktail party for the alumni.

She pulled into the parking lot and cut the engine, rolling her shoulders to alleviate the tension. Deputies Eastwood and Landrum were already on the scene, along with Sheriff Waters and two of his deputies, working to keep the attendees from leaving.

"We've tried to contain the guests, but some left before the call came in," the sheriff said as soon as she and Derrick approached him. "My deputies are already canvassing the guests for witnesses and taking statements."

"Who called it in?" Ellie asked.

"Girl talking to Deputy Eastwood."

"Thanks, Sheriff," Ellie said. "Will check in later."

Inside, she found Shondra consoling a petite redhead. She and the deputy traded an understanding look as Ellie joined them, and Derrick went to look around. She guessed there were about a hundred and fifty attendees, all growing restless and anxious about the police presence, their celebration dampened by a possible abduction of two of their own.

"This was supposed to be a fun night," the girl was saying to Shondra. "Everyone was so excited to see each other again."

Shondra rubbed the young woman's back. "I know, and you're doing great, Dodie. Thank you for calling. We want to find your friends."

Ellie introduced herself. "Tell me what happened."

"Everyone was mingling, having drinks and dancing," she said.

"But Beverly seemed really nervous and kept looking around as if she thought the man who broke into her house might have been here." She shrugged. "I mean, who wouldn't? I'd have been freaked out if it was me."

Did she mention anyone specific at the party who frightened her?"

Dodie shook her head. "No, she just didn't seem in a party mood. And Janie was."

Ellie arched a brow. "How so?"

"She was flirting with different guys and knocking back the drinks." She stopped herself. "But it was a party and we were supposed to be here for fun. You know..." She shrugged. "Relive the college days."

Ellie didn't really know. After high school, she'd attended the police academy instead of partying for four years. That was a different life. "What did you see that made you call 9-1-1?"

Dodie fidgeted with her wedding band. "I saw Janie heading outside with some guy."

"Can you describe him?"

"I didn't see his face, but he was wearing a black shirt, black jeans. Bev was running around looking for her and she chased them outside. So I..." Dodie sucked in a breath. "I thought something was off so I went to the door and then Janie stumbled. Beverly ran after her and then there was a scream..."

"You're doing great," Ellie murmured. "Then what?"

"Then the man shoved them in a car and he took off."

"Can you describe the car?" Ellie asked.

"I don't know," Dodie cried. "It was dark outside and parked in the shadows. Maybe black or gray?"

"A sedan? SUV?"

Dodie inhaled sharply. "Sedan. Does that help?"

Ellie squeezed her hand. "It might. I understand you're upset but if you remember any more details about the man or his vehicle, call me."

Dodie nodded then dropped her head into her hands. Seeing Derrick crossing the room toward her, Ellie met him halfway.

"Witness saw a dark sedan. Man in black clothing. Heard a scream. He forced both women in his car so he must have been armed." She clenched her hands. "Security cams outside?"

"Yeah, but they were disengaged. Whoever did this, planned it, Ellie."

An hour later, Derrick walked Ellie to her door, scanning her property to make sure no one was lurking around. Not that she'd received a personal threat, but being the lead investigator often garnered a target on her back.

And this was a big case.

After interviewing the attendees at the reunion, they still had no specific lead. A few people had talked to Beverly and others confirmed that Janie had been drinking and in a reckless mood. But neither was a crime.

Ellie's porch light was burning, her security system set and as they entered, everything appeared to be in place.

He didn't like the fact that they'd found numerous animal graves though. Most likely, that meant the killer—or killers—had been practicing before they'd graduated to human victims. Who knew what they'd subjected the poor animals to?

His own sister's case taunted him—he had never forgiven himself for her abduction. She'd been murdered by a serial predator who'd gone on to kill numerous little girls. The culprit was just one man.

In this case, he suspected they were dealing with at least

two killers, which could mean that the body count had climbed over the past decade. Ten years of taking victims and escaping detection.

He'd blamed Ellie's father, Randall Reeves—the sheriff at the time—for not stopping his sister's killer. Was he any better now?

"I'm going to take a hot shower," Ellie said, rolling her shoulders as she removed her holster and weapon.

"I'm heading to my cabin to do the same. We'll meet up in the morning."

Ellie gently touched his cheek. "Stay, Derrick. It's been a long day."

Emotions churned through him, rocking him to the core. Ellie was tough but more sensitive than anyone thought. Yet he didn't want her sympathy. Couldn't talk about how this case was getting to him, dredging up memories, the pain and anger of his sister's death. Maybe it was being around Lindsey's kids. The weight and responsibility of playing father when he'd failed as a big brother.

"Not tonight," he said, deciding he needed to be alone. He had to get his head together. Keep focused on the case. Find the killer—or killers—before another woman died.

SEVENTY-SEVEN

WIDOW LAKE

Frank Wahlburg stared through the window of his bedroom. Shadows and ghosts of the past were hiding deep in the dark forest of the AT. The voices of the brothers echoed in his head.

The woods outside held his secrets. The truth that had to stay buried.

His daughter was angry with him tonight. She didn't understand.

He opened his safe and was bombarded with photos and memories. Some so sweet that sometimes he wanted to cry like a baby.

Others so horrible that he wanted to scream in denial.

Lorna Bea thought he'd thrown away all her childhood pictures. That they meant nothing to him. But they meant everything.

Which was why he kept them locked away.

He pulled a small photo album from the midst and thumbed through the shots of her as a tiny little girl.

Her big eyes twinkling as she dug into her birthday cake on her second birthday. Her smile as she climbed on the wooden rocking horse he'd made for her one year. Her look of surprise when they'd hunted for seashells and built sandcastles on Tybee Island.

He'd never thought he wanted children. A family. Or that he'd be a father.

Then she'd come into his life.

The moment he'd looked into her sweet, trusting face, she'd stolen his heart. Her small fingers had latched onto his and something warm and wonderful stirred in his heart. All his sins had faded away. Or at least he'd wanted them to.

He'd sworn to be the best father he could be.

Everything he'd done since had been to protect her.

And he'd do whatever he had to now, to keep her safe.

SEVENTY-EIGHT

Dominique Radcliff sniffed the lavender-scented paper Odessa used for her love letters. Letters he cherished because he knew she would do anything for him.

There were others just like her. Women who wrote him of their undying love and admiration. Some sent gifts like pieces of their hair which they knew he treasured. Some promised to visit and help him escape. Some offered conjugal visits that had sustained him over the years and kept the hungry, horny fellow inmates at bay.

Not that he'd had much contact since they'd put him in isolation. They claimed it was for his own protection.

Hell, he knew better. *They* were afraid of him.

They should be.

Thankfully, he'd found a few followers inside this place. A smile tugged at his mouth. The lights were out for the night. Most of the prisoners probably asleep by now. Guards were cranky and groggy, sneaking away for a smoke or a little side action themselves. As he lay on the ratty thin mattress on the floor, he heard the occasional clang of metal down the hall as a

guard raked his baton along the bars of the cells just to antago-
nize the inmates.

He closed his eyes, his mind sweeping him back to Widow
Lake. The reunion was happening now. The sorority girls
would be gathering to drink and celebrate their achievements.
To brag about their fancy houses and spoiled children and flash
their diamonds and jewels around as if their riches made them
better than the homely girls who'd had to work and scrape to get
by. The girls who the frats used for a night of sex in the dark,
then never spoke to again.

They'd needed to be taught a lesson.

Odessa would no doubt go back there.

He sniffed her letter again, drinking in the scent of her
perfume. She'd done whatever they'd said years ago. She'd kept
her mouth shut since.

Like a puppet on a string, she'd do it all again. He knew it.

"Soon, Odessa," he silently murmured. "Soon we'll be
together again."

Beverly's arms ached from the cuts and from the strain of being strung up, but she was too limp to cry anymore.

But Janie's pitiful sobs boomeranged off the cold concrete walls.

"You'll pay for what you did," the man had growled just before he'd left them. "Think about that."

"Please let us go," Janie had begged.

"I'm sorry for what we did," Beverly yelled as he stalked toward the door.

A menacing laugh was his only response. Then the door banged shut and they were left alone, surrounded by the darkness and the scent of their own fear.

What did he mean? She'd never done anything to hurt him... and neither had Janie.

Janie began to wail. "I don't want to die," she whimpered.

"Hang in there," Beverly whispered. "We'll get out of here."

"No, we won't," Janie cried. "He's going to kill us."

Despair threatened to overcome Beverly. Janie was right.

But Beverly wasn't a quitter.

You quit your marriage.

Maybe so, but what she and David had was hardly a marriage. It had been a farce.

Beverly swallowed back a groan. "Did you recognize his voice?"

"No..." Janie's whimpering faded off. Although she couldn't see her friend's face in the dark, she realized Janie must have passed out.

Alone now with her terror, Beverly struggled to recall the man's voice, to understand what he thought they'd done to him.

If he came back, maybe she could get him to talk. Explain what he meant. Then maybe she could convince him to let them go.

But even as she thought it, she had a bad feeling Janie was right and they were going to die.

EIGHTY

LAKE HAVEN APARTMENTS

Sarah Turner peeked through the front window of her apartment. It was pitch black, but she didn't see anyone in the parking lot. Still anxious over spilling her guts to the cops about the apartment manager, she locked the door and double bolted it.

Her insomnia had grown intolerable the last two months, leaving her exhausted and unable to focus. All because she spent her nights with her eyes and ears wide open listening for an intruder. And worrying that the apartment manager had been inside her place, touching her things.

She poured herself a glass of Merlot then took a sip of the fruity wine, proud of herself for finally speaking up. Hopefully Deputy Eastwood would find out if she was right about Coolidge watching her.

Sure, he'd claimed he'd only been inside to fix the leaky faucet, but her underwear drawer had been rifled through. She'd thrown it all away and bought new ones because the garments smelled like his filthy hands.

The fact that the deputy who'd talked to her was a woman

meant she understood. The few guys she'd told said it was her imagination. Said what harm was it if he didn't hurt her?

Lame, stupid, sexist jackasses.

It *did* hurt. She felt violated even if he hadn't actually physically touched her.

Because she knew he wanted to. He skulked in the shadows like some crazed peeping Tom.

Tomorrow, the cop was coming back to search her apartment for cameras. If they found some, they'd have proof to put him away.

Shivering, she flipped on the lights in every room and began to search herself. First, she surveyed the kitchen, looking at the tops of the cabinets, the corners near the ceiling, moving the cannisters on her counter around to see if one was hidden on the wall.

Next, the living room—again, the corners near the ceiling, then the bookcase and the potted plant, pulling the leaves apart to check. Nothing.

She moved books around on the bookshelf, checked below the shelves, even straightened the painting on the wall. Nothing.

Maybe she was going crazy.

No... She trusted her gut. Her mother had instilled that in her. And her mother was always right. No arguing with Priscilla Turner.

Sipping her wine, she returned to the bedroom.

She ran her fingers along the wall, shined a flashlight at the ceiling corners, laid the framed photographs of her friends face down on the dresser, looking for the tiniest hole or crevice where a camera could have been installed. She'd checked her Alexa and considered getting rid of it but decided if she was in trouble, she could tell Alexa to call 9-1-1 for her.

Odd that she trusted a mechanical device over people. Especially her landlord.

Pulse hammering, she searched the teddy bear she'd kept from childhood for a device, but found nothing. The bathroom came next. The shower, the ceiling, even behind the curtain rods. But she didn't find anything.

Relieved yet frustrated because she was certain they were there, she carried her Merlot to her room, set it on the nightstand and crawled into bed with the light still burning.

Blackout curtains were drawn. Another lock secured on the bedroom door. More locks on the windows.

No one was getting in here tonight.

Her eyelids felt like they were pried open with toothpicks. The light stabbed at her eyes. Her head ached. Her body begged for sleep. She rolled and tossed and stared at the ceiling.

One, two, three... There were four dark spots on the ceiling. Where had those come from?

She blinked. Was she seeing things?

A cobweb fluttered in the wake of the air blowing through the air conditioner vent. The unit rattled. A noise, like scraping or something being dragged across the floor, sounded from above.

The tenant on the third floor? What the hell were they doing?

A noise echoed from the unit next to her. Panic clawed at her. Wasn't that unit vacant?

Eyes wide open now, she strained to hear the sound again.

Threw a look at the door. Still locked. Curtains still drawn. Bathroom door still ajar.

Wait. No. The light went out.

Then there was a louder noise, rattling, from the bathroom.

Alexa was in the living room. Clenching the sheet with sweaty fingers, she reached for her phone to call 9-1-1. God help her, she should have bought a gun.

Another noise, something heavy thudded on the floor next door. Or was it above her... or the apartment below?

A scream caught in her throat and she jumped from her bed to run to the front door. But suddenly someone attacked her from behind, knocking her back onto the bed.

The shiny blade of a knife glinted in the dark as it was raised above her.

EIGHTY-ONE

SOMEWHERE ON THE AT

Radcliff finally felt free again. The prison escape had been a piece of cake. Once he'd enlisted the guard to help, his plans had fallen into place.

He breathed in the fresh mountain air. Only tonight, it was stagnant and so sweltering perspiration trickled down his back.

He smiled at his devoted follower. She'd drugged her husband, snuck out, then taken his car and the cash he kept in his home safe and come to Radcliff.

She'd do anything to help him escape. To feel his hands on her. To give her the pleasure of his company.

He didn't have all night. But he had climbed on top of her and inside her and taken everything he'd wanted. She'd screamed and cried and come, chanting his name as if he'd saved her from her boring pitiful little life.

He smiled in the dark, wrapped her hair around his fingers and tightened his hold.

"Don't leave me, Dom," she moaned. "Please don't leave me."

He traced a finger down her cheek, her pleas warming his

soul. Yet she was sweating all over him and that disgusted him. Women weren't supposed to sweat on their men.

Gritting his teeth, he was kind enough to let her finish, let her think that he loved her. But a boat rumbled in the distance, the lake water churning and sloshing against the bank as it passed, and his need to move on and meet the others took hold.

The clock was ticking. He'd gotten the message.

PT—party time. Again.

She'd served her purpose.

His time was precious. Not to be wasted coddling her pathetic soul.

He'd dreamt about this reunion ever since the cell door had slammed shut in his face.

His days were numbered. Had been for a long time. Eventually, they'd catch him again. The death chamber awaited. He wasn't afraid of death. None of them were.

Living on the edge of it made them feel more alive.

But he wanted to go out shining. One last hurrah. One last time they'd all be together. One last sacrifice of an innocent.

He slid the shank from his shoe, which he'd left on the ground. Lifted her head as if to kiss her neck, then raised the weapon and slashed her ivory throat. Dark crimson blood spurted and flowed down her neck. A beautiful sight.

She collapsed onto the ground, and he sawed off a hank of her hair and stuck it in his pocket. Then he dipped his finger into her blood and painted her lips into a smile.

The boat engine rumbled closer. Night animals skittered in the woods.

He dragged her to the water's edge and left her there, naked and exposed, for the wild animals to enjoy. Wiping his hands on his prison shirt, he hurried to her car, dug out the fresh clothes she'd brought him and changed. He tossed the soiled ones in the lake, not bothering to hide them. He wanted whoever found her to see his calling card.

Seconds later, his adrenaline spiked as he headed toward Widow Lake. He was ready to celebrate.

.

EIGHTY-TWO

WIDOW LAKE

DAY 4

Lorna Bea had written in her notebook half the night, pouring out her anger toward her daddy for locking her in her room. Why come to this lake and force her to stay inside instead of playing or exploring the woods? He'd said they might go swimming, but so far all he'd done was leave each day. And when he returned, he paced and growled like a wild animal.

Even Nana seemed to notice and had been on pins and needles.

When she woke this morning with the sun streaming through the window, Lorna Bea checked the door. Still locked. She kicked it then shuffled back to the window and looked outside. Cade and Betsy were chasing the kitty in the grass, their parents enjoying a breakfast picnic with them.

She wanted to join them, to laugh and play and eat pancakes on a sheet on the ground. But her daddy didn't do picnics.

Fighting tears, she opened the window and climbed onto the tree branch with her notebook.

Cade looked up at her and waved then shouted. "Come down and play!"

Her pulse jumped. Did she dare? "I can't," she called to him.

He looked puzzled, but his father motioned to him with fishing rods in his hands and Cade strutted up beside him. Betsy's mother clasped Betsy's hand and they walked around collecting wild flowers, humming as they went.

A hollow emptiness welled inside her. The stories Cade had told her about the lake stirred her imagination. And she'd read even more about the ghost sightings in that book.

A story simmered in her mind as she wiped at beads of sweat on her neck, and she wrote a horror story about the city of people who'd been buried during the flooding. She made up names of families and how they were trapped by the sudden flooding.

Her hand moved as she scribbled:

They clawed for help, screaming as they were swept below the surface. Gallons and gallons of water swallowed them. The force pushed them deeper and deeper. They tried to hold their breath. Pumped their arms and legs to reach the surface. But another blast of water knocked them down again. Kids reached for their mothers. Mothers cradled their babies. The murky darkness swirled around them. Pain shot through their chests as their lungs burst.

Suddenly a noise at her door jarred her and she tucked her notebook inside her shirt and hurried to climb back inside before it opened. She was too late.

Her father strode toward her. "I told you to stay inside."

"I was just in the tree," she said.

"I don't care. Inside means inside." He snapped his fingers and she climbed back through the window.

"But it's pretty today, Dad, and the other kids are playing and you said we'd go swimming—"

"It's too dangerous out there." He stalked from the room and came back a minute later carrying a box of aluminum foil and duct tape.

She stared in shock as he ripped off sheets of the foil and taped it over the windows.

"But Daddy, it's not fair," she cried. "Why are you doing this?"

"To protect you." He whirled on her. "If you can see out, they can see you."

Coffee in hand, Ellie met Derrick, the sheriff and Deputies Eastwood and Landrum at the office for a briefing.

The whiteboard was filled with information but she had no proof any of it was connected. "Last night Ranger McClain discovered several small graves at a point called Black Snake Cove. Dr. Whitefeather determined the bones in the graves belong to animals. There are no human bones among them."

Landrum rocked back in his chair. "Could be a hunter who decided to bury his kills instead of dressing them."

"I don't think so."

"Lab came back with results on the blood at the Hooper woman's house. It belonged to a deer."

Thank goodness it wasn't human. "That fits." Ellie forced her voice to remain calm, although her mind was racing with sinister suspicions. "I think we may be dealing with another serial predator," she said. "Often killing animals is practice for taking a human life." She paused for effect. "There were eight graves that we found at this point. Who knows if there are others scattered along the AT."

"What does this have to do with Amy Dean?" Bryce asked.

"That's what I'm trying to determine," Ellie said, then she turned to the whiteboard. "At this point we believe that Reuben Waycross, the victim we found in the car in the lake, either killed her or belonged to a group of young men who may know who did." She shifted. "We know for a fact that these guys enrolled in a class on criminology taught by a professor named Dr. Camilla Dansen."

"Nothing illegal about that," Bryce said. "Look at what we all do."

Ellie conceded to that. "Point taken. But we have reason to believe these young men formed a cult-type group where they indulged in dark fantasies. It's possible they planned the murder together and may have committed a string of other crimes." She pointed to the names on the board. "First, this man, Frank Wahlbug, who we've yet to locate. Another man, Professor of Zoology Roland Pockley, was part of the group."

Derrick spoke next. "At the moment, we don't have enough on the professor for a search warrant. But I did a background check on him. He has no record, not even a parking ticket. Grew up in Blackshear, Georgia. Mother deceased. Father was a janitor at the high school he attended." Derrick added the info to the whiteboard. "I spoke to one of his teachers who said he had terrible acne and kids nicknamed him Pockface."

"Sounds like a loner and a bullied kid," Ellie said. "We know how that can manifest itself in a sensitive child." School shooters were often kids who were bullied and mistreated by their families and peers.

"Deputy Eastwood," Ellie said. "What did you learn about him from Pockley's colleagues?"

"Nothing concrete, I'm afraid. Colleagues described him as a little strange, obsessed with his work and research. Keeps to himself and doesn't socialize with the other professors. Never been married and apparently doesn't date, at least not that the staff knew of." She hesitated. "One female professor commented that he showed favoritism to male students. Another said she'd seen him watching females on campus, although she never actually witnessed impropriety."

That didn't mean it hadn't happened. "We have to keep him on our list," Ellie said. "Another person of interest is the manager of the apartment complex where Amy Dean lived at the time of her death. His name is Omar Coolidge, although we have not connected him to Pockley or Wahlburg. He dropped out of college his freshman year."

Ellie turned to Shondra. "What did you and Deputy Landrum learn about Coolidge from the residents at Lake Haven Apartments?"

Shondra's dark-brown eyes gleamed. "Female residents describe him as creepy. A couple mentioned they think he's been in their apartments, touched their personal clothing, especially underwear. A coed named Sarah Turner planned to file stalking charges because she thinks he's been following her. She also said he's made personal comments to her about things that he could only know if he'd listened to her private conversations with friends." Shondra sighed. "She and two other girls agreed for us to search their apartments to look for cameras. I've got warrants."

"Good work, Deputy Eastwood. Make sure she files those charges and if you find cameras in the girls' apartments, use that to obtain a warrant for Coolidge's apartment," Ellie said.

Shondra gripped the edge of the table as she stood. "Copy that. I'll go there now."

Shondra made her exit, and Ellie gestured to Derrick. "What about Frank Wahlburg?"

Derrick pulled a hand down his chin. "Wahlburg is more of a mystery. There's no trace of him since 2013. Seems he disappeared right after Amy Dean did, although no one reported it or thought anything of it, just as no one reported Waycross missing. Where Wahlburg went from there is anyone's guess."

"So he could be dead like Waycross," Ellie said. "Or he could be the killer and he's been on the run since Waycross's death."

Derrick nodded. "Or he may have known who killed Waycross and Amy. He could have witnessed the murder and gone into hiding."

"I guess that's possible," Ellie admitted. But she wanted solid evidence.

"About Wahlburg's background," Derrick said. "He grew up on a chicken farm in North Georgia. Worked in a poultry plant as a teen."

Ellie exhaled. She knew what was involved in that business and it wasn't pretty.

"It gets worse. His father was killed in an accident at the plant and the mother went crazy. Started locking him in the basement while she entertained men."

"A traumatic past like that can lead to violent behavior," Ellie commented. "Maybe a hatred of women?"

"Could go to motive," Derrick agreed. "He's definitely top of our list. I'll keep looking for a paper trail. If we get evidence these men conspired to kill Amy or the other victims we've uncovered, we can squeeze them to give up Wahlburg."

He took a quick break then continued. "On a hunch, Detective Reeves searched for coed murders over the past ten years with similar cause of death. She followed up with the detectives who investigated those cases. Detective?"

Ellie quickly explained about the deaths of Zelda North, Vanna Michaels and Kitty Korley. "Each of these women had their throats slashed. There are enough similarities to warrant further scrutiny."

Derrick's phone buzzed and he checked the number. "I have to take this."

Ellie gave a little nod and he disappeared out the door.

Deputy Landrum twisted his mouth in thought. "You

mentioned a possible cult. I'll see what I can dig up on the internet and the dark web. If the men in question have been communicating the past ten years, that may be how they've stayed connected."

"Excellent," Ellie said, grateful for his tech skills.

The deputies left, then Derrick returned, a muscle ticking in his jaw. "More trouble, Ellie. Dominique Radcliff has escaped prison."

Ellie tugged at the neck of her T-shirt, desperate for relief from the humidity. "I thought Radcliff was in isolation. How did he escape?"

"Someone had to have helped him," Sheriff Waters cut in.

Derrick repocketed his phone. "The warden is looking into that. Prison is on lockdown. Guards and staff being questioned and detained. Security cameras being analyzed." He heaved a breath. "It all started when he was shanked and went to medical."

"How seriously was he injured?" Ellie asked.

"According to the warden, he was stabbed in the thigh. Prison doc started to stitch him up but Radcliff turned on him and sliced his throat. Doc didn't make it."

"Ahh, geesh," Ellie murmured. "Now we have a convicted serial killer on the loose."

"A dangerous one," Derrick agreed. "But the most urgent question is, where is Radcliff going?"

"To revisit the graves of the two women he claimed he didn't kill," Ellie suggested.

"Possibly," Derrick said, then glanced at the whiteboard.

"Or, if he was connected to our persons of interest, he could be headed to Widow Lake to meet them."

Derrick nodded. "The FBI has already issued alerts nationwide, circulating the word to bus and train sections along with airports and border patrols." He addressed the sheriff. "You should alert your deputies in the county and beef up security around town."

Waters stood reaching for his phone. "Of course."

As he left the room, Ellie studied the information on the whiteboard again, in an attempt to connect all the dots.

Ellie's phone buzzed and she connected. "Yes, Shondra?" A pause as she listened. "I'll be right there."

She hung up with a weary sigh. "Sarah Turner's friend thinks Sarah is missing from Lake Haven Apartments."

The timing struck Ellie like a fist in her gut. Sarah planned to file a complaint against Coolidge. She adjusted her weapon and she and Derrick headed from the conference room. Was Coolidge behind Sarah's disappearance?

Or had Radcliff already struck again?

EIGHTY-FIVE
WIDOW LAKE

He stared up at the window where the girl liked to sit and look out over the lake. He'd seen the longing in her eyes when she'd climbed onto the tree branch. He'd willed her to come down and join the boy and the little girl Betsy.

He'd wanted to find a way to separate her from the other kids. But her father had forced her inside.

Now the windows were black. She couldn't see out and he couldn't watch her.

Anger churned in his gut. Frank—who called himself Dwight now—had stolen his pleasure. Had betrayed them all. Had forgotten that he owed them.

But he would teach him a lesson.

The little girl, Betsy, sang "Row, Row, Row Your Boat" while she danced around with the kitty. But it was Lorna Bea he really wanted. He had his reasons.

Laughter mounted inside him as he devised a plan. Get Frank out of the house. Then the girl would be vulnerable.

Though the old lady usually stayed home. But she couldn't weigh more than ninety pounds. She wouldn't be a problem.

And if she was, he'd take care of her. Fast and quick. He

didn't get off on making old ladies suffer. They were too close to death already for it to be fun.

It was the younger ones that made his heart pound with anticipation. Especially this one. She was special. And the perfect way to get to Frank.

EIGHTY-SIX

The walls were closing in around Frank.

He'd known this day would come, but even so, he wasn't prepared. All the lies and moves and changes he'd made to keep Lorna Bea safe might backfire in his face.

She was furious with him now for locking her up.

She would hate him if she knew the truth about who he was. What he'd done ten years ago. The real reason they'd been on the run.

His gut had been in knots for weeks now, just thinking about the reunion. The memories flooded him, drowning him just as the flood waters had buried people alive in Widow Lake. The taste of bloodshed, the muddy water and death blended together, a ripe combination of excitement and disgust.

His mother peered at him through her wire-rimmed glasses. "What's got into you, locking that girl up like that?"

"You want some crazed killer getting your granddaughter?"

"Of course not, but you keep getting harsher and harsher with her. You're going to drive her away one day."

"Don't tell me how to parent," he said through gritted teeth. "It's not like you were the perfect mother. Or wife."

She winced at his statement but forged on with that runaway mouth of hers. "I just want you to let her play, be a normal kid. You're always picking us up and moving us around."

He bit the inside of his cheek and tasted blood. He needed the old lady when Lorna Bea was little and couldn't be left alone. He could do without her now. "If you don't want to go next time, you can stay," he snapped. "But I'll do what's best for my daughter."

Nana's face wilted. "Sometimes you scare me, son. Maybe *you* ought to go and leave her with me."

Rage stormed through him and he raised his fist to shut her up. Her eyes widened and she backed away, then tripped over her basket of knitting. He watched her flail, but she caught herself and fell backward into the rocking chair with a groan.

His boots pounded as he walked to his room, opened the closet and then the large metal safe. He checked to make sure everything was intact then removed the gun he'd bought the day he'd run and shoved it in the back of his jeans.

They'd all come here for a reason. He had his own agenda.

It wouldn't fit into their plans but he wasn't stupid. He had his insurance.

Tonight, he knew where they'd be. He had business to tend to today though. After all, a man had to make a living.

But he'd make it to their little party later. And then he'd be done with them all for good.

EIGHTY-SEVEN

LAKE HAVEN APARTMENTS

Heat blazed the asphalt parking lot, making it feel like it was over a hundred degrees as Ellie and Derrick rushed up to the apartment building. Shondra's squad car was parked in front of the main entrance near the manager's office. Through the window, Ellie spotted Omar Coolidge pacing his office and seemingly arguing with a young blond.

Ellie and Derrick gave a knock, then charged in without waiting for a response.

"He won't let me inside Sarah's," the blond screeched.

"We'll handle this," Shondra said to the near-hysterical woman.

Ellie crossed her arms with an eyebrow raise. "Mr. Coolidge, get the key to Ms. Turner's."

"I can't just let you inside without her permission," Coolidge argued.

"You can and you will," Shondra said.

"We have warrants," Ellie snapped. "And right now, we have to make sure she's okay."

"She's probably just sleeping in. Maybe she *wants* to be left alone," Coolidge said with a sneer.

"Or maybe she's hurt and you're hiding something," Shondra said, going for the jugular.

Ellie cleared her throat and the man jerked his head toward her. "A convicted serial killer escaped prison last night and may be in the area," Ellie said. "Do as Deputy Eastwood asked."

Derrick pushed the warrants they'd picked up on the way into the man's hands. "Warrants. The keys. Now."

Coolidge pulled a childish face, thin lips pursing, then made a show of examining the warrants. Ellie wanted to slap him upside the ears till his head spun off.

"Now," Derrick repeated. "If she's in trouble, every second counts."

Ellie schooled her reaction. They both knew that if the Southside Slasher had gotten to Sarah, she was probably already dead. And if it was Coolidge, he could have easily hidden her body somewhere on the premises.

Shondra curved her arm around Sarah's friend and patted her back as Coolidge retrieved a ring of keys from a hook on the wall beside the door. "It's okay, Rochelle," Shondra told the friend.

Ellie hoped she was right.

Ellie gave Shondra a pointed look. "Stay here with Rochelle while we take a look."

Shondra nodded understanding. If the scene inside Sarah's apartment was bad, the last thing they wanted was for her friend to see it.

Telling herself that if the door was locked, everything might be all right, she and Derrick followed the reluctant Coolidge outside, then down the sidewalk and up the stairs to the second floor.

The air was still and hot, begging for a breeze, the parking lot practically empty as summer semester was winding down. Sarah's apartment was an end unit which meant it shared only one wall. The lights were off next door.

"Anyone live there?" Ellie asked.

"No, new resident moving in next week," Coolidge said.

Ellie scratched her head. An empty apartment. Was there shared access between the spaces?

As she knocked, Coolidge stood back as if he expected this to be a wild goose chase. Anxiety mounted as they waited, but no response.

Ellie pounded the door with her fist this time. "Sarah Turner, it's the police. If you're in there, open up!"

Another awkward tense few moments, and she shook her head at Derrick, then took the keys from Coolidge and inserted them into the lock. The key turned, the lock clicked, but the door wouldn't budge.

"There's a second lock, a dead bolt," Ellie said. "Which doesn't fit the key."

Coolidge shrugged as if perplexed but Ellie wasn't buying it for a second. "You've been inside to do repairs. You knew about the other lock and didn't speak up?"

"I haven't been inside in a while," he said. "She must have just added it. That chick was paranoid as shit."

Ellie ignored his comment and waited as Derrick moved back, preparing to kick the door in. Judging from the fact that the door frame was intact and the lock hadn't been picked, it was obvious that there was no forced entry.

Derrick charged, using his weight, his shoulder and leg to slam the wood. One... Two... Three times before the wood splintered around the doorknob and he maneuvered his hand inside and turned the lock.

Ellie blocked Coolidge from entering. "Stay here. And don't leave the scene."

Cursing, he folded his arms and leaned against the stairwell rail.

She pulled her gun and Derrick did the same as they inched inside the space.

"Sarah Turner, police. Are you here?" Ellie shouted.

The sound of the air conditioner humming full force bled into the silence and the strong metallic scent of blood hovered in the air.

Derrick gestured he'd go left to what looked like the kitchen and living room. She veered right down a narrow hall. The pungent odor grew stronger. The sound of a ceiling fan spinning echoing from the back. She kept her eyes trained, checked the bathroom.

Empty. No signs of trouble.

A few more steps led to the only bedroom. The door stood ajar. She glanced at the interior.

The bed was unmade. Coverlet on the floor. Lamp overturned.

Then she spotted a blood trail from the white sheets to the carpet and drag marks across the floor.

EIGHTY-EIGHT

Ellie paused at the door to Sarah's bedroom, careful not to touch anything. The young woman was nowhere in sight. But judging from the blood and disarray in the room, she'd obviously been attacked and was injured. She just hoped she was still alive. "Derrick, in here!" Ellie shouted.

His footsteps pummeled the floor as he hurried to her, and he muttered a curse as he halted behind her.

"She's gone," Ellie said. "But something definitely happened."

"I'll call an ERT," Derrick said as he pulled his phone.

While he made the call, Ellie snapped photographs of the room, the bedding, floor, and the bloody handprint on the wall. In her mind, a scenario formed—Sarah in bed, a man assaulting her, her fighting. She'd probably clawed at the wall as he dragged her across the room.

Blood streaks were everywhere, a pair of smiling lips painted on the wall similar to the one at Beverly Hooper's house.

Questions nagged at Ellie. If Sarah was dead, why take her body?

She glanced at the window and noted it was closed. Carefully stepping around the blood stains, she crossed to the window and examined it.

The window was locked.

She pivoted, searching the room for signs of how the perp had gained entry. The front door had been locked with multiple locks when they'd arrived. The windows were secure. There was no back door.

"Bloody smiling lips again," Ellie told Derrick as he entered the room.

"Similar to Radcliff's MO but not identical," Derrick said. "Why take her?"

A shiver went through Ellie. "He wanted us to know he struck again so he left his calling card. Now he sits back and tortures her while we hunt."

"Could be," Derrick agreed.

"How did this perp get in and out of the apartment with her?"

"He could have been hiding inside when she got home," Derrick suggested.

"True, but the door and deadbolt were locked from the inside." Curious, she looked up at the ceiling. Nothing there.

Another survey of the room and she saw a vent large enough for a person to crawl through a few inches off the floor.

"The vent screws are loose," Ellie said.

Derrick rushed up behind her. "He crawled through, attacked her, then left the same way."

Ellie scratched her head. "Then he dragged her through the vent?"

Derrick's breath punctuated the air. "It's possible," Derrick said. "Or... once he was in, he carried her out the door, put her in his car then returned. Locked things up and left through the vent."

"And it happened during the night when no one would notice," Ellie added.

Her stomach churned, and she glanced back at the door. They'd ordered Coolidge to stay outside.

"The apartment manager had keys to her apartment," Ellie said. "He could have lied and had a key to the deadbolt."

"Let's ask him and we'll search his apartment for it." Derrick's heels clicked as he turned and strode back through the room, stepping around the blood and the bedding on the floor.

Ellie was right behind him.

But when they reached the door, Coolidge was gone.

EIGHTY-NINE

"He's heading to a truck." Derrick gestured across the parking lot. "I'll go after him."

Ellie followed him to the door, tossed him her keys, and he ran down the steps to give chase while Ellie phoned Shondra. "We're in Sarah's apartment. There's blood and signs of a struggle. It appears she's been abducted." Ellie inhaled. "The apartment manager ran off and Derrick's gone after him. Ask her friend if Sarah mentioned anyone else who may have wanted to hurt her. Maybe an old boyfriend?"

"Copy that," Shondra said.

Ellie wracked her brain for the next steps. "Look in Coolidge's files for a list of empty apartments in the building. It's possible the perp may have left Sarah in one of those."

"On it."

They hung up and she phoned the sheriff and explained the situation.

"Issue an APB for Omar Coolidge. He's driving a black Ford pick-up truck, license plate WV-123-BA. Also, Sarah Turner is missing so alert law enforcement agencies and ask Angelica Gomez to post Sarah's photo on the news."

"Will do," Sheriff Waters said.

"Deputy Eastwood and I are going to search vacant apartments in the complex in case the perpetrator left Sarah in one of them." If he had, Sarah might still be alive.

"You need manpower?"

"That would help," Ellie admitted.

"I'll be right there."

"Thanks. ERT's rolling up now." The forensic van parked and four investigators got out. Ellie called to them and they climbed the steps. While they began documenting and processing the scene, and Dale Harvey took pictures, she went to the apartment next door. Using Coolidge's master key, she unlocked the door then flipped on the light.

At first glance, the apartment was bare. No furniture anywhere, confirming Coolidge's statement that the space was vacant. She walked through the living room and kitchen but it was empty and she didn't see blood. The unit was laid out the same as Sarah's so she found the bedroom. Empty. No blood or sign anyone had been inside.

The bathroom was empty as well but she stooped to examine the vent. The screws were loose here, too.

The perp had entered through this space, crawled into Sarah's and abducted her. Then he'd taken her body somewhere, returned to lock up and left through this unit.

So where was Sarah now?

Derrick swung the Jeep around a curve, pressing the accelerator to keep up with Coolidge, brakes squealing.

Coolidge turned right at the end of the parking lot, then sped onto a winding county road leading into the mountains. Dammit, where was he going?

He rounded curve after curve, swerving to avoid a head-on with a small convertible, and slammed on his horn to keep a group of teens in an SUV from sideswiping him.

Coolidge's truck disappeared for a minute, and Derrick searched the side roads. Dust hurled upward from the man's vehicle. Derrick swerved onto the dirt road that looked as if it led nowhere. Gravel spewed as he rumbled over it, the tires churning. The road was narrow and deserted and wound up into the hills toward Widow Lake.

The Jeep hugged the side of the road, vibrating as he rode the shoulder and he struggled to keep it from going into the ravine below. Coolidge's truck bounced over the ruts and he hit a rock, skidding sideways.

He lost control, the truck fishtailed then slammed into a boulder. Derrick pressed the brake, skidding himself and nearly crashed into the rear of the truck. Dust clogged his vision and he pulled his weapon, then eased open the car door.

Coolidge stumbled from the vehicle then took off running through the woods.

"Stop, Coolidge, it's over," Derrick shouted.

But the man forged ahead, weaving through the brush and trees.

Derrick gave chase, gripping his gun at the ready. He had no idea if the bastard was armed but couldn't take any chances. If he'd killed Sarah, he was desperate.

Coolidge stumbled and Derrick noticed him clutching his side before he slipped and went tumbling down the rocky ravine. His scream boomeranged off the mountain.

Derrick screeched to a halt at the edge of the drop off.

Coolidge had landed on a ledge about thirty feet below. His leg was twisted to the side, his arms thrown out as if to break his fall. Blood seeped from where he'd hit his head on the rocks.

And he wasn't moving.

NINETY-ONE

Ellie returned to Sarah's apartment to update Sergeant Williams.

"We need someone to process the empty apartment next door. I believe the intruder crawled through the vent in there to reach Ms. Turner's apartment. He probably took her out through her own door, left her somewhere close by or put her in a vehicle, then returned, locked up her apartment and the vacant one and off he went. All this while everyone else in the complex slept."

"Don't worry, Detective," Williams said. "If he left so much as a partial print or DNA, we'll find it."

"Radcliff escaped prison so look for signs of him," Ellie said. "We also suspect the apartment manager Omar Coolidge might be involved somehow. Ms. Turner made accusations that he entered her apartment when she wasn't home and touched her things. We have search warrants for cameras in her apartment and his. Also confiscate his keys so we can determine if he had a key to the deadbolt on Sarah's apartment."

"Copy. I'll alert my people to specifically look for cameras,"

Williams said. "We noticed a couple outside. We'll see if they're working."

Ellie inhaled sharply. "Coolidge's prints and DNA are probably in every apartment in this complex, casting reasonable doubt. But if you find it inside that vent, we might be able to use it to nail him."

"Understood," Sergeant Williams said.

"Thanks. My team is going to search the other vacant apartments in case he left Sarah in one of them," Ellie said. "Have them check cars in the parking lot, too."

Williams nodded in understanding and went back to address the team while she hurried to Coolidge's office to meet Shondra.

"I can't believe this is happening," Sarah's friend Rochelle cried. "I knew something was wrong when she didn't answer her phone. She's been so terrified lately that she barely comes out of her apartment. And when she's inside, she calls me crying at night."

"Why was she frightened?" Ellie asked.

"She thought someone was watching her. That the apartment manager was stalking her."

Ellie clenched her teeth.

Coolidge had known Amy Dean. Had he been terrorizing female residents for years? Was he a murderer?

NINETY-TWO

WIDOW LAKE

Lorna Bea felt like ripping the stupid aluminum foil from the windows so she could see outside. Her father had never been this mean before. Ever since they'd come to Widow Lake, he'd gone totally mad.

Remembering his threat about boarding up the windows, she snatched her notebook and began writing a story. She titled it: *The Father Who Kept His Daughter Locked Away.*

A low knock sounded on the door. She went still. Was he back? No... he wouldn't knock. He'd just barge in.

The knock sounded again, followed by a loud whisper. "Lorna Bea, are you in there?" It sounded like Cade.

She jumped off the bed and ran to the door. "Yes, but the door's locked."

"Where's the key?" Cade asked.

"Probably on the kitchen counter."

"I'll go get it." Footsteps echoed as he ran down the steps. A few minutes later, he came back and she heard the lock turning. She twisted the knob and waved him and Betsy inside.

"What's going on?" Cade asked.

Betsy looked up at the window. "Why you got that stuff on the window?"

"My dad did it. He said it's too dangerous to go outside, but I think he's lost his mind." She looked down at the iPad Cade held. "What's that for?"

"There's a prisoner on the loose," Cade said. "He killed a bunch of women and may be headed to the lake."

Lorna Bea's breath sharpened. Maybe her father wasn't totally crazy.

"There's something else," Cade said. "Those bones under the shed were a woman's. They said she had a little girl and they're looking for her."

"That's awful," Lorna Bea gasped.

"It gets creepier," Cade said. "On the news, it showed a picture of the escaped prisoner. And another man they're looking for.

Betsy nodded. "Mama said I wasn't supposed to see it, but I looked anyway."

Cade angled the iPad toward Lorna Bea. "This is him ten years ago. His name is Frank. But he kind of looks like your dad."

Lorna Bea's heart thundered in her chest. The photo was old and grainy. The guy in the picture was a lot younger than her father, had shaggy hair to his shoulders, pale skin and glasses. He was also skinny while her father was heavier.

"That *can't* be him," Lorna Bea said. "I don't think my father went to college."

Cade shoved the tablet under his arm. "Are you sure?"

Lorna Bea shrugged. She wasn't sure of anything anymore.

Cade fidgeted. "Where's he now?"

"I don't know, but if he comes back and finds y'all here, he'll have a fit."

"He's gonna lock you up again?" Betsy asked wide-eyed.

Lorna Bea nodded miserably although the wheels were turning in her head.

It didn't make sense. Neither did moving all the time. But they did that at least every year.

She snapped her fingers and jumped off the bed. "Nana keeps some old pictures in a photo album," she said. "Let me see if I can find them."

She motioned for them to be quiet and follow her, and they tiptoed down the steps. Nana was asleep in her bedroom, so they dashed past her, then Lorna Bea snagged the photo album from the bookshelf and they ran back up the stairs.

In her room, she plopped on the bed with Cade and Betsy and opened the album. Inside were dozens of pictures of her when she was younger, mostly on her birthday and Christmas. She and Nana baking cookies. Decorating the tree. Opening presents.

She flipped further back in search of a picture of her father when he was younger. But several of the pages were empty, the pictures torn out.

And there were no photos of her daddy.

Her thoughts gathered like the gray storm clouds she'd seen moving in. Her father was secretive. Never made friends. Said he did some consulting work for a developer. That he liked the job because it was flexible and he hated staying in one place.

But he was always looking over his shoulder. And he did keep that safe locked.

Cade's words echoed in her ears. The name of the man the police were looking for was Frank.

Her daddy kept changing his name. Their names.

Her stomach cramped. Had he lied to her? Had he been to Widow Lake before? Had he attended college here?

Did he know something about those bodies they found at Widow Lake?

Derrick called a SAR team and an ambulance, then Ellie while he waited for them to arrive. "Coolidge crashed then got out of his truck and ran. He fell over the drop-off and landed on a ledge."

"Is he alive?" Ellie asked.

Derrick used binoculars to get a close-up view of Coolidge. "Hard to tell," Derrick said. "So far I don't detect any movement."

"That's not good," Ellie said. "If he's dead and he's the one who took Sarah, he can't tell us where he left her."

"She's not in his truck," Derrick said.

"Deputy Eastwood, Sheriff Waters and I are searching vacant apartments here and the surrounding property in case he left her on the premises. We'll also canvass residents and ERT is checking their vehicles."

"McClain just got here," Derrick said. "I gotta go."

He hung up and went to meet Cord and the other SAR workers along with the ambulance.

"What do we have?" Cord asked.

Derrick quickly explained. "We think Coolidge may have

had something to do with Amy Dean's death. Last night, another young woman in his complex disappeared. Ellie is at the scene with search warrants and ERT. Coolidge fled the scene."

Cord's eyes darkened. "Then this guy might be a killer?"

"He could be," Derrick said. "But at this point, he's only a person of interest. We need him alive so we can question him."

Cord nodded. "I'll go down and assess the situation, then we'll make a plan to bring him up."

Derrick conceded. Ranger McClain knew what he was doing and had proven invaluable in prior cases.

If Coolidge was alive, there was no one else he trusted to handle bringing him up from the ravine.

NINETY-FOUR

WIDOW LAKE

The girl—Lorna Bea—was alone. Up in her room with the windows blacked out.

And Frank was gone.

He lit a cigarette and inhaled, blowing smoke rings into the hot air as he watched the two other kids sneak into the house. As he inched through the bushes, brush crackled beneath his boots. Sweat beaded on his upper lip as he peered through the window and saw the old lady stretched on her bed, snoozing.

Perfect.

He waited a few minutes, watched to make sure she stayed asleep, then snuck up to the back door. It squeaked as he eased it open and he ran his fingers over the knife he'd tucked in his back pocket, pausing to listen for the granny or the kids.

Voices sounded from the second floor. The kids were in the girl's room.

"When will your daddy be back?" Betsy asked.

"I don't know, so let's be fast," Lorna Bea said. "What else can you find on that iPad?"

He licked his dry lips. Smiled. Then he tiptoed past the old woman's room. He stepped on a loose board that squeaked and heard footsteps.

Dammit. The old woman was awake.

"Who are you? What are you doing in here?" she shrieked.

He pivoted and she came at him, slinging her bony little fisted hands at his chest. He shoved her away and she stumbled backwards then fell against the floor and hit her head on the dresser. For a split second, he held his breath as he watched to see if she got up. No movement.

When she didn't, he closed her bedroom door and crept up the stairs. His pulse hammered with anticipation as he pushed open the door. Betsy jerked her head up, then scooted closer to her brother. Cade wrapped his arm around his little sister, but Lorna Bea jumped off the bed.

"Nana!" Lorna Bea cried. "Nana! Someone's here!"

"Sorry, darlin'," he murmured. "Nana can't help you now."

The boy grabbed his sister's hand and tugged her toward the door. He raised his hand and struck the kid across the face, sending him stumbling to the floor. Betsy screamed.

"Run, Betsy!" Lorna Bea cried. "Run, get help!"

He tried to catch the little girl as she darted toward the open door, but she ducked under his arm and ran down the steps, ponytail flying.

Lorna Bea ran to the boy and shook him. "Cade! Cade, get up!"

He took advantage of the moment, grabbed Lorna Bea around the neck and dragged her down the steps.

NINETY-FIVE

Lorna Bea screamed and kicked, yanking at the man's hand to escape. But he hauled her across the room like she was a rag doll. "Nana!"

"She's gone, honey," he murmured against her ear as they passed the rocking chair. "No use crying now."

Terror clogged Lorna Bea's throat. Nana couldn't be gone. "No!" Her eyes darted to Nana's bedroom. But the door was shut. "Let me go!" she screamed.

The big man slapped his hand over her mouth and drowned out her cries. She dragged her feet, digging her heels in as he hauled her through the door. The humid air hit her and she smelled the awful scent of his sweat and cigarettes. With one arm around her neck, he dragged her toward the woods.

She clawed at his arms as he reached the water, and she used all her might to kick backward. Her foot connected with his knee, and he grunted and loosened his hold long enough for her to bite his hand. He bellowed in pain and she stumbled away from him.

Rage filled his voice as he lunged after her. She ran forward, stumbling blindly. One step. Two. Three.

A sudden wind picked up. A gray cloud rolled across the sky.

"Help!" she screamed. "Someone help me!"

Thunder rumbled. A motorboat puttered past. Her scream was lost in the sound.

Then she heard him behind her. Brush crackling. Twigs snapping. His breath puffing out as he got closer.

She jumped over a log and a broken branch, skidding in a patch of weeds. Briars stabbed at her. Mosquitos buzzed. She ran faster but she tripped over a log and he closed in.

She couldn't give up. Breath huffing out, she snagged a stick and swung it at him. He grabbed at her and she kicked him again then rolled to her stomach to push herself up.

Then something hard hit her in the back of the head. A rock? A gun?

A second later, the sounds grew quiet. The woods darkened. The sunlight faded...

NINETY-SIX

LAKE HAVEN APARTMENTS

While one ERT team processed Sarah's apartment, another searched Coolidge's.

Ellie and Shondra searched the empty apartments while Bryce canvassed the residents in the hope someone had heard or seen something the night before. With ten vacant units, it was a laborious task.

Maybe word about Coolidge's unnerving behavior had spread and they were having trouble renting them.

The first eight apartments were void of furniture or personal belongings, but as she entered the ninth one, Ellie sensed someone had been inside. She motioned to Shondra to proceed with caution and inched into the room, scanning the open living area.

There were dark, reddish brown stains on the carpet. Dried stains that might have been there a while. Mud or blood? It was hard to tell.

The scent of smoke and pungent odor of weed blended with something stronger. She coughed and walked through the room then down the hall to the bed and bath.

No one was inside. No furniture either, although she found

a bong, a ratty blanket and soda cans, some crushed and others used as an ashtray. Empty chip and pretzel bags had been tossed in the corner along with fast food wrappers and three pizza boxes.

"Looks like someone had a party and the munchies," Shondra said, stowing her weapon in her holster.

"Yeah," Ellie said. "Wonder how they got inside."

Shondra went to the window and checked it. "Bottom floor. Window busted out. An end unit that backed up to the woods, easy peasy."

"No sign Sarah or a body was here," Ellie said. "Wait for ERT and I'll check the last unit."

With Coolidge under suspicion, Ellie made a note to report the break-in to the owner of the apartments. For all she knew, Coolidge might have used it as his own private party pad. Covering all bases, she texted Williams and requested someone process the place and take samples of the dark stain.

She wiped her damp neck as she stepped back outside. Black clouds were rolling across the sky. Thunder rumbled as she walked to the last unit. The windows were coated with grime as if the space had sat vacant for a long time.

Using the master key, she unlocked the door and shined her flashlight across the interior. The sense that someone was inside made her pull her weapon.

Then a loud roar rent the air. A wild animal?

No. A man howled then lunged from the shadows and charged her. The force threw her backward, and she struggled to stay on her feet. Her gun flew from her hand and a bullet fired, pinging off the ceiling.

Then he was on top of her, fists connecting with her face.

NINETY-SEVEN

SOMEWHERE ON THE AT

Derrick studied the sharp angles of the ridge as Cord and the rescue team set up their equipment. If Coolidge survived that fall, it would be a miracle. His body had to have bounced off the jagged rocks. The impact against the stone had been hard, had probably shattered his bones.

Heat pounded down, Derrick's skin blistering. Slowly, storm clouds had begun to gather above the spiny branches of the trees. Birds cawed and vultures soared. A slight wind sifted its way through the pungent air, bringing the scent of death.

Cord and his partner harnessed themselves and rappelled down the side of the ridge to examine Coolidge.

Several seconds passed. Derrick wiped his sweaty hands on his pants. His throat felt dry as if he'd been eating dust.

"He's alive," Cord shouted from below. "We'll board him and haul him up."

Derrick signaled his understanding and the rescue team lowered a neck brace and board. Cord and another worker secured Coolidge's unconscious body, harnessed him and brought him up. As soon as they got him on the ground, the medics started to work, taking vitals and calling in to the hospital.

Derrick's admiration for the SAR team rose, along with his respect for McClain's expertise and professionalism.

He crossed to the ambulance and looked down at Coolidge. Blood matted his hair and face. His wrist looked shattered, a bone protruding through the skin. His leg twisted at an odd angle. Skin pasty and white. "How's his condition?" he asked the medics.

"Pulse is low and thready. Head injury, broken leg and probably ribs. Possible internal injuries."

"His chances of making it?"

The young medic shrugged. "I can't say at this point."

"He was fleeing the police during a felony investigation," Derrick said as he handcuffed Coolidge to the gurney. He gestured to Sheriff Waters' deputy who'd just arrived on the scene.

"Ride with him and stand guard," Derrick said. "I'll meet you at the hospital. If he wakes en route, ask him where Sarah Turner is."

The deputy nodded.

Derrick thanked him then addressed Cord. "Thanks for your help today."

Cord's intense gaze met his. Derrick never could get a good read on him. "Just doing my job."

Derrick's phone buzzed. Ellie's boss, Captain Hale.

"Special Agent Fox," he said as he answered.

"Fox, I just got a 9-1-1 call. I tried to reach Detective Reeves but she's not answering. Is she with you?"

Derrick went cold all over. "No. I left her at Lake Haven Apartments where we found Sarah Turner missing."

Cord straightened beside him, worry flashing on his face. "What's happened to Ellie?"

Derrick gestured for him to hang on. "What about the 9-1-1 call?"

"The parents of that little girl Betsy who were staying at Widow Lake claim their kids were attacked by some man at the cabin next door."

The keys to the Jeep jangled in Derrick's hands. "Coolidge is on his way to the hospital but unconscious. Sheriff's deputy is with him. I'll try to reach Ellie and head to Widow Lake now."

"What's wrong?" Cord asked, worry deepening his voice.

"9-1-1 call from Widow Lake. Captain Hale tried to reach Ellie but she's not answering."

Cord un-pocketed his keys. "I'll check on Ellie while you take the 9-1-1 call."

Derrick's gaze met Cord's. His gut instinct told him to run to Ellie himself. But the trouble at Widow Lake might be related to this case and the Turner woman's disappearance, so reluctantly he gave a nod.

"Keep me updated when you get there," Derrick said.

Fear for Ellie nagged at him and he sent her a quick message to fill her in.

Call me when you get this.

Panic threatened when she didn't respond. What would he do if something happened to her?

NINETY-EIGHT

LAKE HAVEN APARTMENTS

Pain shot up Ellie's jaw, her ears ringing. The man's weight had pinned her down but he pushed up to run, his knee digging into her stomach.

She didn't give him a chance to get up. She snatched his arms, then threw him on to his back and climbed on him, straddling him. She raised her fist to pound him in the face then saw his eyelids fluttering, his eyes jerking back and forth. Who was he? Not one of their suspects.

She jerked him by the shirt. "Where's Sarah Turner?"

The man lay dazed, his breathing rattling out, raspy and uneven. Judging from his bloodshot eyes and the way his body was jerking, he was high. His mouth went slack as he blinked to try and focus.

"What did you do to her?" she growled.

He mumbled something incoherent, then his eyes rolled back in his head, his body shaking, then going limp.

Shondra suddenly appeared. "Jesus, what happened?"

"Found him inside and he attacked me." Ellie checked the man's pulse. "I think he's overdosed. Get the NARCAN."

Shondra ran outside while Ellie began CPR. A minute

later, the deputy returned and handed the NARCAN to her. "Call 9-1-1," she said as she ripped open the package.

Shondra did as she said. Ellie took the device, moved her fingers to the bottom of the man's nose, inserted the tip in one nostril then pressed the plunger to release the spray. She did the same with his other nostril then watched to see if he reacted.

"Come on, buddy," Ellie said.

Seconds dragged into a minute. Then another. She thought she'd lost him.

But finally, his body spasmed and he gasped for a breath. Sweat broke out on his skin and his arms jerked, eyelids fluttering rapidly.

Ellie's phone buzzed. She pulled handcuffs and cuffed the man, although judging from his weakened state, he couldn't even walk much less try to get away. She stood and checked the phone. Cord.

"Ellie, where are you?" Cord asked, his tone concerned. "We tried to reach you."

"Apartment five, Lake Haven Apartments."

"Did you find the woman?"

"No." She glanced down at the man who was barely conscious. His hair was ratty, his T-shirt full of holes, his jeans dirty. She had a feeling he was homeless.

And too high to have snuck into Sarah's and abducted her.

NINETY-NINE

Ten minutes later, Cord appeared at the apartment. He took in the scene, then her face and growled, "Dammit, El."

"I'm fine," she said. "He's not though. OD'd. Ambulance on the way."

Emotions flashed in Cord's eyes as he strode to her. He lifted his hand and cupped her jaw, angling her face to examine her. "Looks like it hurts."

"Like hell," she said with a small smile.

He didn't return the smile. Instead, anger streaked his face. He opened his mouth to say something but they'd played this song and dance before and knew better.

"Don't," she said. "It comes with the job. And I'm okay."

Cord's labored breathing rattled in the silence. He looked away for a long minute before it finally steadied. "Coolidge is on his way to the hospital."

A siren wailed and Shondra hurried to meet them.

"How is he?" Ellie asked.

"Unconscious. Broken leg, ribs, head injury. One of the sheriff's deputies is escorting him and standing guard."

"I hope to hell he survives," Ellie said. "And that he knows something about Sarah Turner."

The medics appeared and Ellie waved them over. "He OD'd. Administered a dose of NARCAN and revived him."

"Do you know what he took?" one of the medics asked.

"No idea," Ellie said. "Shondra, take a look around."

Shondra searched the kitchen then disappeared down the hall. When she returned, she was carrying a syringe and empty vial.

"Looks like heroin," Shondra said.

The medics stooped beside the man to check his vitals. "What's his name?"

"Don't know. We were searching the apartments for a missing woman and he charged me. Think he's homeless and been using this place for shelter."

One medic checked the man's pockets for an ID and pulled out a driver's license.

"Expired," he said. "But his name is Willie Hager. He's twenty-five."

Ellie glanced at the deputy. "Text Deputy Landrum and ask him to see what he can find out about Hager. If he has next of kin, notify them."

"Copy," Shondra said.

Ellie's phone buzzed. Sergeant Williams.

"Found cameras hidden in Sarah Turner's in her bedroom vent," he said when she connected. "We also found a hub of cameras in a secret room behind some bookshelves in Coolidge's living room." Derision laced his tone. "Sicko was spying on all the female tenants."

Ellie silently cursed. "Son of a bitch. Confiscate them all and send them over."

Her phone buzzed with a text just as she hung up. Actually, there were two. First she read Derrick's.

Then saw her captain's.

Get up to Widow Lake stat. Twelve-year-old girl has been abducted.

ONE HUNDRED

SOMEWHERE ON THE AT

Present

Lorna Bea paced the dungeon-like room, then crossed to the window and stared at the stormy sky and the shadows of the forest. It was so stuffy and hot her stomach felt queasy.

Where in the world was she?

That mean man had hit her. And then... she remembered. She was blindfolded, in a car bumping over rocks and ruts in the road. It seemed like they were driving for hours but was probably only a little while, then he stopped, dragged her from the vehicle and threw her in this dungeon.

Cold fear seeped through her bones. What was he going to do to her?

Tears gathered in her eyes, but she blinked them back. She had to be strong like the characters in her books.

Her daddy cared about her. Loved her. When he found out someone had kidnapped her, he'd come and find her. He would.

And he'd take care of that monster.

But doubts niggled at her. Her daddy was a liar... He lied to everyone about their names. What else had he lied about? Did he know the man who'd taken her?

She rubbed at her eyelids where they still burned from the blindfold. He hadn't wanted her to see where she was going. And she hadn't.

The room was dark. Through the window, all she could see for miles were massive trees and woods. She was not at Widow Lake. Or anywhere she'd ever been before.

She tried to remember some fun times with her father like the way Cade and Betsy and their parents picnicked and fished and the mama read stories to Betsy at night. The way the kids built forts in the woods and skidded pebbles across the lake. The way they even held hands and said a prayer before they ate.

Things a real family did.

But her mind was a big black hole filled with nothing but packing empty boxes and running.

She closed her eyes, struggling.

One memory finally worked its way to the surface. When she was five, she'd begged her father to take her to the carnival.

They left Nana at home making a blueberry cobbler, and Daddy drove her to the carnival. The bright colored lights and rides and noises made her heart thump. Music echoed around her. Kids laughed. Clowns did tricks. Vendors called out, selling funnel cakes, popcorn and cotton candy.

She'd never seen anything so exciting! They rode the Ferris wheel around and around. It went so high, she giggled and squealed. Then they stopped at the top and she got dizzy and a little scared they'd never come down.

"It's all right, girl," her daddy said as he curled his arm around her. "I'll always keep you safe."

She huddled close to him and knew he meant it. She smiled. Finally, it moved again and they climbed off, then got cotton candy and played games and he won her a giant panda bear. Then a clown came up to them with his painted face and big red nose. His mouth was painted into a big red smile but it was scary... She trembled.

The clown looked down at her, peering at her oddly, "Hey, honey, what's your name?"

Her father snatched her hand. "Come on. We have to leave."

"But my panda bear," she cried.

"Forget about it," he snarled as he dragged her away. "I'll buy you one." Suddenly, he rushed them to the car and tore from the carnival.

She cried as they left all the pretty lights and the rides and the panda behind.

ONE HUNDRED ONE

WIDOW LAKE

As Derrick swung the Jeep into a parking spot at Widow Lake cabins, Ellie phoned. "I got your message."

"You okay?"

"Yeah. Where are you?"

"I just arrived at the Hammersteins' cabin."

"Be there in a few. I'm on my way."

He hung up and hurried to the door.

The father opened up, his expression distraught. "Thanks for coming."

Derrick identified himself and the man did the same. "Ken Hammerstein. My wife is Gina and our kids, Cade and Betsy."

The names teased his mind. Betsy was the child Ellie had looked for when they discovered the bodies up here. "What happened?" Derrick asked as he followed Mr. Hammerstein inside.

The ceiling fan whined, and soft crying echoed across the room from the sofa. The mother was sitting on the couch holding Betsy in her lap. The boy was huddled beside her, staring at the toes of his high-tops with a dull expression.

"Shh, it's all right," the mother whispered to the children. "The police are here now."

"The kids went to see Lorna Bea, the girl in the cabin next door." Mr. Hammerstein's breathing was choppy. "Apparently her father locked her in her room. Cade found the key and unlocked it."

"Her daddy covered the windows with foil," Cade said.

That disturbing image made the hair on Derrick's neck prickle. "Did she say why he covered the window?" Derrick asked.

Cade bit his lip. "He told her bad people were out there. That they could see in."

That definitely raised suspicions. "Was he at the house when you went over?" Derrick asked.

The boy shook his head. "We waited till he drove off."

Derrick swallowed hard. "Then what happened?"

Mr. Hammerstein rubbed his son's shoulder. "It's okay, Cade. Tell him."

Cade's eyes widened in fear. "This man came in and tried to take Betsy."

Anger hardened Hammerstein's voice. "My brave boy Cade grabbed her hand but the man knocked him down."

"Lorna Bea yelled at Betsy to run and she did," Cade added.

"Betsy came in screaming." The father wheezed a breath. "Then Cade ran home and told us what happened."

Cade's chin quivered. "He dragged Lorna Bea out the door and I couldn't stop him."

Derrick knelt in front of the boy. "Hey, man, you did great. You protected your sister and you ran for help. That was the smartest thing you could do."

The little boy's tormented face indicated he was still beating himself up.

"Are you okay?" Derrick asked. "Did he hurt you?"

"His face is bruised," the mother said protectively.

The boy shrugged and put on a tough face. "I got worse when I fell out of the tree."

Derrick patted his leg. "You're a brave kid, buddy. Can you describe this man?"

"He was a monster," Betsy whispered.

Derrick's heart squeezed. "Was he tall? Heavy?"

"He was big, I mean tall, but skinny," Cade said.

"What color was his hair?" Derrick asked.

Cade's nose wrinkled as he thought about it. "I don't know, he had a mask over his face and head."

A ski mask, Derrick realized.

"How about a car or truck outside?" Derrick asked.

Cade shook his head. "No, but I heard a boat."

So that was how he'd escaped.

"I'm sorry this scary thing happened," Derrick said. "But both of you are being very helpful."

Mr. Hammerstein motioned for Derrick to step aside with him, then lowered his voice. "Do you think it was that escaped prisoner?"

How could Derrick answer that? "I don't know, sir. Radcliff didn't abduct or hurt children." That they knew of. "His victims were all college-aged students."

Although, serial killers had been known to change their MO and victim profile, so he couldn't rule out the possibility. But if Radcliff wasn't responsible, who had kidnapped the girl? And what did he plan to do with her?

As Ellie and Cord rushed to the door, Derrick met them and quickly summarized what had happened.

"Where was the girl's father?" Ellie asked.

"He wasn't home. Cade said he heard a boat," Derrick said. "But I think the girl's father knew Lorna Bea was in danger. He covered her window so no one could see inside."

Ellie clenched her teeth. "We need to find him and get Lorna Bea's picture on the news."

"Let's go next door and see what we're dealing with," Derrick said.

Ellie texted Captain Hale.

Issue Amber Alert for twelve-year-old Lorna Bea Jones. Will send photo soon. Checking out the house situation now. Need an ERT.

Cade's father walked over with Cade beside him. He shifted back and forth anxiously. "Agent Fox, Detective Reeves, this may be nothing, but I thought you should know everything," Mr. Hammerstein said.

The young boy's chest rose and fell as he drew a breath for courage. Then he indicated the iPad in his hand. "We heard about that body in the lake and those bones you found. I looked it up online and saw that picture of a man you were looking for."

He handed the tablet to Ellie. She checked the photo. "Yes, we did post that. His name is Frank Wahlburg. He's wanted for questioning."

"I know," Cade said. "Me and Lorna Bea like mysteries and since she was at the shed, I figured she'd want to see the story about the bones you found there. I showed her the picture of this man you're looking for..." He dug the toes of his sneakers into the floor.

"Go ahead, Cade," Mr. Hammerstein encouraged.

"He kind of looks like Lorna Bea's father."

Ellie's lungs tightened.

Derrick patted the boy's shoulder. "Thank you for telling us this, Cade. Like I said, you're a brave young man."

Ellie angled her head toward Mr. Hammerstein, "Do you know how to reach Lorna Bea's father?"

Mr. Hammerstein shook his head. "We didn't exchange numbers. He said his name was Dwight Jones, but he wasn't exactly friendly. The grandma looked kind of afraid of him. We should have known something was off then."

"What does he look like?" Ellie asked.

"He's about six feet, short brown hair, brown eyes," Mr. Hammerstein said. "Probably early thirties, give or take a couple of years."

"He has scars on his arms," Cade added.

Ellie offered Cade a warm smile. "Thanks for your help, bud. You might be a detective in the making."

Cade relaxed for the first time since she'd arrived, and his father gave him a hug.

"Do you think that man will come back for Betsy?" Mr.

Hammerstein asked.

Derrick cleared his throat. "I don't know. But we'll have a detail guard your house until we figure it all out."

Ellie nodded. "For now, stay inside and lock up. We're headed next door."

"Don't worry, we won't be letting the kids out of our sight," Mr. Hammerstein assured them.

She and Derrick left the family and joined Cord who was staring out over the lake. Muggy air swarmed around as rain clouds gathered.

Cord crossed his arms, his body rigid. "What can I do?"

"Organize a team to search the area for Lorna Bea and her abductor. He's probably long gone but..." She let the sentence trail off. She knew they probably feared the same thing she did —that the man had killed the girl and dumped her body in the lake or woods.

Cord agreed with a grim expression.

"Look for tracks and see if anyone else in the area might have seen something," Ellie told Cord. "We'll get a crime team here ASAP."

Cord nodded and headed in the direction Cade had pointed.

"What the hell's going on?" Ellie asked as they pulled their guns and walked toward the cabin next door. The dog days of summer had been bad before but nothing like this insanity.

"This kidnapping, Sarah Turner's disappearance, the break-in at Beverly Hooper's, Amy Dean and Reuben Waycross's murders, Radcliff's escape... They must be connected."

"According to Cade, Lorna Bea's father covered her windows so no one could see in," Derrick said. "He warned her there were bad people out there."

Ellie's skin prickled. "If he thought she was in danger, why didn't he come to the police?"

The obvious answer hit her. Because he'd done something illegal himself. Was he the killer they'd been hunting?

ONE HUNDRED THREE

SOMEWHERE ON THE AT

Beverly roused from unconsciousness, weak and disoriented. For a moment she thought she'd had a nightmare where she'd been abducted and attacked.

She blinked, forcing her heavy eyelids open, and squinted to focus. Reality returned with sickening clarity as she realized the nightmare was real. She and Janie... at the reunion... Janie going outside, crying for help... someone jumping her from behind.

She surveyed the dark room. Concrete walls. No windows. One door, which was locked—she'd heard him turn the key when he'd left.

She yanked at the ropes around her wrists. She couldn't get up anyway. He'd untied her from the ceiling but tied her to the wall now. Dear God, what was he going to do to her? Did anyone even know she and Janie were missing? Was someone looking for them?

"Janie?" she said in a raw whisper. "Janie, are you here?"

But her friend didn't answer. "Janie?" she cried.

Nothing but silence. And the sound of her own ragged breathing.

Please, God, help me. I don't want to die.

ONE HUNDRED FOUR

WIDOW LAKE

Ellie and Derrick approached the Jones' cabin with caution, the afternoon heat burning Ellie's neck. Brittle twigs snapped and crackled as they walked over them, the hum of a boat on the lake puttering in the silence.

They grew quiet as they reached the front door. The heat was cloying. The sense that something bad had happened here permeated the air.

Ellie gripped her gun at the ready and eased open the front door. The wood floors squeaked as they eased inside. The air conditioner whirred, a clock ticking in the silence.

The curtains fluttered from the air blowing through the vent. Dust motes danced in the dim light slanting through the living room window. The furniture was non-descript. Plain dark-green sofa. A rocking chair. Basket of knitting yarn and needles beside it.

She glanced at the kitchen but it was empty. A half full pot of coffee sat on the counter. A mug on the wood table.

Where was the grandmother?

Derrick checked the hall closet and end tables for a phone.

Ellie noted another room to the right. She paused to listen at the door. Silence.

Instincts on alert, she eased the door open. Her heart stuttered. The grandmother lay on the floor, her graying hair torn loose from her bun, her eyes wide, blood pooling beneath her head.

Chest tight, Ellie stooped and checked for a pulse. The woman was dead.

ONE HUNDRED FIVE

"Derrick, in here," Ellie shouted.

Derrick came running, then cursed at the sight of the poor woman. "Lowlife," he muttered. "Bad enough to take a child but to kill a little grandmother, too."

Ellie fought her own anger and revulsion. "Look around in here while I call it in." Derrick knelt to examine the doorway and floor while she phoned Captain Hale.

"We definitely have a kidnapping. Grandmother was murdered," Ellie said. "Girl's father is not on the premises but we need to find him. He goes by the name Dwight Jones, although we have reason to believe he's actually Frank Wahlburg. Run a background check on the name Dwight Jones. See if he has other family or a permanent residence."

"Will do."

"Send Dr. Whitefeather and a forensic team," Ellie said. "Ranger McClain is searching outside. Agent Fox and I will look for a photograph of the girl to text you."

After hanging up, she took pictures of the dead grandmother and the crime scene. A scenario formed in her head as she noted the woman's fingernails had broken off, probably in a scuffle when she'd tried to save her granddaughter. The kidnapper must have shoved her, then she'd fallen and hit her head. Poor woman.

If she'd made physical contact with him or scratched him, hopefully she'd gotten some DNA.

"Did you find a phone?" Ellie asked.

"No. No bills or checkbook or anything personal either, not even a photo," Derrick said.

"There weren't any personal family photos in this room either," Ellie said, thinking that was odd as she glanced around the room.

"This was just a vacation rental. Maybe there are pictures at their personal residence," Derrick suggested. "I'll search the father's bedroom."

"I'll check upstairs." Ellie yanked on latex gloves and carefully stepped around the blood-stained rug. The stairs creaked as she made her way up. The sight of the aluminum foil covering the window made her stomach revolt.

She photographed the room, noting the empty walls, the plain bedspread, a few books on the bookshelf and a cardboard box in the closet. No suitcase. No kids' or preteen toys. No phone, laptop or video games.

She checked the dresser and found two pairs of jeans, T-shirts, shorts and underwear. No frilly ribbons or hair products.

The bedding was ruffled where it appeared Lorna Bea had sat on it, the covers askew. A photo album had fallen to the floor. She photographed it, then picked it up, hoping to find pictures of Lorna Bea and the father to compare to Frank Wahlburg's.

There were no school pictures, which struck her as odd. Didn't schools have picture day every year?

She found some photos of Lorna Bea when she was small, maybe five or six, at Christmas and on her birthday. None of birthday parties with other children or relatives. Her grandmother was in several pictures but oddly her father wasn't included in any of them.

There were several blank pages as if they might have been torn out at one point.

Finally, she found a more recent shot of the girl which could have been taken in the last year or two. She took a screen shot then texted it to her captain.

She went to the closet and rummaged through the cardboard box inside it, surprised the girl had very few mementos or treasures with her. Just a seashell, an arrowhead, some rocks and a map. Then a blank notebook.

Ellie smiled at that. As a child, she'd lived her life by maps when she and her father took trips together. She'd had her life planned out. Grow up and become sheriff like her father.

Except her father had endorsed Bryce for sheriff instead of her. A seed of bitterness resurfaced. Later, she'd learned he'd done it for her own protection. It still stung though.

The corner of the bed caught her eye, and she noticed something jammed beneath the mattress. Curious, she pulled it out and realized it was a small diary like notebook that Lorna Bea had hidden.

Maybe it would hold some answers.

She glanced at the aluminum foil covering the window again. Lorna Bea's father claimed he was protecting her.

Who was he protecting her from?

ONE HUNDRED SIX

Derrick searched Dwight Jones' closet and found jeans, T-shirts, a pair of sneakers and boots, and several pairs of disposable gloves.

The dresser drawers were practically empty. No personal items in the room. In the bathroom, he did find a toothbrush and comb, which they'd test for DNA. ERT would dust for prints.

He moved on to the closet where he found a large metal safe. Locked. A code was necessary to open it.

What was inside? Dwight's will? Money? A gun he wanted to keep away from his daughter?

Outside, a car engine rumbled and he went to the door. The ERT had arrived along with the ME. Ellie was coming down the stairs.

"No sign of the girl but the kids were right about the foil covering the window. Something bad was definitely going on here. I found a notebook Lorna Bea had hidden beneath her mattress," Ellie said. "Maybe she wrote something in there that will help."

The knock at the door halted their conversation and Ellie let the ME and ERT in. She relayed their findings while

Derrick made his call, then the investigators started processing the house.

"Poor lady," Laney said as she stooped to examine the body. "She didn't have a chance."

"I know. Thank goodness the door was closed and the neighbor's son and daughter didn't see this," Ellie said. "Hopefully Lorna Bea didn't either." Ellie indicated the woman's broken fingernails. "Looks like she fought her attacker. Check for DNA."

She left Laney to do her job and carried Lorna Bea's notebook outside. The stench of death followed her, mocking her with the fact that she had a child to find and another murder to solve.

And she felt like she was running in circles.

ONE HUNDRED SEVEN

WIDOW LAKE

Radcliff wondered if they'd found Geraldine Woodall yet. Not that he cared. She had been dispensable. By now, the moron cops knew he'd escaped. He smiled at the thought of them seeing his latest handiwork.

Still, he needed to lay low until night. He drove past the college and stashed the car in a wooded section. Then he slipped into the tunnel entrance and made his way through it until he entered the sanctuary where the brothers had convened. His killing spree had begun before theirs, and ended when theirs was just getting started. But he'd been thrilled to provide them inspiration. His chest swelled with pride.

Later, after his trial, he'd learned Dr. Dansen had added his case to her curriculum. That had made him even more famous.

He'd looked forward to returning here for years. Every night, as he lay on the mattress in his cell and counted the cracks and spider webs on the ceiling, he imagined the reunion. The worst part about being locked away was being cut off from the brothers. He desperately wanted to hear about their deeds in detail. Although, each year his following had grown and he'd managed to receive a few messages, so he knew the body count had risen.

But Frank had not made contact once. Not with him or the others. He'd entertained equally as sadistic thoughts as the rest of them, but he'd disappeared from Widow Lake after the first killing and hadn't checked in. That had been part of the Brotherhood pact. They'd agreed to communicate yearly. They'd also taken precautions to make certain no one talked.

Using the burner phone, he called Odessa. She'd been a constant lifeline to the past, visiting and writing him and offering herself to him in any way he wanted.

She answered in a breathy tone. "Hey, lover boy. I've been waiting. Where are you?"

"On the way. You?"

"I'm here. Things are heating up already."

"We'll celebrate when I get there."

"I can't wait," she purred.

He grinned. She had no idea what he had in store for her.

Just as the ME and ambulance left to transport the grandmother's body to the morgue, Angelica Gomez arrived. As usual, she looked professional in a black dress that accentuated her figure, her dark eyes and coppery skin.

Her cameraman, Tom, trailed her as Angelica walked toward the cabin.

Ellie gestured for them to wait. "You can't go inside," she said. "ERT's still processing and I have to find the man who lives here and notify him of his mother's murder."

"What was cause of death?" Angelica asked.

"It looks like the kidnapper pushed her and she fell and hit her head." Ellie exhaled, trying to wash the image from her mind. "We suspect Jones is involved in all this and may be Frank Wahlburg, the man we've been looking for in relation to the Amy Dean and Reuben Waycross murders. But that's off the record. We'll frame it so we're looking for him to notify him about the kidnapping."

"Got it." Angelica lifted her microphone, then gave Tom the signal to begin. "This is Angelica Gomez, Channel Five News,

294   RITA HERRON

coming to you live from Widow Lake." She tilted the mic toward Ellie. "Detective Reeves."

Ellie forced a calm voice. "An Amber Alert has been issued for twelve-year-old Lorna Bea Jones who was abducted earlier today by an unknown assailant at the cabin where she was staying with her father and grandmother. A witness described the kidnapper as tall, thin and wearing a ski mask. He is considered armed and dangerous." She hesitated a beat. "We are also looking for the girl's father, Dwight Jones, who is in his early thirties, described as muscular with short brown hair and brown eyes. If you hear this message, Mr. Jones, we want to reunite you with your daughter and need your help." She offered a sympathetic look as if she was speaking directly to him. "If anyone else has information regarding this abduction, please call the Crooked Creek Police Department."

Angelica's expression remained stoic as she recited the phone number. She signaled Tom that the interview was over and he went back to the news van.

"Do you think that escaped prisoner kidnapped her?" Angelica asked.

Fear gnawed at Ellie. "I pray not," she said. "But it's possible. The witness didn't see his face."

"I'd like to interview the witness," Angelica said. "Is he or she inside?"

Ellie lowered her voice. "No. The witness was another child, Angelica. He's pretty shaken up and the family's concerned for their safety."

Sympathy softened her eyes. "Understood."

From the doorway, Derrick cleared his throat. "Ellie, come here. You have to see this."

"I'll be right there." She turned to Angelica. "I'll let you know when we can report the murder. For now, let's concentrate on finding the missing girl."

Angelica agreed and walked back toward the van while

Ellie climbed the steps again. Judging from Derrick's troubled expression, he'd found something disturbing.

"What is it?" she asked.

"You have to see for yourself."

Worry for Lorna Bea mounted as she trailed Derrick to the father's bedroom.

"I got that safe open."

At first, she wasn't certain what she was looking at. There were plastic bags and boxes labeled neatly. One held a knife, one a scalpel, another fingernails, another hair, another teeth. Names were listed on each item.

Ellie's heart slammed in her chest.

Dear God. Dansen had said that Frank was into murder-abilia. These were souvenirs from murder victims.

Frank Wahlburg handed his client his merchandise and accepted the payment, smiling at how much people were willing to pay. Long ago, he'd established his side business, dealing with memorabilia that catered to those on the dark web.

The private chat room he'd established for his business had drawn followers and collectors from all over the world. Orders were shipped, although there were a few items he could not send through the mail. Those required personal meetings.

Another reason he traveled across the country.

Tonight, he had to meet the brothers though. Satisfy the agreement, even though he'd deviated from it ten years ago. They still didn't know the truth. And they never would.

He secured the box he'd brought with him for the reunion, locking it in the secret compartment he'd had installed in his SUV. As he drove, he turned on the radio.

"This is Cara Soronto with your local weather. It's been another scorcher today, folks, with no relief in sight. Brush fires have popped up along I-16 toward Savannah and a mandated no watering restriction is in place. Already six deaths from heat strokes have been reported across the South and these record temperatures will remain in the high nineties for the rest of the week. Please do not leave your children or pets in a locked car with no ventilation!"

Next came the news. "Angelica Gomez from Channel Five news here with this breaking story. An Amber Alert has been issued for twelve-year-old Lorna Bea Jones who was abducted from a cabin where she was vacationing with her family." She paused, then continued, "Police are also looking for the girl's father, Dwight Jones, who is in his early thirties, described as muscular with short brown hair and brown eyes. If you hear this message, Mr. Jones or if anyone has information regarding the abduction, please call the Crooked Creek Police Department."

Frank pounded the steering wheel with his fist and cursed. He'd done everything he could to protect his daughter. But now *they* had her. He knew it in his gut.

Cold fear seized every cell in his body. He stepped on the accelerator. No telling what they'd do to Lorna Bea. They'd tell her everything.

He had to save her. She didn't deserve to suffer for what he'd done.

ONE HUNDRED TEN

SOMEWHERE ON THE AT

Pretty Sarah Turner didn't look so pretty anymore. Not like she had when she'd socialized with her friends. Or undressed in her apartment.

He'd watched her for months now. Liked the way her silky hair draped her shoulders and the wind tossed the strands around when she jogged.

She was a fitness fanatic and worked out a like a fiend. The treadmill. Running. Even yoga at the park in her tight yoga pants and sports bra that revealed the finest cleavage he'd seen in years.

But she'd looked right past him as if she didn't even see him.

As if he was invisible.

Just like he'd always been.

He hauled her unconscious body across the grounds to their meeting place. He was prepared for the celebration.

Tonight, the moon would be full, heightening the apprehension in the air and his anticipation.

They'd chosen this place ten years ago because it was abandoned and secluded. Though it was supposed to be a healing place, plenty had died within the walls and ghosts haunted it.

Nobody knew it still existed.

He'd get her ready, then he'd wait for the brothers to join him.

ONE HUNDRED ELEVEN

CROOKED CREEK

Fear for Lorna Bea tied Ellie's stomach into a thousand knots as she drove toward Crooked Creek.

Who exactly was this man and how had he raised a daughter? Did he know she was missing? Was he responsible?

Had he killed his own mother and then left with Lorna Bea?

No... Cade said there was another man who'd broken in. A man in a mask.

Maybe he was the man Betsy had mentioned she and Lorna Bea had seen the night she chased the kitty into the woods. A kitty that could have been planted there to lure her away from her parents...

Ellie pressed her hand to her racing heart.

This man could be connected to Dwight Jones... could be the one he was worried might be endangering his daughter.

If Dwight was in fact Frank Wahlburg, the evidence inside that safe could prove they'd worked together. Her mind spun with it all.

Although it was late, the glow of the moon looked almost

eerie as it streaked through the tree branches overhanging the lake.

Cord had search teams combing the woods now. The grandmother's body would be autopsied and with a smidgen of luck, they might find DNA, but Ellie doubted it. That would be far too simple for this mind-reeling case.

She and Derrick left the ERT collecting the souvenirs in Jones' safe and processing the crime scene, but she'd brought the notebook she'd found hidden in Lorna Bea's room to examine it.

"I need to call Lindsey," Derrick said as Ellie dropped him at his cabin. "And I'm going to dig deeper into all our persons of interest. See what each of them has been doing the last ten years."

Ellie nodded, knowing they both needed sleep and a shower. She had a feeling her dreams would be tormented with the pieces of the puzzle she hadn't yet managed to click into place.

They said good night, and she wound through town to her bungalow, eyeing her property as she always did before parking and going inside. Grateful for the light she kept burning on her front porch and the golden moon illuminating her yard, she swung into the driveway, and got out.

Once inside, she did a quick search of her house, poured herself a vodka and carried it to the den. She settled on the couch and thumbed through Lorna Bea's notebook.

As she skimmed the entries, chill bumps cascaded up her spine:

All I want is to have a nice house, a home. Friends. And to go to a regular school.

But my life is lived in boxes. The boxes we move every time we change towns.

"You can only take what you can fit in the box," Daddy says. But even then he looks at what I pack and removes anything too personal. No phone or computer. No souvenirs of where we've been. No notes or postcards or pen pal letters with friends.

Not that I have any friends. Daddy says I can't talk to anybody. That people are dangerous. We have to stay inside. Stay on the run. That there are bad people out there. That they might get me.

But he won't tell me who they are. Or why they'd want to hurt me.

My box is the only thing I have. Sometimes we don't stay in one place long enough for me to unpack it.

He has boxes, too. Boxes that hold secrets. He takes a smaller metal box with him when he goes places. He never tells me where he goes or who he sees or what he does. Or what's inside the box.

He has a big safe in his bedroom that he moves with us, too. I don't know what's inside that either, but I know I'll be in bad trouble if I get into it.

I keep this notebook hidden from him. But I've kept a running list in my mind of where we've been. And the names we've used. When I was little, Nana called him Frank. Then it was Daryl and Marvin and Hugh and... there were more, so many I can't keep track of them.

That's another thing. We change our names every time we pack up. He used to call it our adventures. But adventures are supposed to be fun.

Only the way he acts is scary.

Ellie rubbed a bead of sweat from her forehead, her heart aching for the twelve-year-old. Her life in boxes, like an orphan being shuffled here and there.

Lorna Bea had admitted they'd changed names. And her father had once been called Frank.

Which suggested Jones was actually Wahlburg as they suspected.

She skimmed the list of places they'd moved along with the dates. In the morning, she'd share it with Derrick and see if crimes had been committed in those cities around the time Wahlburg and Lorna Bea had lived there.

If they had, he could be a killer.

ONE HUNDRED TWELVE

CROOKED CREEK POLICE DEPARTMENT

DAY 5

Gritty-eyed from lack of sleep the next morning, Ellie carried her third cup of coffee with her to the conference room to meet the rest of the team—Derrick, Cord, Deputies Eastwood and Landrum, Sheriff Waters and her captain. All night she'd tossed and turned, wondering what might be happening to Lorna Bea. Who had her and what were they doing to her?

She felt sick to her stomach at the thought of that child being hurt.

Judging from the team's grim expressions as they filed in the conference room, the case was wearing on all of them. Derrick looked almost as tired as she felt.

She began by filling them in on what they'd found at the Jones' house. "Grandmother murdered in cold blood. Jones, aka Wahlburg, MIA. Daughter, Lorna Bea, taken." She added the information to the whiteboard. "We have several persons of interest who may be connected to one another. Professor Roland Pockley, our victim Reuben Waycross and Frank Wahlburg who we've been looking for.

We now believe the father of our kidnapped child who is currently using the name Dwight Jones is Frank Wahlburg."

Derrick gestured toward a file box on the table. "We also found several fake IDs in his safe. Frank Wahlburg has been on the run and changing identities ever since the night Amy Dean and Reuben Waycross died."

A collective unease splintered the air.

Ellie continued, "He told Lorna Bea that bad men were out there. Maybe he thought his cohorts might come after her for some reason. But why?"

"He had a kid. Maybe they were afraid he'd get soft and talk," Derrick offered.

"That's possible," Ellie agreed.

"Any word on Radcliff?"

"After reviewing camera footage, the prison warden believes a female guard named Geraldine Woodall helped him," Captain Hale replied.

"Do we know where she is?" Ellie asked.

"No, she didn't call or come in to work, and she's not at her mobile home." Captain Hale popped a mint into his mouth. "Locals in Trion looked into her. It appears she'd packed a suitcase and had depleted her bank account the day before. She and Radcliff could be anywhere by now."

Ellie shook her head. "My gut tells me he's somewhere around Widow Lake."

"That would be crazy," Bryce muttered.

"Maybe not," Derrick interjected. "He attended Widow Peak College and also took Dr. Dansen's criminology class but was not in the same class with the others. When he was arrested in early 2013 and his trial was all over the news, the professor led discussions about his case with her students. It's possible these guys met Radcliff on campus somewhere and knew what Radcliff was up to before he was arrested."

"And he shared the details about the hair and bloody lips," Ellie said.

It took a minute for everyone to digest that. "Perhaps the group is having their own reunion this week."

"Exactly."

"Any word on Omar Coolidge?" Ellie asked.

"Still hasn't regained consciousness," Derrick said. "But I viewed cam footage from his computers last night. He was definitely watching the female residents in his building for years. I found one of the night Darla Loben was attacked by spiders. There was an empty apartment next to hers. Someone put them in the vent."

"Same way Sarah Turner's abductor got into her place." Ellie thought on that. "Coolidge had access. But as far as we know, there's no connection between him and the other suspects. He dropped out of college his freshman year and definitely wasn't in Dansen's class."

"Maybe he'll wake up and confess," Deputy Landrum said.

Fat chance of that, Ellie thought. "The hospital is supposed to notify me if he regains consciousness." She inhaled. "Shondra, any info from Professor Pockley's colleagues?"

"Nothing concrete. Just that he liked biology, especially dissecting animals. His colleagues also said he was awkward around women, and that he didn't handle rejection well."

"Thanks, Deputy Eastwood. Good work. The dissection of animals could lead back to those animal graves we found."

Shondra smiled and continued, "If he asked Amy Dean out years ago and she rejected him, it could go to motive."

"We'll keep that in mind," Ellie said. "Now let's talk about Wahlburg. Dr. Dansen mentioned that Frank was obsessed with murderabilia," Ellie said. "We found evidence of that in Jones' safe." She filled them in on the contents, and a ripple of unease rumbled throughout the room.

Deputy Landrum raised a finger, indicating he wanted to

speak. "I found a private chatroom on the dark web which could be how they've been communicating. Aliases are used, but one guy is into collecting and selling murderabilia."

"Dr. Dansen said Wahlburg wrote a paper on that topic," Ellie said.

"What is the name of this chatroom?" Derrick asked.

"The Brotherhood."

Ellie considered that.

Deputy Landrum continued, "In the chatroom, participants share fantasies about mutilation, dismemberment of victims, torture and murder."

Ellie exhaled. "My God."

"Maybe the Bureau's cyber team can track the IP addresses and identify the members," Derrick said. "If our suspects are part of it, they may have referenced crimes they committed in that chatroom."

ONE HUNDRED THIRTEEN

Derrick used a separate section of the whiteboard to list each of the persons of interest starting with Frank Wahlburg, then Professor Roland Pockley and Dominique Radcliff.

"I did some research last night and compiled a timeline of where each of these men have been the last ten years. We've established that Frank Wahlburg disappeared after Amy Dean's and Waycross's deaths."

Ellie interjected, "I can fill in a few of those blanks. In Lorna Bea's journal, she said they moved around at least once a year, changing their names with each move." On the whiteboard, she listed the states Lorna Bea had mentioned along with the dates they'd moved.

"That helps," Derrick said. "Let's talk about Professor Pockley. After college he earned his master's in zoology and for a while worked at the Atlanta Zoo before returning to Widow Lake to teach. Since then, he's been a guest lecturer at other universities and conferences."

Derrick listed the dates and places, chronicling the man's career.

"Now let's move on to Dominique Radcliff. Radcliff went

the tech route and became a phlebotomist at a community hospital in the suburbs of Atlanta. After his arrest, he claimed he intended to study criminal investigation, focusing on blood spatter analysis." Derrick listed Radcliff's victims that they knew of, the dates the bodies were found and the two other missing women they suspected he'd murdered.

"Radcliff had a tumultuous upbringing. His mother was bipolar and had multiple affairs. One night Radcliff's father went crazy, slashed his wife's throat and killed the lover. His father painted her lips with blood. Blood spatter analysis was used to expose the truth."

Ellie sifted through that realization. "So he hated his mother and chose to kill other women as a replacement. The bloody lips mimicked what his father had done." She snapped her fingers. "Did his father hack off his mother's hair?"

"No, we think he did that to destroy their beauty." He paused a beat. "We know Amy Dean was killed in Widow Lake in 2013. That same year, two other coeds were murdered. A young woman named Zelda North, ten days after Ms. Dean disappeared. Two months later, on Halloween, Kitty Korley was killed in Brunswick, Georgia. And a third—Vanna Michaels from Dawsonville. We think these murders may be connected, either committed by one of our suspects or the group."

After he allowed time for everyone to absorb that information, he continued, "Radcliff began his killing spree in 2008. First with a young woman named Pamela Louis. He was caught early 2013. It's possible a copycat or accomplice adopted his MO and went from there."

Ellie nodded. "I found a list of four other similar crimes across the states. However, in looking at those dates, Radcliff was already incarcerated," she said, adding their names to the board. "Pockley was speaking at a conference at the time a coed named Judy Zane was murdered. We don't know the whereabouts of Frank Wahlburg at the time which means he could be culpable," Ellie said.

Sheriff Waters rolled a pen between his fingers. "According to those dates, no single suspect was in each place at the time of all of the murders."

Ellie breathed out, her theory of a conspiracy mounting. "Because we aren't dealing with just one killer. These men conspired to kill and covered for each other by copying the others' MOs, to throw off the police so we wouldn't make a connection.

"The bloody smiley lips were found on Beverly's mirror, not her body, which could also point to a conspirator or copycat," Ellie pointed out. "But he did hack off some of her hair."

"Maybe he panicked when she screamed but he still wanted us to know he was there," the sheriff said.

"Possibly," Derrick said. "Currently we have four possible victims, who are missing. Beverly Hooper, Janie Huggins, Sarah Turner and Lorna Bea Jones."

"The timing of the reunion is key," Ellie said. "What if they're meeting in one place for a grand finale?"

Derrick drew a question mark on the board. "My thoughts exactly. But where are they meeting?"

Ellie aimed her response at Shondra. "Deputy Eastwood, contact the counselor at the prison and Dr. Dansen. See if either of them can find something specific on a place the men might have mentioned."

"On it," Shondra said then left the room.

Captain Hale's phone buzzed and he stood, stepping out to answer.

Deputy Landrum started tapping on his computer. "I'll search this chatroom and see if they mention a physical location."

Captain Hale returned, his expression stony. "We've got another body."

A restlessness vibrated through the room and Ellie rubbed her temple. Who now? Ellie thought. This case was like dominoes, one body falling after another.

"They found the guard who helped Radcliff escape," the captain said. "Throat slashed, body left naked and exposed in the woods slightly north of Widow Lake. That road is en route to Widow Peak College."

"Definitely Radcliff's MO," Derrick said. "And fits with our theory about the reunion."

"Sheriff, why don't you get up there to the crime scene," Captain Hale said.

Bryce stood, his keys in hand. "On my way."

As he left the room, Ellie stood and gestured to the map on the wall. "That would be here," Ellie said, her mind sorting through the information.

Landrum spoke up, "In the chatroom, the men mentioned a bar called Knights where they played chess. They also made references to a hospital."

Ellie grabbed her laptop and began a search, looking for places that might fit the descriptions. A minute later, her pulse jumped. "There's a bar on campus named Knights. It sits over a tunnel in the mountain."

Ellie rubbed her temple as she studied the whiteboard then moved to the map on the wall. "The prison counselor said Radcliff fantasized about killing and putting body parts together to create a person." She studied the map. "Look, there's an old abandoned hospital north of campus."

Cord interjected, "I've worked SAR in the area and know the location. The building's still there but it's been abandoned for years."

"We need to divide up," Ellie said. "Agent Fox, take Deputy Landrum with you to the bar. I'll take McClain with me to the hospital."

With a plan in motion, they rushed out the door.

ONE HUNDRED FOURTEEN

SOMEWHERE ON THE AT

Janie was so cold, her fingers and toes were numb. Her wrists hurt from struggling to free herself. The room was dark and she smelled chemicals that might be used in a lab. Or maybe a morgue.

Terror filled her.

Why was this monster doing this to her?

And where was Beverly? Had he already killed her?

Tears filled her eyes and ran down her cheeks. Just a few days ago, she'd been so excited to reconnect with her friends at the reunion. To take a break from her stuffy life. Have fun again and not be tied down.

Her husband's face flashed behind her eyes. Rick was a great guy. Smart. Hard-working. Ambitious. Those were the reasons she'd married him.

But he'd become so self-absorbed and career-driven; work always came first. The romantic dates they used to enjoy had turned to business dinners that kept him out till all hours of the night. If she didn't know better, she'd suspect he was having an affair. But sex seemed to be the last thing on his mind. Building his portfolio took priority.

Still, he loved her and the kids. He'd even promised to take them on a cruise for Christmas.

And her little girl and boy... What would they do without a mother?

Sadness blended with icy fear, and she doubled over and sobbed. Forget the cruise. All she wanted now was to go home, cuddle her kids and sleep in her own safe bed. Take a walk with Rick and tell him she still loved him. Make him the homemade chicken curry he liked so much.

She blinked to clear her vision from the tears. She had to think. Find a way to get out of here.

She turned her head to look around for a way to escape. A sliver of light wormed through the bottom of the doorway. Dingy concrete walls surrounded her. Shadows closed in.

And silence. The kind of eerie silence that came before a terrible storm. The kind of silence that made her think that she'd never see her husband or children again.

Cord knew the location of the hospital, so Ellie let him drive. She needed time to sort through the dates and times again of the unsolved cases she thought related to the current ones.

Cord picked up his SAR dog from his cabin, hoping Benji would be able to help them locate possible victims if they were being held at the building.

Dark storm clouds threatened, the trees starting to shiver in the wind. Hopefully the rain would hold off until they could search this place.

She explained her conspiracy theory to Cord. "We know Jones, AKA Frank Wahlburg, kept souvenirs. If Pockley was in on it, he may have kept something, too."

She texted the captain:

Get a warrant for Professor Pockley's home and office, including his computer, files and any video footage he may have kept.

Copy that.

A text appeared from Shondra next.

Talked to Dr. Dansen. She confirmed that Waycross was especially interested in ritualistic behavior, that he wrote a paper about cult and gang initiations.

Ellie responded:

Thanks

She texted Derrick her theory about the initiation. "Cord, gang initiations often involve committing a crime or murder. Some of our witnesses suggested these guys formed a cult. What if their initiation required them to take a life?" Her thoughts raced. "The reunion is the anniversary of the beginning. Ten years ago, Amy Dean was murdered. Now they could be celebrating that day by taking new victims."

ONE HUNDRED SIXTEEN

SOMEWHERE ON THE AT

Déjà vu struck Frank as he parked in the woods. He had to be strategic, couldn't rush in guns blazing.

The brothers had been his friends, had shared his obsessions. They were the only ones who understood the demons that crawled through his mind like a flesh-eating virus.

The damn heat had made him crazy back then. It was making him crazy again. The thick trees of the AT stood so close together that it was suffocating him. The branches with their spiny leaves shot out tentacles, choking him. Invisible hands pushed him to the steep edge of the cliff where he looked down at the haunted lake and saw the dead buried, Waycross's body parts floating on the surface.

He closed his eyes, taking deep breaths as the chanting began in his mind. The rumble of thunder above the mountain thrust him back in time to that night.

The pact they'd made.

The minute the challenge had been issued, he'd known who he'd take. She'd been so beautiful, so quiet. Unaware of his draw to her.

Like the others, she'd ignored him. He'd asked her out but she'd looked right past him and given him a hard no.

That hard no sealed her fate.

He'd waited until midnight. The moon had been full then, too. Then he'd snuck into her apartment. He could still see the fear in those big beautiful blue eyes. Hear the shrill lilt of her scream as she'd tried to get away.

He hadn't known she had a child.

The woman screamed. The baby in the crib screamed.

He'd raised the knife...

ONE HUNDRED SEVENTEEN

KNIGHTS

Derrick contemplated Ellie's theory about an initiation as he parked at the bar where the suspects met to play chess.

Now they just had to prove that theory. And find the men responsible before the body count climbed higher.

The gray stone building was set on the top of Widow Peak overlooking one of the highest parts of the mountain. It reminded Derrick of a castle in ancient times. Woods shrouded the property, adding to the ominous feel, but the parking lot was packed with cars, SUVs and trucks.

"You don't actually think they'd meet in a public place like this, do you?" Deputy Landrum asked.

"Hiding in plain sight could be part of their game," Derrick said. "Or a place to stalk new prey."

Landrum nodded, quietly scanning the lot as they walked up to the entrance. Derrick didn't know the deputy well but according to Ellie, he was a whiz with the tech side and that skill was invaluable, especially with social media and so many crime scenes to analyze.

Inside, the bar was dark and gloomy with the scent of cigar smoke drifting through the vents. The décor looked like something out of ancient times itself. Artwork displayed scenes of the Knights of the Round Table, with framed articles describing the legends and history of King Arthur. Others featured medieval knights—Richard Lionheart, the middle-ages warrior king, William Marshal, England's greatest medieval knight, and Joan of Arc.

A full-sized replica of a knight in shining armor anchored the place with historical details, yet oddly the music piped from the speakers on the wall was contemporary.

A few of the students took notice of him and the uniformed deputy, and Derrick realized they were leery of cops.

"Canvass the room and show pics of our suspects," he told Landrum. "See if someone's seen any of our persons of interest. I'll talk to the bartender then take a look around."

Landrum nodded and accessed the photographs they'd all downloaded on their cells. Derrick crossed the room, then gestured to the bartender and—judging from the plaque on the wall—the owner, Antwaun Drake. The guy was in his thirties and looked a little rough around the edges, with choppy brown hair, tats of medieval symbols snaking up and down his arms and a Celtic knot earring on his left earlobe.

"You drinking or asking questions?" the bartender asked with a skeptical frown.

"Asking." Derrick angled his phone toward the guy. "Do you recognize any of these men?" First, he showed him a picture of Dominique Radcliff.

"Sure. He's that escaped serial killer," Drake said. "Haven't seen him though or I'd have called the cops."

Next, a picture of Professor Pockley. "What about this man? His name is Roland Pockley. He's a professor of zoology at the college."

The bartender gestured around at the clientele. "College staff usually don't hang out here. Bad for business."

"Drake, the beer?" a customer called.

Drake filled a mug and Derrick glanced at a thin man with glasses staggering toward the corner in the back.

"How long have you run the bar?" Derrick asked after Drake slid the beer to the customer.

Drake's green eyes reminded Derrick of a feral cat's. "Opened it about twelve years ago. College needed a place for students who weren't jocks or into the Greek scene." He shrugged, revealing a crooked front tooth, as he indicated the packed bar. "Turns out I was right."

Derrick showed him a photo of Waycross. "Do you remember this man?"

Drake cut his eyes toward the picture. "Waycross, he's the fella you guys found dead in the lake."

"Yes, he is," Derrick said. "And the reason I'm asking about his friends at the time. They were interested in true crime."

"Well, we do draw some true crime nuts. Inspired me to add décor about serial killers and murders downstairs, where the chess players meet."

"Were Pockley or Waycross among those?"

"Maybe. There's been hundreds of guys in here over the years. I can't remember them all."

"How about this man?" Derrick showed him the ten-year-old picture of Wahlburg. "His name was Frank."

A waitress pushed an order slip in front of Drake and he grabbed a bottle of vodka, a jar of olives and a shaker and shook his head. "Like I said, I can't remember everyone who came in here."

"What's downstairs?" Derrick asked.

"Pool table, medieval furniture, cigar bar. Set up for poker games and chess matches."

Derrick thanked him, threw a five-dollar bill on the counter then headed toward the rear where he'd seen the drunk guy staggering. A narrow, spiral stone stairway led down into a smoky space that had a speakeasy type feel. He counted seven young men smoking cigars and playing poker. Tables of two were seriously intent on their chess games.

Photographs of most wanted criminals in history hung on another wall with articles describing their deeds, creating a morose feel. A sword was attached to the wall along with a glass case housing various kinds of hunting knives. A framed sketch of a torture chamber along with illustrations of people being tortured and mutilated dominated the far wall. Posters of horror movies, including *The Silence of the Lambs*, occupied another.

Derrick's skin prickled.

Had the men met here to plan murder ten years ago?

ONE HUNDRED EIGHTEEN

THE HOSPITAL

The brothers gathered, humming as they had ten years ago in this very spot. Viewing screens were set up in one central station, so they could watch their victims.

The morgue was ready. The other bodies, they'd kept embalmed and preserved, tucked in their drawers. Shortly after they started the game, they'd realized that dumping the victims might lead the police back to them, so they'd created their own private graveyard here.

Police had questioned the others. But he'd managed to stay off their radar.

On one screen, he watched Radcliff lead Odessa toward the wall and string her up.

"You wanted to play," Radcliff said. "You like to live on the edge, don't you, my love?"

"Yes," she whispered. "Anything for you, Dom."

That look of fear excited him the most. Radcliff raised his knife and slashed Odessa's clothes, shredding them as he would her skin. But first he'd toy with her as he always did.

Her clothes hung in pieces off her pale body, which quivered with his touch.

While Radcliff played with her, pricking her back with the tip of the knife, she began to shake and whimper.

He turned to the next screen where the woman named Sarah Turner lay limp, helpless and terrified.

In another room, Beverly Hooper, and another, Janie Huggins.

Then there was the young girl. Frank called her Lorna Bea. He watched her huddle in the dark cold room, knees pulled to her chest, big eyes wide with fear as she trembled.

His heart pounded.

Her innocence would turn to horror when she realized why he'd taken her.

ONE HUNDRED NINETEEN

Ellie parked in the woods, secured her weapon, then she and Cord grabbed flashlights. Cord had taken back roads to keep from alerting the perps, if they were indeed at this location, so they had to hike in.

He led the way onto the path. An owl hooted in the distance and the hum of the wind stirring filled the air, bringing the scent of rotten moss.

Shadows plagued the woods, reminding Ellie of the time she got lost as a child. Was Lorna Bea out here somewhere? If she escaped her abductor, how would she find her way?

The thought of the child being hurt made her stomach twist. But she pushed her fear away. That little girl needed her to be tough. So did the other missing victims.

"Watch your footing," Cord said as he pointed out a section of briars and poison ivy. She hiked around it, avoiding stepping into a hole. They maneuvered through the line of trees and around downed limbs, climbing a hill and passing a ravine with a drop-off so steep it made Ellie dizzy to look down.

Cord held her arm to steady as they walked along the ledge. "Careful," he murmured. "It's slippery here."

Ellie inched her way, sticking close to Cord until they were on level ground again. They paused for a moment to catch their breath and Cord aimed his flashlight directly north. "It's about a half mile that way."

Ellie breathed out and forged ahead. They fell silent as they hiked, senses honed for sounds of someone who might be keeping watch. As they ascended the hill, Ellie spotted a building in the distance.

It appeared to be deserted, surrounded by overgrown weeds and brush. A tree had fallen on one side against the roof and kudzu climbed the grimy walls.

Cord panned his light across the property. "There's a van nestled in those trees."

"Someone is here." Ellie's heart started to hammer. She assumed the lead, gripping her weapon at the ready as she maneuvered the terrain. When they reached the clearing, she hunched low, and Cord followed, taking cover behind bushes flanking the sides of the building.

She paused to listen, but the concrete walls buffered any sound. Inching around to a rear door that had probably once been used for services and deliveries, she peeked through a window and saw a dim light inside, followed by some movement.

Dwight Jones, AKA Frank Wahlburg, was inside, creeping down a long, shadowy hallway.

ONE HUNDRED TWENTY

KNIGHTS

Derrick searched for a secret safe or wall leading to another room, some place where the group might have left evidence. But there was nothing behind the photographs and along the walls. He lifted the corner of the rug and checked beneath it, earning curious stares from the patrons inside.

"Excuse me a minute, guys," he told the chess players as he checked beneath the table. Again, nothing.

"What the hell are you doing?" one of the chess players asked.

"Searching for evidence in a crime investigation." He lifted his phone to show them the photos of the suspects, but his phone rang before he could question them.

"I think they're here at the hospital," Ellie said in a low whisper when he answered. "Frank Wahlburg is inside."

"Wait for me," Derrick said. "I'm on my way."

"I'll just take a look," Ellie said. "Scout out how many—"

Suddenly, the line went dead. Derrick's pulse pounded and he charged up the stairs to get Deputy Landrum.

Dammit, Ellie had been cut off. She might be in trouble.

ONE HUNDRED TWENTY-ONE

THE HOSPITAL

The room was dark and a horrible smell filled the air. Lorna Bea's stomach roiled. Something squeaked from the corner. A whine sounded in the distance and something rattled.

The man who took her was the one in the black hoodie she'd seen before.

If she ever got out of here, she'd write a story about him. And the girl he took. Only she would not be afraid. She'd have superpowers and turn invisible and slip past him into the woods.

Men's voices echoed from the other side of the wall, jarring her. It sounded as if they were arguing. Then she heard her father's deep voice. "You took my daughter."

She breathed out. Yes. Her father was here! He'd save her. Make that bad man pay for taking her.

"You broke the rules," the bad man said in a deep voice.

"Daddy!" Lorna Bea screamed. She wanted to run to the door but her wrists were bound and a rope tethered her to the wall. She twisted her hands to try and free them but the ropes cut into her wrists.

A sliver of light snaked through the room as the door opened. Her father's boots pounded the floor as he entered.

"Daddy, help! He killed Nana!"

Her father glared at the other man and cursed. "Was that necessary?"

"What? You don't like to have fun anymore," the other man hissed.

"I'd hardly call killing an old woman fun," her father snapped.

Lorna Bea's throat clogged with fear. What kind of fun was the man talking about?

The other man chuckled. "Don't worry. I spared her the knife. *She* wasn't the one I wanted."

"Don't do this," her father said in that sharp tone that made her stomach turn upside down. "Lorna Bea's just a child, an innocent in all of this."

"No, she's not. She's the reason the damn cops are crawling up our asses."

A knife glinted in the darkness as the man waved it around.

Terror ripped through Lorna Bea. Was he going to kill her?

"We know what you did, Frank," the bad man said. "We finally figured it out. All this time we thought Waycross left town to hide out, but he was dead."

"Daddy, what's he talking about?" Lorna Bea cried.

"Be quiet," he snapped. "I'll handle this."

The other man stalked toward her, then lifted a hank of her hair and chopped it off with the knife. She yelped, trembling with fear.

"Leave her alone," her father growled. "We'll find a replacement."

"No, it has to be her. And it has to be tonight."

ONE HUNDRED TWENTY-TWO

The sound of brush crackling behind Ellie startled her and she dropped her phone and whirled around. Two men in black masks lunged at her and Cord. She threw her arm up to deflect the blow but was too late. One of the men struck her on the side of her head. Pain shot through her temple. Stars swam behind her eyes. The world spun.

She heard grunting and an angry howl as Cord and the other man fought. "Get off her!" Cord shouted.

Cord knocked the second man down and stormed her attacker. He flung Cord backward. The second guy recovered, charging Cord from behind. Ellie tried to fight back, but he raised a knife to her throat and went still. The tip of the knife pricked her skin. Images of former victims with their throats slashed swam in her head. She dared not breathe.

Cord howled. Out of the corner of her eyes, she saw him fall to his back. A knife was lodged in his stomach. Blood spurted.

Ellie screamed in rage, then grabbed her assailant's knife hand and they fought. He twisted her arm behind her back. Sharp pain splintered her shoulder as she felt it being wrenched from the socket. A dizzy spell swept over her, and she went limp.

"Looked forward to this celebration for ten years," he growled.

Ellie recognized his voice. Pockley.

"She'll be our grand finale." Radcliff.

She'd been right about them. They were in this together.

Where was Wahlburg?

Questions bombarded her, nausea climbing to her throat as the men dragged her and Cord through the door. He was limp, bleeding badly, unconscious.

Fight, Cord, dammit, stay alive. We have to save that little girl. I have to save you.

In the hall, the concrete floor was hard and rough. Cord groaned.

Seconds later, a door opened and she was hauled inside. Radcliff forced her into a chair and tied her arms behind her, her wrenched one throbbing so badly the world began to fade. No, she had to stay conscious. "Cord..."

No answer. Panic seized her. Then they dragged Cord away down the hall.

Lights blinked, nearly blinding her. Suddenly, Radcliff swung her chair around to face a sea of screens. Ellie gasped in horror as she realized what she was looking at.

Different rooms, all in shadows. Each one holding a prisoner—one of the missing girls.

Odessa Muldane was in another. Her blood-soaked body hung from the ceiling. Lips painted in that ghoulish smile with blood. It was too late for her.

But the others were still alive: Sarah Turner. Beverly Hooper. Janie Huggins. And Lorna Bea.

Dear God. They were planning a killing party.

Tree branches swayed in the wind. Dried leaves and twigs tumbled across the road. The scent of impending rain mingled with the cloying humidity.

Derrick called Ellie's number three more times as he flew around the switchbacks. No answer. With each call, his fear intensified.

Dammit, Ellie. She should have waited on him. What was happening?

A knot seized his chest. They'd dealt with twisted killers before but this time there was more than one. She couldn't possibly fend off an army of psychos.

McClain is there, he reminded himself. *She's not completely alone.* And she was a fighter. Resilient. And well-trained.

She was also a woman he cared about.

Deputy Landrum studied the GPS for exact directions and the shortest route. Using his hands-free system, Derrick phoned Cord, but his phone went straight to voicemail. Frantic, he pressed the sheriff's number.

It rang four times before Waters picked up. "Sheriff, it's Agent Fox. Ellie's in trouble."

"What the hell now?" Waters growled.

"We think our suspects are meeting tonight at the old Widow Peak Hospital. Ellie called to report that Wahlburg was there, but the phone got cut off."

Waters grunted. "Knowing her, she charged in."

Exactly what he was thinking. "McClain's with her, although he doesn't have a firearm," Derrick said. When this was over, they'd find a way to rectify that issue.

"He usually carries a hunting knife," Waters said. "Maybe that'll help."

"Maybe." The ranger would be a fighter, especially if it meant protecting Ellie. They seemed to have some kind of special bond that went way back. Sometimes he wondered if there was more...

"On my way," Waters said, cutting off his thought. "I'll bring back-up."

As he disconnected, Landrum pointed out a side road that had them climbing the mountain. A lightning bolt struck in the gray sky. The college faded to a blur as they left it in the distance. A sign announcing the reunion flew past.

Derrick's fingers tightened around the steering wheel. It was a reunion all right. A reunion of killers.

And Ellie was caught right in the middle.

ONE HUNDRED TWENTY-FOUR

Ellie struggled not to pass out as she studied the screens. Beverly's shrill cries echoed in her ears. Janie was unconscious.

A groan brought her head to another screen. Cord lay on the floor, not moving, blood pooling beneath him. A sob caught in her throat. "Hang in there, Cord. I'm coming for you."

Don't you dare die on me.

The sound of Lorna Bea's voice drew her to yet another screen. A dim light glowed from a bulb overhead, enough for her to see the terror on the girl's face. She sat on a low cot, her hands tied, the rope attached to the wall.

Wahlburg was in the room. And another man.

Shock stole her breath. It was Harvey—the photographer who worked with their very own ERT.

A sense of helplessness mingled with rage.

"Let her go," Wahlburg said as he untied Lorna Bea's hands. "She has nothing to do with this."

"Daddy, what's he talking about?" Lorna Bea cried.

"She has everything to do with it," Harvey barked. Then he turned to the girl. "You think you know your father but you don't. This man made a pact with us. We all made our choices and he chose your mother."

Lorna Bea turned a confused look toward Wahlburg. "What?"

Wahlburg started toward the man, jaw tight, fists clenched. "Shut the hell up."

But Harvey grabbed Lorna Bea around the neck. She shrieked and the monster laughed.

"He's not your father," Harvey spat. "He killed your mother and was supposed to kill you, too. That was the deal. Leave no witnesses behind."

"She was only a toddler," Wahlburg snapped. "I saw her birthday picture on the table and couldn't do it."

"You chicken shit," Harvey growled.

"She was a baby," Wahlburg said this time. "She wouldn't have remembered anything. She *doesn't* remember anything now."

Ellie frantically struggled to loosen the knots around her wrists. Her shoulder throbbed and was practically useless, but she clenched her teeth at the pain. Now she had some answers.

Wahlburg had killed Amy Dean. Lorna Bea was Paisley, the missing child.

"You ran because you knew she could be linked to us, to her mother's death. And when they found Amy's body, they'd start digging."

"You killed my mother?" Lorna Bea asked in a strangled voice.

Emotions colored Wahlburg's face. "I'm sorry, honey," he said, regret in his tone. "It was a long time ago. We... I was in a dark place. We... were all experimenting with drugs."

Ellie twisted the rope and finally felt it loosen slightly. Nausea clogged her throat as she kept working the knots.

"You killed Waycross, too," Harvey said. "He was one of us."

"I didn't set out to kill him, only to get the little girl away. But he fought me."

"And you killed him then put him in the car and forced it into the lake."

"I had to, to protect all of us. He was going to dump Paisley in the lake." Wahlburg began to pace, clearly agitated. "I didn't sign up to kill babies."

"You agreed to the pact."

"I kept the pact, and all your secrets the past decade." Wahlburg whirled on Harvey and drew a gun from the back of his jeans. "Let her go. I protected her all these years and I'm going to protect her now."

Harvey gripped Lorna Bea by the hair and raised the knife.

Ellie's heart thundered. She had to hurry.

Desperate, she searched the room for a weapon. Nothing. No window. No bathroom. The door looked heavy and was locked. But the cameras...

She rocked herself back and forth in the chair, scooting it closer to the screens. Inch by inch, she scooted. She pushed too hard and the chair tumbled over. Pain slammed into her back with the force. She sucked in a breath to stifle a scream, and dragged herself another inch, then two, then another until she reached one of the screens.

Using her feet and upper body, she tried to upright the chair. Frustration mounted as she made it halfway then fell again. Gritting her teeth, she tried again and again. On the fourth attempt, she managed to get the chair back up on four legs. Her breath panted out.

Lorna Bea's screams pierced the air. Wahlburg jumped in front of her to protect her.

Ellie sucked in a breath and slowly shifted the chair so she could reach one of the monitors. Using her elbow, she swung backward until the glass shattered. Pellets of glass sprayed. Three larger chunks hit the table the monitors sat on. She pivoted her body and strained to get hold of one. The sharp corner stabbed her palm and blood seeped from the cut. Biting back a moan, she used the piece of glass to saw back and forth until the ropes gave way.

Sweat beaded her skin and trickled down her face. Taking deep breaths, she managed to untie her ankles, then stood. She swayed, dizzy, and grabbed the table for support.

Wahlburg and Harvey were shouting. Lorna Bea crying. She glanced at the screens again. At Cord. God, she wanted to go to him. To save him.

But Lorna Bea needed her and she could not let that bastard kill her.

Fear sparked her adrenaline and Ellie hurried across the room. The door was unlocked. She hesitated for a second, wondering if they were watching. If they'd left it unlocked to lure her into a trap.

The door squeaked as she opened it and she peered into the dark hallway. This place smelled old and musty, of death and darkness. She paused to listen then walked a few feet, searching for the room where Lorna Bea was being held.

A gunshot rang out, and she ran in the direction of the sound.

Derrick and Landrum met the sheriff and Deputy Eastwood on the main road leading to the old hospital and parked beneath a canopy of trees to camouflage their arrival. Weapons drawn, the four of them crept through the brush and trees until they reached the building.

Kudzu and years of grime covered the concrete, and the windows were crusted over. "I think there's at least three perps inside," Derrick said. "Wahlburg, Pockley and Radcliff."

His gaze scanned the property, but he didn't see anyone outside. Still, there were plenty of places to hide cameras so the men could be watching.

"Consider them armed and extremely dangerous," Derrick warned. "If this is their big celebration, there may be several victims inside. The girl Lorna Bea, Sarah Turner, Beverly Hooper and Janie Huggins." His throat thickened. "They also have Ellie and McClain."

The deputies and Waters nodded understanding.

"The last thing we want is to give them more hostages. Once inside, let's divide into teams," he said. "Landrum, you're with me. Deputy Eastwood with the sheriff. And keep your mics on so we can communicate."

Scanning all directions, Derrick led the way to the front door and eased it open. The place was dark and smelled musty as if there had been water damage. Cobwebs dangled from the corners and somewhere a clock's loud ticking echoed through the cold corridor.

They fanned out, checking the closest rooms and finding them empty. Derrick led the way to a stairwell and crept down it, the others following, ears and eyes alert.

The stairs led downwards into what must have been the morgue. There, he found a room with the door open. He glanced inside and his chest tightened. A wall of screens ran live footage from various rooms.

Coolidge's spy cameras were disgusting but this set-up was mindboggling. It was central station to a bad horror show, except the horror here was very real. Odessa Muldane hung from the rafters in one room, blood soaking her naked body, her head lolled over. Sarah Turner, Beverly Hooper and Janie Huggins were tied in separate rooms.

"Oh, my God," Deputy Eastwood whispered.

"Sophisticated equipment," Deputy Landrum commented.

"Where's Ellie?" Sheriff Waters asked.

Derrick turned in an arc and spotted another room where McClain lay, also bloody and unconscious. In another, he found Lorna Bea.

Wahlburg was there, another man holding a knife to the girl's neck. He pivoted slightly and Derrick recognized him. One of the crime scene investigators, the photographer Harvey.

A gunshot blasted the air—Wahlburg. The shot missed Harvey, but he charged Wahlburg. The two of them traded blows, fighting for the knife. The gun went off again and Harvey collapsed.

Suddenly, on camera, the door to the room burst open and Ellie stormed in.

Derrick cursed. "Deputy Eastwood, phone for ambulances. Let's divide up and find the victims. I'll find Ellie and the girl."

ONE HUNDRED TWENTY-SIX

Ellie froze as she entered the room. Harvey was on the floor bleeding out, his body convulsing. Wahlburg had shot him in the chest.

In the struggle, Wahlburg lost his gun. But Lorna Bea had it in her shaking hands. The gun bobbed up and down, her eyes glazed with horror. "You killed my mother!"

"I'm sorry," Wahlburg said, emotion thickening his voice.

"You're a monster," she cried.

Ellie gestured for Wahlburg to let her handle the situation, and she inched closer to Lorna Bea. "Hey, sweetie, it's Detective Reeves. I know you're upset and you have every right to be, but please lower the gun."

A crazed look darkened the girl's expression and she shook her head wildly. "He lied to me all my life! He killed my mother and lied to me and changed my name and made us move all over the place and never let me have any friends." A sob escaped her. "I hate you!" she said, pointing the gun toward Wahlburg.

Ellie held her breath. "Listen to me, Lorna Bea," Ellie said softly. "What he did was awful. I understand what it's like to be lied to by a parent, I do. But you don't want to shoot him."

"Yes, I do," she screamed. "He killed Mommy!"

"I'm so sorry, sweetie," Ellie murmured as she eased closer. "He deserves to pay for what he did. I promise you he will."

"Lorna Bea, please give the detective the gun," Wahlburg said calmly. "You don't want to live with killing someone." His voice cracked. "Trust me... it eats at your soul."

"Trust you?" she screeched. "You're a murderer and a liar."

His shoulders sagged. "I am, but I swear to you I regret what I did." Guilt laced his gruff tone. "I wish I could take it back. I... thought by protecting you, by taking care of you, that somehow I could make up for it."

"You can't!" Tears streamed down Lorna Bea's cheeks. "You can't bring my mother back."

The poor girl was trembling so hard, the gun wavered all over the place. Ellie lifted one hand and slowly slid it over Lorna Bea's. "Let me take him to jail," she whispered. "I promise you he'll go to prison and never get out."

Wahlburg raised his hands in surrender. "I will go to prison, Lorna Bea," he said. "Just give the detective the gun. You can still have a good life."

Ellie cut him a look, not trusting that he wouldn't pounce on her if given the chance. "He's right. He deserves to be punished, and you deserve a future." Ellie gently pushed the weapon downward.

Lorna Bea began to wail and Ellie trained the gun on Wahlburg. He lunged at her and the gun went off in the tussle. A grunt followed and the bullet pierced his chest. A shocked gasp, then he collapsed onto the floor, blood spurting.

Lorna Bea screamed. The door swung open and Derrick raced in. "Ellie?"

"I'm okay," she said, angry as she realized Wahlburg had intentionally jumped her to force her to shoot him.

A second later, Wahlburg's breath rasped out then his body went slack.

Ellie silently cursed. But she would not feel guilty over his death. Not when he was a cold-blooded killer. Not when he'd stolen this girl's mother from her.

ONE HUNDRED TWENTY-SEVEN

Ellie pulled Lorna Bea against her, her injured arm hanging limply by her side as the girl sobbed against her.

Derrick called Landrum to report in.

"I'll get Lorna Bea outside," Ellie said. "Look for the others. Sarah, Beverly and Janie are all here." Her voice wavered as the fear resurfaced. "And Cord. I'll come back for him."

He gave a nod, and she gently coaxed Lorna Bea from the room. By the time she made it outside, she saw Deputy Eastwood. "Stay with her until the ambulance arrives," Ellie told her.

Shondra gave a nod, and Ellie knelt in front of Lorna Bea. "Honey, it's going to be okay. I'll be back, but for now wait here with this nice deputy. There are others inside that need my help." She brushed the girl's tear-soaked hair from her cheeks. "Okay?"

Lorna Bea trembled, her chin quivering. Then she gave a tiny nod.

Ellie addressed the deputy, "Once the ambulance gets here, make sure they stay inside the vehicle. We don't want innocents caught in crossfire."

"Copy that."

Ellie turned and darted back inside to find Cord.

Armed with the weapon she'd taken from Wahlburg, she followed the corridor to the camera room. It was empty so she went in and studied the monitor showing the room where Cord lay. She searched for a clue as to its location in the building. But it was so grainy and dark, all she could make out were concrete walls.

She darted out the door and located the staircase. But just as she entered the doorway, something hit her from behind. Pain splintered her head and she pitched forward, lost her balance and tumbled down into the darkness.

Seconds later, she felt herself being dragged across the floor. Then a door screeched and she was dragged inside. She fought to stay conscious and smelled fresh blood as the man dumped her and left.

Although she was disoriented and dizzy, she managed to open one eye. Blinking as she peered around, she spotted Cord. It took every ounce of her grit to crawl to him.

She called his name or at least she thought she did. Nothing from him in return. No movement. She couldn't even tell if he was breathing.

She nudged his arm but it was limp and heavy. Fear clenched her chest and she collapsed against him. His body felt so cold, she tried to shake him. But the darkness pulled her under.

ONE HUNDRED TWENTY-EIGHT

Derrick found a morgue in the basement. He spoke into his mic to the others, "Downstairs. I hear voices."

He eased along the concrete wall, careful to stay in the shadows as he waited for Landrum and the sheriff.

"We'll have to move the other bodies."

Derrick's pulse hammered. That voice. Radcliff.

"We'll dump them in the lake and no one can trace us here," Radcliff said.

"What about that detective?" Pockley asked.

"We'll get rid of her," Radcliff said. "I can't wait to see her scream when I slash her throat."

Laughter erupted and Derrick saw red. He was about to race in, gun drawn, when he saw the sheriff and Landrum creeping down the hall. He signaled to them that the suspects were inside and they joined him, weapons drawn.

Derrick burst through the door and they rushed in. Radcliff and Pockley spun around, caught off guard.

Then Radcliff laughed, raised a gun and fired.

All hell cut loose. Waters charged Pockley, who pulled a knife, and Derrick raced after Radcliff.

He caught the sociopath just as he tried to slide out the door. The bastard made a run for a Jeep in the woods, but Derrick was faster and fired his gun.

The bullet struck Radcliff in the shoulder, then the storm clouds unleased. Thunder and lightning zipped across the tree-tops. Radcliff darted through the trees and Derrick gave chase up the mountain. The gunshot wound was slowing Radcliff down, and Derrick followed the blood trail through the brush. Limbs cracked and fell as a gust of wind picked up. Leaves swirled. Radcliff crushed weeds in his haste then neared a ridge.

Inching toward him, Derrick raised his weapon. "It's over, Radcliff. Give it up."

Radcliff halted at the edge of the ravine, his breath panting out as he pressed his fist to his bloody shoulder.

"Put your hands in the air," Derrick ordered.

Radcliff simply smiled at him then shook his head. "I'm not going back to prison."

Derrick took another step closer and Radcliff inched backward. "Don't you dare jump, you coward."

Another inch though, and Radcliff's laugh boomed. Then he lifted his arms to his side, windmilling as he stepped off the ridge. Derrick ran forward to grab him, but he was too late.

Radcliff plunged into the jagged rocks below.

ONE HUNDRED TWENTY-NINE

Cord stirred from unconsciousness. On some level, his body ached, yet a blinding numbness had begun to replace the pain. He'd been stabbed, he knew that.

Where was he now?

Suddenly he felt a warm weight against him and forced himself to fight through the numbness. Breathing, low and shallow, echoed through the fog in his brain. A soft hand lay against his cheek. A voice... He'd heard Ellie whispering his name.

Panic jumpstarted him back to life. Ellie... She was here with him.

Groaning, he raked his hand sideways on the floor and tried to turn over. She was curled against his back. He had to see if she was all right. Slowly, he managed to shift, but with every tiny movement, he felt more blood seeping from his stomach.

"Ellie?" he croaked. "El?"

He pressed his hand over hers and finally turned to face her. Their noses touched. Her shallow breathing bathed his face.

Dammit, he would not let her die.

"El," he managed to groan out the word. "Wake up."

The air felt foggy. Smelled funny. His lungs strained for air.

The truth dawned quickly. Gas... He smelled it.

Forcing low even breaths, he shook Ellie. "El, wake up, honey, we have to get out of here."

She moaned softly, and he shook her again. "Gas is coming in. I'm going to find a way out of here."

Finally, she roused. "Cord?"

"I'm here," he murmured. "But we have to do something or we're going to die. Let's look for the door or a vent."

She coughed, raised her head and looked around. He dragged himself across the floor to the wall and raked his hand across it.

Ellie pushed herself up, holding her left arm to her side, and he realized she was injured. His gut clenched. He couldn't stand to see her hurt.

But now wasn't the time for a lecture. It wouldn't do any good anyway. Ellie had a mind of her own. It was one thing he loved about her.

The stubborn independence drove him crazy, too.

Slowly he managed to drag his body along the one side, leaving a trail of blood as he went. Ellie's short breaths echoed through the room as she crawled.

"Cord," she rasped. "There's a vent over here."

His pulse hiked and he hurled himself forward as fast as he could.

"If the gas is coming through it, maybe it's connected to the other rooms. Bang on it and maybe someone will hear."

"Derrick's up there with back-up." She began to beat at the vent crate and shout for help.

Cord coughed and clutched at his wound to stop the bleeding.

But he was weak, his own breathing turning shallow. His lungs strained for air. And he felt himself losing the battle to remain conscious.

ONE HUNDRED THIRTY

There was nothing Derrick could do for Radcliff. The fall was at least a hundred feet. His body lay twisted and broken, blood seeping onto the rocks. The SOB had taken the coward's way out.

But he had others to find. Ones he could save. The victims. McClain. And Ellie.

He ran back through the trees and down the hill then rushed into the lower level where he'd left the others.

By the time he reached the room where Radcliff and Pockley had been, the sheriff was cuffing Pockley. The man looked shell-shocked as if he couldn't believe they'd finally been caught.

"Let's find the victims," Derrick told Landrum. "Waters, do you see keys to the rooms?"

The sheriff searched Pockley and found a key ring at the man's belt. He tossed them to Derrick then pushed Pockley to the door to escort him to his squad car.

Derrick and Landrum hurried down the hall. He came to three doors and heard crying inside. He unlocked the first door and raced in to find Beverly Hooper sobbing.

"Check next door," he told Landrum.

Landrum disappeared and Derrick rushed to Beverly. "Hey, it's okay," he said gently as he knelt to untie her. "You're safe now."

Tears choked her voice. "He was going to kill me," she wailed.

"I know, but you're safe now." He finished untying her ankles and helped her stand. She staggered and held onto him, and he scooped her up and ran outside to the ambulance.

The medic took over, and he ran back inside just as Landrum carried a weeping Janie Huggins out the door. One more room. Sarah Turner was here, too.

He checked another room, but no one was inside. In the fourth room, he found Sarah. She'd lost blood and was unconscious. He checked for a pulse. Low but she had one. He quickly lifted her and carried her down the hall and outside.

Another ambulance had arrived and he rushed her to them. They immediately helped her onto a stretcher and began checking her vitals.

His heart thundered.

The women were safe. Pockley was in custody. Radcliff, Wahlburg and Harvey dead.

Time to find McClain and Ellie.

Derrick left the sheriff with Pockley who'd totally clammed up in the backseat of the squad car. Deputy Eastwood was working to comfort Lorna Bea and the other victims.

"Landrum, get ERT, the ME and a recovery team to bring up Radcliff's body from the ridge where he jumped," Derrick said. "I think there might be more bodies in the basement. I'm going in for McClain and Ellie."

"Copy that. Let me know if you need back-up."

Derrick nodded and hurried back inside. He searched the same area where he'd found the victims but found empty rooms. Fear driving him, he turned and jogged down another corridor, combing the downstairs halls. Finally, he heard a banging sound. Then shouting.

Ellie. "Help!"

Even with his raging heart, he forced himself to stand still. To focus on the direction of the sound.

"Ellie!" he shouted. "I'm on my way. Where are you?"

Her voice again. "In here!" she cried. "We're locked inside."

He raced down the hall, following the sound until he made

a turn and reached what looked like a dead end. Then he heard coughing.

Pulling a handkerchief from his pocket, he covered his mouth and nose as he jiggled the doorknob. It was heavy and secure but three more tries, pushing all his weight against it, and he managed to open it.

The door screeched and Ellie fell forward at his feet, gasping for air.

"Come on, I've got you." He stooped down to help her up.

"The other victims?"

"We got them all out safely."

She pushed at him. "I can walk. Help Cord. He's been stabbed."

Derrick hesitated, holding onto her. Saving Ellie was all that mattered to him at the moment.

"Do it!" she shouted as she pushed herself up. She groaned in pain as she staggered forward, and he saw McClain collapsed on the floor.

He ran to the ranger, hauled him up from the floor and draped McClain's arm around his neck, then dragged him from the room. Ellie stood outside against the wall, heaving for air and coughing.

"Lean on me," he said, then slid his free arm about her waist. He slowly helped both of them down the hall to the outside where they could breathe.

"What about the perps?" Ellie asked, coughing.

"Pockley's in custody. Radcliff threw himself off a ridge."

Lights twirled in the night sky, and another ambulance, the ME and ERT drove up. He spotted the sheriff beside his squad car, guarding the prisoner inside, and Deputies Eastwood and Landrum leading medics to the victims.

"Over here!" he shouted.

Another set of medics rushed to them, one helping McClain to a stretcher, the other assisting Ellie.

Derrick followed them and watched as a medic took her vitals and called it in. Minutes later, they loaded her and McClain in the back of the ambulance.

Two hours later, Ellie rolled over in the hospital bed, wincing. Bruises covered her body, a headache blurred her vision and her arm and shoulder throbbed like a mother. It had been dislocated but the doctor had reset it.

She looked down at herself in frustration. The stupid sling had to stay on for a while. Dammit, she couldn't shoot like this. Couldn't be effective. And crime wouldn't stop just because she was injured.

She'd tolerate it a week or two, then she'd shed the damn thing and get back to business.

But she was more worried about Cord than herself. She hated this helpless feeling. Hated that she couldn't wave a magic wand and make him better. Not that Ellie Reeves believed in magic.

Shondra came into the room and handed her a cup of water with a straw in it. "You look like hell."

"Thanks. I needed that," Ellie said wryly, then drained the water. Shondra took the cup and Ellie's gaze caught sight of a sparkling stone on her hand. A single solitary onyx glittered on a gold band.

She jerked her friend's hand toward her. It was on her ring finger, left hand. "Oh, my God. Is that what I think it is?"

A smile tilted Shondra's lips. "It is. Julie proposed. Said she was terrified when she heard about this case and what we've been working on."

Ellie admired the stone. "It's beautiful, Shondra. I'm so happy for you." She reached out her arms and Shondra gave her a hug.

"I'm happy, too. Julie's a keeper."

Tears stung Ellie's eyes. Good grief, she wasn't a crier. Her mother once accused her of not having a sentimental bone in her body.

But ever since her friend Mia had gotten married on Memorial Day weekend, she'd had seconds, just tiny flickers, of imagining what it would be like to tie the knot herself.

"Have you set the date?" Ellie asked.

Shondra twirled the ring around her finger with a wide grin. "No, not yet. But we want it to be small and intimate."

"That sounds lovely, Shondra," Ellie said and meant it. "Hope I'm invited."

"Are you kidding?" Shondra said with a sparkle in her eyes. "I want you to be my maid of honor."

Unexpected tears blurred Ellie's eyes. "Of course."

Shondra gave her another quick hug. But Ellie's mind was already turning back to the case. Rescuing Lorna Bea and the other victims. Searching that hospital in case there were other bodies.

"How's Lorna Bea?"

"Traumatized, but a child psychologist is with her now. They've already called Emily Nettles." Emily was head of the Porch Sitters, a local prayer group, and also a foster parent.

"Good," Ellie said. "Emily will know what to do." She always did. "What about Beverly and Janie and Sarah?"

"They're all emotional, bruised and dehydrated but they'll make it."

Ellie clutched the sheet with clammy fingers. So far no one had told her anything about his condition. "And Cord?"

Shondra gave her an understanding smile. "He sustained a head injury. Docs ran a CAT scan and MRI. Waiting on results. But the surgery went well. He lost a lot of blood. They've patched him up and are putting him through the ringer with pain meds and antibiotics."

Ellie pushed at the covers and threw her legs over the side of the bed. "I have to see him."

"He's still unconscious and heavily sedated," Shondra said. "You need to rest yourself. The staff is taking good care of him."

"Maybe so, but I need to see him." Ellie's stubborn streak kicked in and she brushed Shondra's hands aside and stood. For a moment, she felt dizzy and wobbled slightly but righted herself quickly. "Get my clothes."

Shondra didn't bother to argue. She opened the dresser drawer in the corner and pulled out Ellie's clothes. Ellie shrugged off the hospital gown, her body throbbing as she dressed.

Cord had always been there for her. Although occasionally his overprotectiveness grated on her, he was never demanding. Never smothering.

Tears pricked her eyes again. He was her rock and he needed to know it.

Shondra guided her down the hall to Cord's hospital room and opened the door. Machines beeped and whirred. He looked pale and so still that, for a second, Ellie could barely breathe.

Pull it together, girl.

Taking a deep breath, she shuffled toward him. Her heart in her throat, she pulled a chair up next to him and laid her hand over his. "Cord, you listen to me. You're the toughest guy I know. You fight and get yourself back here, do you hear me?"

She waited, hoping for a response, but he didn't move or even squeeze her fingers.

The doctor entered the room, his expression guarded. "How're you doing, Detective?"

She ignored the pain in her body. "Fine. I'm just worried about Cord."

The man gave a nod. "I'm afraid it'll take time for him to heal. I know it's difficult, but patience is your best friend right now."

She barely resisted a smirk. He didn't know the first thing about Ellie Reeves. Patience was not in her skill set.

ONE HUNDRED THIRTY-THREE

THE HOSPITAL

Derrick shook his head in shock as he watched recovery teams carry the remains of four more women from the morgue in the basement of the hospital.

His pulse hammered. This group of men had been killing for years and gotten away with it. Now Waycross, Wahlburg, Harvey and Radcliff were dead.

A search team was at Pockley's house now and another would search his office as soon as the building was open in the morning. Another team was searching Harvey's home and computer as well. The photographer had not only taken part in the murders but shown up as an investigator and relived the glory by filming the crime scenes right under their noses.

That stung.

Dr. Whitefeather looked pale as she exited the building. "I'll get you IDs on the victims as soon as I can," she said. "But this may take a few days."

"I'll search missing person's reports and send over what I find."

She pushed her hair behind one ear. "Thanks. We need to speak for these young women."

Yes, he wanted justice for them all.

Leaving Williams, the ERT and the recovery workers to do their jobs, he drove to the police station where the sheriff had taken Pockley.

He still had unanswered questions. And Pockley was the only one left who could answer them.

A few minutes later, Derrick strode into the interrogation room and the sheriff brought Roland Pockley from the holding cell. He and Waters hadn't always gotten along, but they were on the same side today and he gestured for him to sit in.

Pockley's acne scars were highlighted by the reddening of his skin. He fidgeted, eyes darting all over the place, anywhere but at Derrick. His thin lips were tight, his leg jiggling up and down.

"You know we have you on first degree murder and conspiracy to commit several others," Derrick said bluntly. "Police are searching your home as we speak and come daylight will be all over your office." He paused and let that sink in. Hopefully they'd find enough to nail him. "It's only a matter of time until we identify the victims we found at the morgue."

Pockley's bony shoulders lifted in a tiny shrug.

"Tell me who the leader was," Derrick said. "Radcliff?"

A faint smile tilted his mouth. "He was our inspiration."

"So you, Wahlburg, Waycross and Harvey met in Dr. Dansen's class, then formed a chess club and called yourself the

Brotherhood. There you made a pact and planned your first kills."

A smug smile pulled at Pockley's face.

"What I want from you now, is to know who was responsible for each woman's death. And names of the other victims we just found at the hospital. Their families deserve closure and to give them a proper burial."

Pockley rocked back in the chair. "Why would I tell you all that?"

"You wanted to be famous, didn't you? After all, serial killers want a name, to be important, to garner the attention of the press," Derrick said. "You were a loner as a kid, bullied, made fun of. You were invisible to the women."

"Not invisible," he said through clenched teeth. "They laughed at me."

"And that pissed you off," Derrick said. "Is that the reason for the bloody lips?"

Pockley shrugged. "Radcliff started that. But who's laughing now?"

Anger seethed inside Derrick. He saw the faces of the victims, the bodies being carried out. The terrified twelve-year-old whose mother was a victim.

"And Harvey was part of it from the beginning?" Derrick asked.

Pockley fiddled with his glasses. "He filmed mock murders back then. But that got boring after a while."

"So he filmed the real thing?"

Pockley grinned. "It made things more exciting."

Derrick leaned closer. Those videos could help confirm that every victim was accounted for. "Now, names and dates."

"Why would I tell you all that?" Pockley asked.

"If you don't, I'll bury you. No one will know your name or that you were part of this elaborate plan." His tone was icy, condescending. "You won't be famous at all. You'll just be another loser inmate who'll die in prison."

Pockley's eyes turned to steel. He took several deep breaths, wheezing out his frustration and twitching as he debated what to say. Finally, he stilled and looked at Derrick dead in the eyes.

"Get me some paper and I'll write it all down. But you have to get me an interview with that pretty reporter, Angelica Gomez." A smile lit his eyes. "The whole world is going to know Roland Pockley."

ONE HUNDRED THIRTY-FIVE

Derrick had no intention of giving Pockley an interview with Angelica Gomez. He didn't bargain with killers.

But he had to play along.

While Pockley made the list, Derrick took a break in Ellie's office and researched Harvey.

He'd never been arrested and had no traffic violations. Mother died when he was two so raised by a single father. His father worked at a fish camp off the AT and died eleven years ago.

The timing of that could be significant. He'd lost his hunting partner and had to find another.

He'd accomplished that by meeting the others in Dr. Dansen's class. From there, he'd attended a crime scene investigations program. He'd worked in Savannah for a while before moving to Widow Peak, where he'd joined local law enforcement, and had been working in the area for the last few years.

Derrick phoned Sergeant Williams, head of the ERT. He seemed just as shocked as Derrick and Ellie that Harvey was not only a killer, but he'd documented the crimes for his own personal collection. With his training, he knew how to protect himself from detection.

"Did you ever sense anything was off about him?" Derrick asked.

"No," Sergeant Williams said. "He paid great attention to detail which made him good at his job. Although, he wasn't social with any of the other investigators and definitely was a loner." He paused. "We found recordings of each murder in a safe in his house. I'll send them over.

Derrick thanked him and ended the call, then went to see if Pockley had finished his list.

As he entered, Pockley was thumping the pen on the table. He pushed the list toward Derrick with a smirk.

Derrick examined it and was satisfied that Pockley had detailed dates and names. Pockley had killed the two women Derrick had questioned Radcliff about.

Derrick would compare the list to the tapes Williams was sending over.

It was mindboggling that this conspiracy had gone on for a decade and no one had put it together.

On the table, Derrick laid a photo of the graveyard of animals McClain had discovered.

"This was your doing?" Derrick asked.

"Actually, that was Harvey's idea," he said. "His father was a hunter and took him with him in the woods when he was a kid. He talked about the thrill of lying in wait, stalking his target, then striking."

"But you all participated in it?"

Pockley nodded. "It was practice. We kept score on how many each one of us killed just as his father made him do. His father filmed him pulling the trigger his first time when he was ten."

That must have been how Harvey got the idea to film the murders.

"So his appetite for murder was whetted at an early age," Derrick commented.

Pockley nodded. "The animals were fun but after a while we decided to up the game. Then Harvey told us about the time his father kidnapped a woman. He let her out in the woods and told her to run. Then he tracked her down and shot her."

Derrick swallowed hard at the image that formed in his mind. One sadistic killer had bred another.

ONE HUNDRED THIRTY-SIX

BLUFF COUNTY HOSPITAL

Lorna Bea twisted the hospital sheet in her hands, the devastation of learning what her father had done crushing her. No, she could *not* call him her father, not ever again.

His name was Frank Wahlburg and he was a monster. He'd murdered her mother in cold blood. And he was supposed to kill her.

The fact that he'd chickened out made no difference. He'd taken her mother from her and kidnapped her, then lied about who he was.

A sob welled in her throat. The pain was so deep, she thought she was going to die. All these years she'd wanted a real home but she'd been living with her mother's killer.

Where would she go now? How would she survive?

Nana—who wasn't actually her grandmother—was dead, too.

She had nobody.

She rolled to her side in the bed and stared at the blank wall. For so long, she'd been on the run. Carried her box from place to place. Followed that monster around. Thought he loved her and was protecting her.

But he'd been protecting himself from getting caught. She'd been a loose end.

Now she was on her own. All alone.

She knew what happened to orphans. They got shuffled around to strangers' houses. Sometimes the people wanted them. Sometimes they didn't.

But they wouldn't be a real family.

And once the people found out about Frank and what he'd done, they wouldn't want her to stay. Especially if they had other kids. They'd probably be afraid she'd turn out to be a monster, too.

Tears burned her eyes and she cried into the pillow. Now she'd never have a real home or a real family. She'd never get to be normal.

DAY 6

It was five a.m., and Derrick had been up all night. He'd checked on Ellie and learned she was stable, so he'd focused on the case. Something was still bugging him. He wanted all the evidence he could find to give the victims' families closure.

He met a forensic team at the small cabin Odessa Muldane had rented on a dirt road named Buzzard Trail. The cabin was set in an isolated section of the woods, offering privacy and access to the AT.

The woman had no family. At one time she'd worked as a court reporter, but she'd been fired for taking copies of criminal trials home with her. He'd also learned she was a patient of Dr. Morehead's and being treated for hybristophilia.

Although Odessa hadn't survived Radcliff's torture, Derrick was determined to know if she was simply a victim or if she was culpable in any of the murders.

The cabin was dark inside, with dusty furniture that smelled of weed and must. He started in the kitchen and found the cabinets practically bare and the refrigerator almost empty.

An old Afghan hung over the back of a dark-green sofa and a woodstove appeared to serve as the heater. Window fans jutted from the windows, a sign the cabin did not have central air conditioning.

He searched the drawers in the cabinet and found silverware and a junk drawer holding rubber bands and plastic baggies. In the desk in the living room, he found blank envelopes, stamps and a vial of sickeningly sweet perfume that she might have used to scent the letters she wrote Radcliff in prison.

He looked for return letters but didn't find any, so he went to the bedroom. A black comforter covered the bed, the windows shrouded with blackout curtains. He flipped on a light and looked in her dresser drawers. Sexy lingerie was stacked neatly, a combination of black and red. He searched the closet and found a camera stand and camera, hinting that she might have photographed herself, perhaps to send the pictures to Radcliff.

Moving on, he returned to the hall and noticed a door leading to a basement. He shined his flashlight down the steps and heard water dripping from somewhere. When he reached the bottom floor, he looked around and found a trunk filled with old clothing.

Then he found a secret room and kicked it open with his foot. Using his flashlight, he crept inside. Shelves lined the wall holding decorative cardboard boxes like you'd find at a craft store. He pulled one down, looked inside and found dozens of handwritten letters. A quick shuffle and he realized they were letters from Radcliff while he was incarcerated.

Another box held letters from various inmates. Some names he recognized as serial killers or men who'd been on the FBI's Most Wanted list.

He opened one envelope and skimmed it:

My Love,

You understand me like no one else. When we're together, I have more details to tell you about my kills.

He moved onto another.

My Sweetness,

Thank you for sharing stories from the brothers. I live vicariously through them, knowing they've honored the pact and continued the calling.

There were several more, but he'd have them bagged and sent to the lab. They would determine if there was useful information in them.

On the next shelf, he found a decorative jewelry box. Odessa didn't seem the type to wear expensive jewelry. When he opened it, he saw that was not what was inside.

There were individual plastic bags, each containing a single item of jewelry: a necklace, pair of earrings, a plain gold chain... Nothing looked expensive.

But the names on the bags were familiar.

Amy Dean, Kari Bernard, Jordie Nixon, Zelda North, Judy Zane. Vanna Michaels...

After ERT processed Odessa Muldane's house, Derrick had to see Ellie.

Once he'd downloaded Harvey's videos to his computer, he drove to the hospital so they could study them together.

He was surprised she was dressed yet not surprised she was arguing with the doctor, demanding to be released.

"Detective Reeves..." the doctor said, looking flustered.

"I have to work," she said stubbornly.

"You need to stay here for observation for twenty-four hours."

Ellie jerked her head toward Derrick as he entered. "Then he can observe me, can't you, Agent Fox?"

Well, that was a loaded question. He almost smiled at the doctor's frustrated face. "You might as well release her," Derrick said. "If you don't, she'll just find a way to leave without the papers."

The doctor huffed, shook his head then left the room to get them.

Ellie pulled her hair back into her usual ponytail, wincing

as she raised her arms to do so. A second later, a nurse hurried in and handed Ellie the release papers for her signature.

"Did we get what we need to lock up Pockley for good?"

Derrick nodded. "Forensics found the bodies of Haley Worth and Judy Zane deep in the basement of the old hospital. There are two other bodies Laney is working on. But Pockley gave up names so that should help with the identification process."

"Zelda North's boyfriend has been serving time for her murder," Ellie said.

"We should have enough forensics and evidence to exonerate him," Derrick said. "While you got your beauty sleep, I reviewed some of the tapes we confiscated from Harvey's house."

Ellie rolled her eyes at his wry comment. "What did you find?"

"They're pretty horrific," Derrick said. "I thought we'd look them over together. Something's bugging me about them."

"What?"

"I'd rather not say until you take a look."

Ellie headed to the door. "Then let's get out of here. All this cleanliness is making me ill."

Derrick chuckled and followed her outside. When they got in his sedan, he asked, "How's McClain?"

Worry darkened her eyes. "Still unconscious."

"He's a fighter, Ellie," Derrick said quietly.

She nodded and clenched her jaw. "Let's pick up breakfast on the way."

He stopped at the Corner Café and got them coffee and their usual breakfast sandwiches, while she waited in the car. Ten minutes later, they parked at her bungalow and she went straight to shower.

The temptation to join her niggled at him but first, he had

to figure out what was missing about the case. If he was right about his hunch.

He set the coffee and food on her kitchen island and placed his computer between the bar stools.

Once Ellie was out, she sucked down the coffee and sausage-cheese biscuit as if she hadn't eaten in days. He polished his off, deciding they needed to eat before watching the gory videos.

The first video was of Amy Dean's murder. The air in the room grew charged with emotion as they watched Frank Wahlburg attack the young woman with a knife. She screamed and so did her little girl, and blood spattered everywhere.

"Kill the girl, too!" Waycross ordered. "We can't leave any loose ends behind."

But Wahlburg had refused and charged Waycross. They fought and Waycross grabbed Paisley and ran out the door. Wahlburg gave chase but the footage stopped when they got outside.

"They all this bad?" Ellie asked.

He nodded. "Never easy to watch someone lose their life to violence." Except these men had fed on it.

ONE HUNDRED THIRTY-NINE
CROOKED CREEK

By the third video, Ellie felt ill. She had to erect a mental wall to protect herself from breaking down. The footage of the young coed posed in front of the Coastal College in Brunswick was especially disturbing. Next, footage of Haley North's murder, one of the victims Radcliff had denied killing.

The image caught on the camera was blurry, but the stature wasn't Radcliffe's. This guy was thinner, taller, wore glasses. "That's Pockley," Ellie said.

Derrick nodded. "He confessed to the two murders we asked Radcliff about."

"Wait," Ellie said. "Replay it."

He rewound it and ran it again, his pulse jumping.

"There's someone else there," Ellie said. "I... think I heard another voice. Can you enhance the sound?"

Derrick did and watched her reaction. "I heard it, too. But it's difficult to distinguish if it's male or female."

Ellie sipped her coffee. "Odessa Muldane?"

Derrick gave a non-committal shrug and played the video of the initiation. Each man had brought a souvenir from their first kill. Odessa had been watching in the shadows. "The Muldane woman was there in the circle with them." Next, he played the video of the attack on Sarah Turner. "Coolidge didn't attack her. But Harvey was definitely there."

And so was someone else.

Although the voice was muffled and she couldn't tell if it was male or female.

Derrick's phone buzzed with the hospital number and he connected. "Special Agent Fox."

"You asked me to call when Omar Coolidge regained consciousness. He has."

"I'll be right there." Derrick hung up. "Omar Coolidge is awake. Maybe he can fill in some blanks." He pulled his keys from his pocket. "Why don't you study the remainder of the videos while I question him?"

Ellie nodded. "Sounds like a plan."

He rushed outside, hopped in his sedan and sped toward Bluff County Hospital. Traffic was minimal, the roads still damp from the storm the night before. Mid-morning sunlight was already shimmering through the clouds, the temperature slightly cooler today, hinting that fall was around the corner.

He turned the images in the videos over in his mind as he drove. Exhausted from staying up reviewing the tapes and trying to tie up loose ends on the case, he rolled his shoulders as he parked, then got out, entered the hospital and found Coolidge's room. The deputy was still standing guard and would be until Coolidge was transported to jail to await his trial.

He opened the door and went in, noting the IV and heart monitor beeping. Bandages peeked from the man's hospital gown, where his chest had been wrapped. His leg was in a cast, his arm in a sling and bruises and scrapes marred his hands and face.

After knowing how he'd tormented the tenants in his building, Derrick found no sympathy for the lowlife.

He cut straight to the chase as he approached. "We have you dead to rights on illegally taping and stalking several residents in your apartment building. Other charges will follow."

Coolidge's eye was so swollen it was half shut. He said nothing.

"We confiscated the tapes and cameras in your apartment and know you've been doing this for years. Did you witness Amy Dean's murder on tape?"

Coolidge released a heavy, defeated sigh. "No. But I can tell you something about that that night."

Derrick maintained a cool expression. "We know who killed her. We found tapes of her murder done by the killer. We've already made an arrest and other perpetrators are dead."

Coolidge's eye twitched. "Those weirdos took that criminology class together."

"I also know that," Derrick said. "Tell me something I don't know."

The man's bruised fingers curled around the sheets. "That teacher visited Amy Dean."

"You mean Professor Pockley?"

Coolidge shook his head. "No, the chick."

Surprise hit Derrick. "Dr. Dansen came to Amy's apartment?"

Coolidge nodded. "The day Amy was murdered."

Ellie refused to take serious painkillers, but she downed two aspirin with water. The doorbell rang, and she frowned.

She'd called her parents from the hospital to assure them she was okay, but knowing them, they'd rushed over to see for themselves. She was not in a mood to be hovered over.

Pasting on an *I'm fine* expression, she walked to the door and checked the peephole. Not her parents.

Dr. Dansen.

Had she heard the news about the arrests? They needed to thank her for her help.

Ellie opened the door with a smile. "Dr. Dansen, I wasn't expecting to see you."

"I know, and I'm sorry for just dropping in," she said as she followed Ellie into the living room. "But I saw the news last night and wanted to make sure you were okay."

"I am," Ellie said then gestured to the coffee pot. "Would you like some?"

"Sure," Dr. Dansen said.

Ellie poured them both a cup and they seated themselves at

the breakfast bar. Dr. Dansen glanced at Derrick's open computer and Ellie quickly closed it.

"Do you have creamer?" she asked.

"Of course." Ellie turned her back to get it from the fridge then carried it to the bar and set it in front of the woman.

"I still can't believe some of my students conspired to commit all those murders." She poured the creamer into her mug and stirred. "Who would have thought they'd get away with it all these years?"

"They were smart," Ellie said. "Covering for each other."

"Did they share details?"

"Some," Ellie said. "Although they didn't have to. We found enough evidence to prove their culpability. Agent Fox and I have been reviewing the tapes Harvey made of the murders."

"Harvey?"

Ellie nodded. "He was the student who filmed the mock murders," Ellie said.

"I thought he'd moved away and attended film school."

"Apparently not. He became a forensic investigator."

"And you have those tapes?"

"Yes," Ellie said. "That, and souvenirs the men took from the victims."

Ellie's phone rang. Derrick. "Excuse me, I have to take this. Agent Fox is at the hospital questioning the apartment manager now. We think he may know something."

Dr. Dansen pursed her lips and Ellie turned and walked to the door to the patio. "Derrick?"

"Yeah. Listen, Coolidge said Dr. Dansen was at Lake Haven Apartments the day Amy Dean was murdered."

A chill went through Ellie.

"I'll find her for questioning," he said.

"No need," Ellie said, striving for a calm voice. "Here."

The floor creaked behind her and Ellie spun around. The woman was walking toward her with a .38 in her hand.

ONE HUNDRED FORTY-TWO

Derrick pressed the accelerator, taking the turns on two wheels. Had Dansen known the men's plans? Had she orchestrated everything through her criminology class, choosing susceptible subjects, studying them and guiding them to pursue their secret dark fantasies?

The muffled voice he and Ellie had heard on the tape must have been hers. When they'd asked her about the class, she'd mentioned the guy who'd filmed the mock murders had moved away as a misdirect, so they wouldn't look for him.

The college had supported her program. Law enforcement agencies had counted it as a prerequisite. Even the FBI had respected her knowledge and asked her to guest speak at conferences.

The implications of who and how many she'd affected—even inspired, as her followers would probably say—was staggering.

And now she was at Ellie's.

Derrick pounded the steering wheel with his fist, cursing the fact that he'd left her alone.

Like any game with intelligent participants, Harvey and

Dansen had gone virtually unnoticed. Insinuated themselves in the investigation by willingly offering information to appear to be helping them.

A classic move.

One he should have considered.

His mistake.

And now Ellie might pay for it.

ONE HUNDRED FORTY-THREE

CROOKED CREEK

"You should have drunk the coffee," Dr. Dansen said. "That would have made it so much easier and less painful, Detective. But I do admire your work." She waved the gun in Ellie's face. "You've been the most interesting and challenging opponent." Her laugh tinkled through the air as she gestured toward the steaming mug. "I shall truly miss you. Now suck it down and we can avoid the mess."

The woman was insane if she thought Ellie would go down without a fight.

Dammit. She should have recognized the signs. Dr. Dansen had known each of their suspects. Though there was no evidence she'd been in touch with Radcliff while he was in prison, it was possible she had kept contact through the others.

The calculating intricacy of her manipulation went deep. She'd damn well set them up.

"Why?" she asked.

Dr. Dansen stepped closer to Ellie. Her breath stalled in her chest. Where was her own weapon?

Derrick had probably taken it last night when she'd been transported to the hospital. It might be in evidence now.

All she had was herself.

She had to stall. Keep her talking. Get answers. Derrick would be here soon.

"Tell me about you," Ellie said. "What's your story? Why would an attractive, intelligent woman resort to murder?" Ellie asked. "I know female serial killers are rare. Did you just want to stand out?"

Dansen raised a brow. "You think you're so smart. But you deal with murder every day so I could say the same about you. That you have a dark side of your own."

"I try to save lives, not take them or inflict pain," Ellie said flatly. No way was she going to allow this twisted woman to get inside her head. She crossed her arms. "Most serials have a sad sack story? What's yours? Your mother beat you? Father kill her? Or did he molest you?"

Dansen's nostrils flared and Ellie knew she was close.

A second later, Dansen lifted her chin. "He killed my mother and my sister and brother. Massacred our entire family. I'm the only one who survived." Bitterness laced her voice. "But I didn't really survive. Everywhere I went, people knew about it. Other girls wanted nothing to do with me."

Ellie swallowed hard. She had to make certain the same thing didn't happen to Lorna Bea.

Her eyes darted to the counter in search of something to use to protect herself. The knife block was too far away. Coffee pot as well. A cutting board was propped against the backsplash. Maybe she could reach that.

"Special Agent Fox is on the way," she said. "We heard a muffled voice on Harvey's videos and knew someone else was there. It was you, wasn't it? You were at Lake Haven Apartments the day Amy Dean died. Even if you kill me, Agent Fox will track you down and you will go to prison."

A maniacal laugh punctuated the air. "No matter. I've taught my students well over the years."

Ellie's blood ran cold. Was she implying she'd trained a new wave of killers?

"Give it up, Dr. Dansen, there's no need for you to die," she said calmly.

Another eerie laugh. "Oh, I'm not going to die. I'll live on through my apprentices. But you, Detective Reeves, are going to hell."

Suddenly, Dansen charged like a caged animal. Ellie grabbed the mug and threw it at her. Dansen screamed as hot coffee sloshed in her face. But she was quick and raised the gun.

Ellie threw her arms up in defense, snatched the cutting board and swung it upward to deflect the blow. The gun went flying.

Dansen quickly recovered and jumped Ellie. Ellie fought with all her might, pushing Dansen away and going for the knives in the knife block. Before she could reach it, Dansen caught her from behind, and she stumbled forward. Ellie's head hit the corner of the cabinet. Pain ricocheted up her temple and the world spun.

She grappled to remain upright, lost the battle and went down. Then Dansen was on her, strong and bellowing like a rabid animal.

Ellie saw Lorna Bea's face in her mind. Heard the words in her journal—living her life in boxes. Always on the run. Wahlburg had killed her mother because of this woman.

Rage fueled her adrenaline, and as Dansen scrambled for the gun, Ellie delivered a swift blow to her wrist just as she was about to snag it.

Dansen fought, the two of them rolling and banging against the side of the cabinet, trapping her. Then Dansen lurched up and grabbed a knife from the knife block. Ellie cursed as the woman charged her. Ellie dodged the attack, then dove at Dansen.

Her breathing panted out as they struggled. Dansen shoved

Ellie to the floor, then dug her knee into Ellie's thigh as she climbed on top of her. The knife wavered above her heart.

Ellie groaned, ignoring the pain as she punched Dansen in the face, then used her body to flip Dansen.

"Paisley did not deserve to lose her mother," Ellie snarled. She used every last ounce of strength she possessed and swung the knife down into Dansen's chest.

The woman's shocked gasp filled the air. Her eyes widened with a mixture of disbelief and euphoria as if she'd imagined this moment before. Her breath puffed out. Blood was spurting.

Suddenly her door bust open. "Ellie!"

Derrick was there, looking down at her as Dansen gasped for a breath.

"Call an ambulance," Ellie shouted.

She did not intend to let this woman get off easy by dying. She pressed her hands over Dansen's wound to stem the blood flow.

She wanted Dansen to suffer in prison. She would make sure she was in solitary confinement, too.

Then her teaching would come to an end.

ONE HUNDRED FORTY-FOUR

BLUFF COUNTY HOSPITAL

Lorna Bea sat stiffly on the edge of the bed. Ms. Emily had come and talked to her about foster care, and she'd thought she'd stay with her for a while. She seemed nice and had four kids of her own so that might not be bad.

But her sympathetic eyes made her feel like a lost orphan, like Annie in the movie.

Because she was exactly that. She wasn't a little kid. She knew what would happen and that social worker and Ms. Emily seemed to realize she knew, because they didn't beat around the bush with some lame promises that everything was going to be all right.

Nothing was going to be all right, not ever again.

Tears threatened again, but she blinked them away. She was twelve. She had to be brave.

She'd be in the system until she was eighteen. She wondered how many boxes she'd have to pack the next six years and how many cities she'd live in and how many houses there would be and if the people would be nice to her or treat her like she was a psycho because she'd lived with one.

A rainy mist streaked the window of the hospital room. As

she watched the raindrops trickle down like teardrops, she wiped at her own damp eyes. The gray clouds were shadowy blobs of black in the sky.

Her box sat at her feet, her notebook inside where Ms. Molly had left them earlier.

She'd looked worried and had taken a phone call, saying she'd be back later. Maybe with some news.

Don't get your hopes up, Lorna Bea reminded herself.

When people find out about your daddy, they won't want you.

Ellie finished the press conference and headed to her office, hoping the people in the area felt safe again.

Her shoulder throbbed and she rubbed her arm, which was still in a sling, a constant reminder she wasn't as strong as she wanted to be. That Cord was still fighting for his life.

There, she found Emily Nettles waiting along with the social worker in charge of Paisley's case.

"How's Lorna Bea?" she asked without preamble.

"Still traumatized and confused," Emily said. "It'll take time, Ellie. But we've arranged counseling and she's talking. She even wants to go by Paisley, the name her mother gave her."

"That's a good sign," the social worker commented. "We also found a home for her. One where she should be happy."

Ellie had been consumed with worry over what would happen to the girl. "With you, Emily?" she said hopefully.

Emily gave a small shake of her head. "No. The Hammersteins want her to live with them. Without her bravery, they said they might have lost their little girl Betsy."

Ellie's heart thumped. "She did save her, didn't she?"

"She did," Emily said.

Ellie's chest eased slightly making it a little easier to breathe. "They know about Frank Wahlburg and what he did? About Paisley being dragged across the country, living out of her boxes?"

"Yes," Emily said. "They've already met with the counselor and are committed to supporting her through therapy."

"It won't be easy," Ellie said. "She may suffer long-term trauma and PTSD."

"They're aware and they're all in, Ellie," Emily assured her. "They're good people."

"Have you told Paisley?"

Emily and the social worker exchanged looks. "We thought you might want to," Emily said.

Ellie smiled. "Yes, I want to see her." An idea struck her as she remembered reading the girl's journal. "But first I need to pick up something on the way."

Paisley needed a new journal, one with clean pages where she could write a new story.

Hopefully this one would have a happy ending.

ONE HUNDRED FORTY-SIX

BLUE JAY LANE

Paisley sat in the back seat of the car, her arms wrapped around her box. Ms. Ellie had picked her up and was taking her to her new home, although she hadn't told her anything about it.

But she had given her some new notebooks to write in.

So far, all she'd done was look at the blank pages, thinking they were as empty as the road in front of her.

Ms. Ellie turned the car down a street lined with small houses, in a neighborhood that looked like it had a lot of kids. Bikes and toys were in the yards, a plastic blow-up, baby swimming pool in another, and a basketball goal sat in a cul-de-sac where two boys and a girl were outside, shooting hoops.

The houses looked nicely painted and flowers dotted the yards. Ms. Ellie veered into the drive in front of a blue house with white shutters and marigolds dancing in the breeze in the window boxes. Rocking chairs and a porch swing were front and center and a "Welcome" sign hung on the yellow front door. The house looked cheery and pretty like a fairy tale house and made Paisley want to cry.

Ms. Ellie cut the engine and turned to her with a sympathetic look. "We're here, Paisley. I think you're going to be surprised when you go inside."

Paisley didn't like surprises. She'd had too many of them lately.

She gritted her teeth though and simply nodded, then retrieved her box from the floor.

"I'll get your books," Ms. Ellie said, pointing to the second box in the back seat.

Paisley climbed out, her legs rubbery, her body numb with fear and uncertainty.

Swallowing back emotions, she followed Ms. Ellie up the front porch steps. Next door, she saw two girls pushing doll strollers in their yard and a boy and girl were kicking the soccer ball in another.

Ms. Ellie knocked and Paisley held her breath as they waited. Like a fireball suddenly shooting through the sky, the sun burst through the dark clouds overhead and lit up the porch.

Paisley gripped her box with sweaty hands. The urge to run took hold. She wanted to hide. Come back and do this another day.

But then the door opened and the entire Hammerstein family stood there, smiling and looking at her. Mr. and Mrs. Hammerstein, Cade and little Betsy and the kitten.

Her heart stuttered.

"Come in, come in," the mother said.

Mr. Hammerstein gave her what looked like a real genuine smile. "We've been getting ready for you all day."

"Lorna Bea!" Betsy cried.

"Hey," Cade said.

Paisley looked back and forth at all of them then up at Ms. Ellie. "It's okay, let's go inside," Ms. Ellie said.

"We're so excited you're here," Mrs. Hammerstein said.

Ms. Ellie gently coaxed her forward and Paisley clenched

her box like a lifeline and shuffled over to the sofa where everyone found a seat. Cade and Betsy plopped at her feet and stared up at her with goofy expressions.

Had they just stopped here to say hello? If so, why would Ms. Ellie bring Paisley's books inside?

"Lorna Bea," Mrs. Hammerstein said.

Ms. Ellie cleared her throat. "She wants to be called Paisley," Ms. Ellie said. "That was the name her mother gave her."

"Of course." Mrs. Hammerstein reached out and touched her hand. "Paisley, you can call me Gina."

"And I'm Ken. We have so much to thank you for," Mr. Hammerstein said. "You saved Betsy the first time when she fell in the shed. And you saved her when... when that man broke into your cabin."

The memory made Paisley's wooden body feel like it was cracking. "I'm sorry for what he did." Her voice quivered. Tears threatened to steal her voice.

"Oh, honey, none of this is your fault," Mrs. Hammerstein said softly.

"Without you, we might have lost Betsy," Mr. Hammerstein said.

Paisley looked at him and realized he meant it. Betsy shivered for a minute and crawled into her mother's lap.

"We understand you've been through a lot," Mrs. Hammerstein said. "And Ms. Ellie told us that you don't have other family."

Betsy wiggled. "So we wants you to be in ours."

Paisley fidgeted with a tattered corner of her box.

"She's right," Mr. Hammerstein said. "We've fixed a spare room up for you."

"Well, we didn't decorate it too much," Mrs. Hammerstein added. "I thought you might want to go shopping with me and pick out some bedding and curtains." She gently stroked Paisley's hair. "And we can get you some hair ribbons and new clothes and shoes. You have a nice closet in your room."

Paisley hugged the box tighter. "I just keep my stuff in my box so it's ready to go when I have to leave."

Mrs. Hammerstein pulled Paisley's hands in hers, squeezed them. "Honey, I don't think you understand. We want you to live with us and be part of our family. To stay here. Forever."

"Forever," Betsy added.

"You can keep your box if it makes you feel better," Mr. Hammerstein said. "But you won't need it anymore. You'll have your own dresser."

Paisley studied each of their faces, searching for a sign they were joking. Then she looked at Cade and he grinned.

"I told Mom you like mystery books so we picked you out some at the library," he said.

They got her books? Nana and her father—Frank—made fun of her for reading. "Always got your face stuck in a book or one of those books," he said.

"We heard you like to write stories, too," Mrs. Hammerstein said.

Paisley gave a little nod, too afraid they'd laugh and say it was silly like everyone else did.

"I love to read, too," Mrs. Hammerstein said. "Cade's into sci-fi and Betsy likes books about puppies and kittens. We read every night at bedtime."

"Say you'll stay," Cade said.

"I always wanted a sister," Betsy said.

Paisley's eyes misted with tears. Did they really want her?

Cade jumped up. "Come on, we'll show you your room."

"Then we can go out and play," Betsy said.

"We're building a fort in the woods with the neighbor kids," Cade said.

Paisley felt hope tug at her insides. She hugged her arms around her box and followed the family into a bedroom next to what had to be Betsy's. Dolls and stuffed animals were everywhere.

In this room, there was a white four-poster bed and a desk with paper and notebook and a jar full of ink pens and markers. A bookshelf held a whole shelf of novels. And there was a dresser and closet just like the Hammersteins said.

"Look," Betsy said as she pointed to the nightstand. "Mommy gots you a silver hairbrush just like mine."

Paisley remembered watching the mother counting strokes as she combed Betsy's hair and wanted to weep.

"Let's go play," Cade said.

"Why don't we let Paisley put her things away and settle in first?" Mrs. Hammerstein said. "We can get some cookies and lemonade ready for y'all to take to the fort while she does that."

"Yay, cookies!" Betsy squealed.

As they all left, Paisley turned in a wide circle and studied the room. She went to the window and looked out and saw the woods and the sunshine streaking the treetops, and the other kids playing. There was even a pond out back and ducks were waddling to the water.

All she'd ever wanted was a real home and a family and friends to play with.

She hurriedly unloaded her box and put her books on the bottom shelf. Then she thumbed through the ones the Hammersteins had chosen for her.

Excitement built in her chest. They were all mysteries!

Then she glanced at the notebook Ms. Ellie had got her. All the blank pages that she could fill in with her words and ideas. She couldn't wait to get started.

It would be about a girl who wasn't locked away. One who was free. One who could go outside and feel the wind on her face and climb trees and look up at the clouds without anyone yelling at her.

Birds twittered outside and she heard Betsy and Cade laughing downstairs.

An odd feeling tickled her tummy. She felt almost... giddy.

She set the books and notebook aside. They could wait. So could her writing.

The empty box mocked her. They said she wouldn't need it. She hoped not. Still, she shoved it beneath the bed anyway.

Smiling, she hurried downstairs to the living room. Ms. Ellie said goodbye. Betsy had a bag of cookies and Cade waved her to the back door and then they were running toward the woods. Other kids were there, laughing and playing and dragging sticks and straw to make a fort, and suddenly the empty blank road seemed bright and sunny—like it might be going somewhere.

ONE HUNDRED FORTY-SEVEN

BLUFF COUNTY HOSPITAL

One week later

"Cord..." Ellie whispered as she clung to his hand.

He was pale, his breathing shallow, the respirator doing its job to keep him alive while he was under the hospital-induced coma.

"You can't leave me, so hang in there, do you hear me?" Her voice caught on a sob, the hospital scents nauseating her. Her head and body throbbed, but she'd come out lucky this time. Only Cord was hanging on by a thread.

She stroked his hand. "I don't know what I'd do without you."

She felt his fingers twitch. Slightly. Or was she imagining it? Could he hear her?

The doctors straddled the fence about that. Some claimed a comatose patient didn't hear anything around them. That they remembered nothing, not about what had happened to them to put them in the hospital, not about experiencing pain or having visitors. Some had amnesia, temporary or long term. Others had to relearn basic skills like talking or walking.

Other doctors claimed it was possible for comatose patients to remember vivid details of what happened. Conversations from loved ones who visited. Even a specific song they heard playing.

She stroked his hand again. "Can you hear me, Cord? If you can, please show me a sign."

But his hand lay limp in hers and he lay motionless. She lifted it and kissed his palm then pressed it to her cheek where the tears had started to fall.

Suddenly, she felt someone in the room. She closed her eyes to compose herself then opened them and looked over her shoulder to see Derrick standing behind her. His body was rigid, concern in his eyes and some other emotion she couldn't quite define.

His breath heaved out, then he spoke so softly she almost didn't hear it. "You're in love with him, aren't you?"

Ellie's breath caught. "Derrick—"

His phone rang and he checked the number. She recognized the ring tone. Lindsey. "I have to go. I'll give you time to figure it out."

She squeezed Cord's hand and then stood to follow Derrick, but confusion, pain and worry stole her voice.

And then he was gone.

ONE HUNDRED FORTY-EIGHT

Cord's body felt weighted down. Pain clawed at his muscles and head and he couldn't open his eyes. But he'd heard a voice. Soft and silky. Muffled. Upset.

Ellie...

He struggled to recall what had happened. If she was okay. The darkness kept pulling him under. Only a sliver of light bled through the black.

Was he dying?

He remembered bright lights. The cold steel table. The hushed voices. The needles and the... sound of voices. Doctors and nurses.

The years rolled back and he was at the mortuary. His foster father with the dead bodies. The sick, perverse things he'd done.

The way he'd tried to force Cord to do the same...

He'd run from that life. Hadn't cared what he'd had to do to escape.

But there was Ellie. And he hadn't told her. She'd never seen all his scars.

Ellie... he thought she was here. Wasn't she? He tried to say her name, but something was stuck in his throat, his tongue thick, and he couldn't move his hand to reach for her.

He'd never told her how he felt. He had to fight, to come back and tell her. Maybe his love for her would redeem him.

Another sound, a door closing then opening?

Then another voice. A woman. Ellie again?

God, he didn't deserve her. But he wanted to hold her hand.

"Cord," the voice murmured. "It's me, Lola."

His brain swirled with confusion. Too many lights and sounds. A machine beeping. A wheezing, pumping sound.

Then he felt something warm on his hand. A soft caress.

"I know we took a break," Lola said. "But you have to hang in there, Cord. You cannot die."

Her voice sounded odd. Far away. Pleading. Full of tears.

The dark gave way to a light. He wanted to go to it. But she tugged at his hand and he felt himself jolt back to the emptiness.

"Stay with me," Lola whispered against his ear. "I have something important to tell you."

He didn't understand. The light was fading. More darkness. Then Lola again, "Please, Cord." His hand was being lifted. Pressed between hers.

"I'm pregnant, Cord," she murmured. "I need you. And so does our baby."

Cord felt his world rock. He was going to be a father?

The lights blinked erratically. The darkness sucked at him. The machines went crazy, beeping and chirping and whining. He searched for Ellie's voice.

Instead, he heard Lola sobbing as she buried her head against his chest, and he disappeared into the black abyss.

A LETTER FROM RITA

Thank you so much for reading *Widow Lake*, the eighth book in my Detective Ellie Reeves series! If you enjoyed *Widow Lake* and would like to keep up with all of my latest releases, you can sign up at the following link. Your email address will never be shared, and you can unsubscribe at any time.

www.bookouture.com/ritaherron

I'm thrilled to continue the Detective Reeves series with *Widow Lake*, a supposedly haunted lake based on legends surrounding Lake Lanier in Georgia. This man-made lake was created years ago when the government decided to build a much-needed dam. Unfortunately the dam flooded, burying entire communities below the water and causing countless deaths. Marked and unmarked graves sit at the bottom of the lake, and people have reported seeing and feeling body parts floating in the water.

When a body turns up in Widow Lake, Ellie uncovers decade-old secrets that lead to a band of killers called The Brotherhood. Will she survive or will she join the ghosts of Widow Lake?

I hope you enjoyed Ellie's journey in *Widow Lake* as much as I enjoyed writing it. If you did, I'd appreciate it if you left a short review. As a writer, it means the world to me that you share your feedback with other readers who might be interested in Ellie's world.

I love to hear from readers so you can find me on Facebook, my website and Twitter.

Thanks so much for your support. Happy Reading!

Rita

www.ritaherron.com

facebook.com/authorritaherron

twitter.com/ritaherron

instagram.com/ritaherronauthor

ACKNOWLEDGMENTS

A special thanks to my editors, Christina Demosthenous and Lydia-Vassar Smith, for their insight and guidance in adding this one to the Detective Ellie Reeves series. I will truly miss you, Christina!

Thanks also to the entire Bookouture team for the great title, cover and support for the series.